WHEN YOU
Blush

New York Times and USA Today Bestselling Author
KRISTEN PROBY

&
AMPERSAND
PUBLISHING, INC.

When You Blush
THE BLACKWELLS OF MONTANA

KRISTEN PROBY

&
AMPERSAND
PUBLISHING, INC.

WHEN YOU BLUSH

A Blackwells of Montana Novel

Kristen Proby

Copyright © 2025 by Kristen Proby

All Rights Reserved. This book may not be reproduced, scanned, or distributed in any printed or electronic form without permission from the author. Please do not participate in or encourage piracy of copyrighted materials in violation of the author's rights. All characters and storylines are the property of the author, and your support and respect are appreciated. The characters and events portrayed in this book are fictitious. Any similarity to real persons, living or dead, is coincidental and not intended by the author.

No part of this piece of work was made utilizing artificial intelligence.

*This is for every single one of you who puts yourself last.
Who cheers on everyone else, and would drop everything in
the middle of the night for those you love.
Who never wants to be a burden, or be in the way.
Please take care of yourself. You can't pour from an
empty cup.
Be a good girl and let Blake remind you just how deserving
you are.*

Spicy Girls Book Club
TBR

Reading List:

Steel by Eva Simmons
Camera Shy by Kay Cove
Breathtaking by Bella Matthews
Slap Shot Surprise by Melanie Harlow
The Way We Score by Tia Louise
The One I Didn't See Coming by Piper Rayne
Sunlight by Devney Perry
Crazy Love by Willow Aster
All Too Well by Corinne Michaels
Wild Side by Elsie Silver

Content Warnings

Your mental health always comes first! There are some elements in this book that may be triggers for some.

You can find a comprehensive content warning list at the following link:

https://www.kristenprobyauthor.com/potential-trigger-content-warnings

Kristen

Prologue

HARPER

Two Years Ago

One time when we were in the kitchen, and he was getting water out of the fridge, he growled at me like he was a wolf and I was the bunny.

He literally stood there, glared at me as his water bottle filled, and *growled*. Not in a sexy way.

In a ridiculous, I almost laughed way.

He sleeps on the couch, mostly because he knows I hate that. He knows I hate the silent treatment, too.

And he hasn't spoken to me in three weeks. Not a single word.

Why is he behaving this way? What stunt did I pull that was so egregious that it earned this behavior from the one person in the world who's supposed to love me more than anyone else?

Because I picked up an extra shift at the hospital and couldn't go with him to his buddy's party earlier this month.

That's all. I went to work.

I'm a nurse, and we were short-staffed, so I picked up a shift, and to punish me, my fiancé hasn't spoken a word to me in almost a month and treats me like I'm the shit on his shoe.

Honestly, the silence has been great.

And his ignoring me has created the space I need to plan my exit strategy.

Because after three years of putting up with his mood swings, lectures, body shaming, and cheating on me with just about anyone with a heartbeat, *I'm over it.*

I've been over it for a while but didn't have anywhere to go.

Okay, that's not *entirely* true, and Ava, my best friend since we were twelve, would be appalled and likely slash my tires for even *thinking* that I couldn't go to her. But her family has already done so much for me.

I can't run to the Hendrix family every time life gets hard.

Now, if Nathan—*not Nate. He hates nicknames.*—can just hold on with his silent treatment for three more days, I can leave while he's gone for a work trip this weekend, and it'll all be over.

Am I a chickenshit for packing up and leaving when he's none the wiser?

No. I'm not. Because Nathan can be a violent asshole, and I don't want to chance that this will be the first time he hits me and holds me hostage in our house. Make that *his* house. Because when we chose and bought the pretty little bungalow just outside of Portland, he refused to put me on the mortgage. It's only in Nathan's name, which works well for me.

I have no responsibilities here.

In three more days, I will fly out of Portland to Charlotte, where I've taken my first traveling nurse assignment.

A new life.

Freedom.

Anything but what I've been living.

I'm sitting on the couch with my laptop, looking at used car listings in Charlotte, when Nathan walks into the house, glares at me, and paces into the kitchen.

He often comes home on his lunch breaks. I used to think it was because he wanted to hang out with me, but now I know it's because he's checking in on me. He doesn't trust me. Not because I've ever done anything to betray his trust—aside from planning my escape—but because Nathan himself isn't trustworthy. So he comes home every day on his lunch break to make sure I'm where I say I am.

I refuse to share my location on my phone.

He doesn't say a word as he makes himself a sandwich, and I continue staring at my computer.

"We need to talk," he says, startling me.

I don't immediately look his way. My heart is thumping. *Shit.* He couldn't have continued his tantrum for three more freaking days?

"Did you fucking hear me, dumbass?"

I scowl and look his way. "So talk."

His blue eyes narrow on me in malice. "You're such a piece of shit. You know that, right? You're a mediocre nurse at best. No one besides me can even stand to be around you."

His eyes move over my body in disgust.

"Christ, do you ever get off that couch?"

Fuck you.

Fuck you up the ass with no lube.

It's amazing how kind and sweet and tender he is with me when we're around other people, but when it's just the two of us, the monster comes out to play.

And I can already see where this is going. He's decided to move on to the lecture, torment, make-me-feel-smaller-than-a-snail part of his agenda. He does this often. Several times, he's locked me in a bedroom and *screamed* at me for hours on end.

But not today.

Not ever again.

Slowly, I close the laptop and stand, pushing my feet into my shoes. Over the past week, I've packed most of my clothes and the few sentimental items I own, which isn't much at all, and shipped them to Ava in our hometown of Silver Springs, Montana.

She'll forward them to me when I need them.

There's nothing here in this house that I can't replace.

Including Nathan.

"What the fuck are you doing? I told you we need to talk, so sit your lazy ass down."

Without a word, I walk to the front door and loop my handbag over my head and across my body. I still have my car because I'm not selling it to the buyer I found until Friday, so I grab my keys and open the front door.

"WHERE THE FUCK DO YOU THINK YOU'RE GOING, HARPER?"

I stop and look back at him. Once upon a time, I thought he was so handsome. He's tall with all that thick blond hair and bright blue eyes, and he has a body that most of us drool over.

But he's fucking rotten on the inside.

"You don't get to speak to me ever again."

I push out of the house and walk to my car, get inside, and start the engine.

He doesn't follow me.

He's probably still standing there with his mouth hanging open.

And finally, for the first time in three years, I'm free of him.

It feels amazing.

With shaky hands, I drive to a nice hotel closer to the airport, and when I approach the desk, the receptionist smiles.

"Good morning. How can I help you?"

I clear my throat. "I just left my piece-of-shit fiancé, and I need a room for two nights, please."

The woman—Monica, according to her name tag—

tilts her head to the side, her smile gone, looking at me with sharp eyes. "Are you okay, honey?"

"I'm way better than I was thirty minutes ago."

She nods, types on her keyboard, then offers me a half smile. "One presidential suite for the basic room rate coming up. I'll send up some champagne in thirty."

I blink at her, and for the first time in a long time, I feel like crying.

The kindness of this stranger is what finally breaks me?

Pressing my lips together, I take my credit card and driver's license back from her and nod.

"Thank you."

"It's my pleasure. Congratulations, Miss Newman."

Chapter One

BLAKE

"It's wild to me that Bitterroot Valley is so socked in with fog and snow that we can't land there, but it's not bad at all here in Missoula."

With her hand still clutched in mine, the gorgeous woman next to me stares out the airport windows to watch the snow drift down softly as we wait for our luggage.

She's not my girlfriend.

She's definitely not my wife.

This intriguing woman is a complete stranger to me, but I absolutely do *not* want to let go of her hand.

The minute she stepped foot on that plane, I felt it. An immediate attraction. A connection. And not simply because she's gorgeous.

I met her less than two hours ago on a flight from Denver to Montana, thanks to a medical emergency mid-flight with another passenger.

I was asked to help because I'm a doctor, and she was

sitting next to the patient. She couldn't have been better with him. She knew exactly how to calm him down, how to keep him engaged and his mind off being scared.

I loved that she told us about how sad she gets after losing a patient of her own. And when it was time to leave the plane, I knew I couldn't leave her behind.

All I know about her is that her name is Harper, she's a NICU nurse by trade, and with all that dark hair and gray eyes, she's so fucking beautiful. I can't take my eyes off her.

But when she tried to walk out of my life at the end of that tarmac, I told her she'd be with me and I offered her my hand.

It wasn't a question or a request.

And she didn't argue. If Harper were *my* sister, I'd punch myself in the face. But she's not. She's a beautiful woman, and I'm not ready to say goodbye yet.

We're stuck in Missoula for the night, thanks to the early winter storm happening at home in Bitterroot Valley.

And I plan to make the most of it.

"Are you okay?" she asks, peering up at me with those gray eyes.

I'm fucking fantastic. Never better.

"I'm fine. And you? Will your family be upset if you don't make it home in time for Thanksgiving?"

Yes, this is my way of asking about her family. *Mine* will not be thrilled that I won't make it home in time for dinner.

"They'll be okay." She shrugs a shoulder, then points

when she sees her black-and-red suitcase with a bright yellow ribbon on the handle come around on the carousel. "That's me."

I muscle it off the belt for her and set it on its wheels. Then I spot my own luggage, and before long, we're walking away from baggage claim.

"I could just rent a car," she says thoughtfully as we walk, each one of us rolling our bags, still holding hands. "It's only a couple of hours from here."

"In a storm," I remind her, shaking my head. "Let's find a hotel for the night."

She lifts an eyebrow, and her lips tip up with humor. Gray eyes flash. "Wow. Does that line work on all the nurses you pick up on rerouted flights, or am I just the lucky one?"

I grin at her. Christ, she's pretty. Even dressed so casually in leggings and a hoodie, with her hair up in a messy bun and in her glasses.

No makeup.

Absolutely fucking perfect.

And I can tell that she's attracted to me, too. This isn't one-sided. She's still letting me hold her hand, for fuck's sake.

"Two rooms," I reply, shaking my head. "I'm not trying to be a creep or anything."

"Good to know. I'll order an Uber."

"Already done," I reply, chuckling when she narrows her eyes at me. "And you're welcome to join me."

Now, she bites her lip. "Okay, I'm going to be brutally honest."

"Please do."

"You don't seem like a serial killer."

"Glad to hear it."

"But, Dr. Blackwell, I don't even know your first name."

I smile at her, nodding. "Blake. Thirty-four. Family practice and ER doc from Bitterroot Valley. The middle child out of five, I *will* likely catch some shit for not making it to dinner tomorrow, especially from my niece, Birdie, who is six and the apple of my eye. I'm not married or otherwise attached."

She's blinking at me, listening with wide eyes, and nods slowly.

"Your turn," I tell her.

"Uh, let's see. Harper I'm-Not-Telling-You-My-Last-Name. Thirty. NICU nurse, as you know. No siblings. Hell, no parents."

I tighten my hand around hers, but she doesn't seem to notice.

"My best friend and *her* family will miss me tomorrow, but like I said, they'll be chill about it. I like your niece's name."

I grin at that.

"We're all B names. My parents thought it was fun."

"Totally fun," she agrees with a nod. "You know, you could have made all of that up and could still be a serial killer."

I sigh and purse my lips. "You're right. I could have. Well, I guess you'll have to trust me."

"Or I could say goodbye and go fend for myself like the grown adult I am."

I lean into her, not touching her, and press my lips to the soft skin just below her ear.

Fuck me, she smells good.

"You don't want to do that, do you, Harper?" I pull back and hook a loose piece of her hair behind her ear. She licks her lips. *Yeah, she's fucking attracted to me.* "I promise I'm not a danger to you."

She huffs out a laugh. "Why not live on the wild side, right?"

My Uber pulls up to the curb, and I load our suitcases into the trunk. The ride to the hotel is quiet as we take in the snow around us, getting heavier by the minute, and then we're pulling up to the hotel.

Harper walks next to me as we approach the front desk.

"How can I help you?" the receptionist asks.

"We need two rooms, please," I tell her, and she types away on her keyboard.

"Do you have a reservation?"

"No," I reply.

She hums, wrinkling her nose. "Well, with it being the day before Thanksgiving and so many flights canceled, we only have one room left. However, it *is* a suite."

I glance at Harper, who shrugs.

"We'll take it." I nod and pass her my credit card, just as Harper offers her credit card as well. "Don't worry, I've got this."

"No way—"

"You can buy dinner," I tell her, and she frowns at me as I get the room squared away with the nice receptionist.

On the way up to the room in the elevator, I glance down at the woman beside me. She's worrying her bottom lip between her teeth.

"I'll take the couch," I inform her. "Just laying that all out there now so there's no awkwardness later."

"You're super tall," she reminds me, and then her eyes skim over my chest and shoulders. "And ... *broad*. I should probably take the couch."

"Let's see the room before we make any decisions," I suggest as the elevator comes to a stop, and we walk out onto our floor.

Our suite is at the end of the hallway. I open the door, and Harper slides past me, pulling her suitcase behind her.

"Well then." She whistles and looks around the spacious space. "Big room."

A couch and chair are arranged in front of a television, and the dining room table along one wall sits six.

Through a doorway is the bedroom with a king bed, and the bathroom is big enough for a soaking tub *and* a standing shower that would easily accommodate both of us.

I'm not going to lie. I'd love to fuck her in that shower.

"I'll fit on that couch," I inform her, although I

sincerely hope that by the time it's time for bed, I'll be in the king with her.

Harper is gorgeous, smart, and completely fuckable.

And I've recently had a dry streak when it comes to sex.

I don't do relationships. Ever. My schedule is too messy, and I'm married to the hospital. No woman should feel like she's secondary to anything, especially a job, and that is unapologetically my priority in life.

But I have casual sex down to a science.

"Are you hungry?" she asks, and I lift an eyebrow.

Harper rolls her eyes, making me laugh.

"For *dinner*, Romeo. I didn't grab anything before the flight. There's a restaurant downstairs."

"Then we'd best go get some dinner," I reply with a nod.

"Hold that thought." She raises a finger and pulls her phone out of her pocket. "I have to let Ava know that I won't be in tonight."

I nod and give her privacy. I use the bathroom and freshen up from the flight. When I return to the living room, she's just finishing her call.

"I know, it sucks, but I can't control the weather, you know. Yeah, I'm safe." She turns and looks at me and bites that plump lip again. "I promise I'll keep you posted. I don't have a return ticket, remember? You'll get plenty of time with me. Jesus, Ava, you're fucking needy."

That makes me chuckle, and Harper smiles back at me.

Fuck, that smile.

"Yeah, yeah, love and blah, blah." I lift an eyebrow, and she rolls her eyes. "Yes. Yes. No. Okay, *Mom*, eat some turkey for me. I'll be there as soon as I can, clingy girl. Okay, bye."

She lets out a gusty exhale, closes her eyes, and shakes her head.

"That girl needs a boyfriend. Hold on, I'm going to wash my hands."

She strides into the bathroom, and I shove my hands in my pockets.

Jesus. I like her.

When she's finished, we walk back down the hallway to the elevator.

"This place isn't bad at all," she says as we climb on the elevator, and I hit the button for the lobby.

"Do you stay in a lot of hotels?"

"Actually, yeah. I do." She shrugs and leans back against the wall. "I'm a traveling nurse. I usually only stay in one place for about a month. Lots of hotels. Not all of them are awesome."

"I bet they're not."

Traveling nurse. I'm intrigued. I can't imagine being in a new place every month. That's a lot of moving around.

"What made you decide to go the traveling route?" I ask after the hostess leads us to a table and leaves us with the menus.

Harper sighs and sips her water, eyeing me, and I can tell she's trying to decide how much to tell me.

I'm a perfect stranger.

But I want to know everything I can find out about her in our short time together.

"I had a piece-of-shit ex who I needed to get away from."

Fire.

Fire rolls through me at that admission, but she keeps talking, oblivious to the fact I'd like to hurt the idiot who made her feel that she had to run from him.

"That was two years ago." She shrugs that shoulder again and looks down at the menu. "I like the job. And it's not like I have anything permanent to get back to, so going where I'm needed is rewarding."

She bites her lip as if she's said too much.

"I think I'll get the chicken Caesar." She pushes the menu away and watches me for a minute through those glasses.

"Are you originally from Bitterroot Valley?" I ask. I don't think she is. It's a small community, and I know for a fact that I've never seen her before, even in passing.

"Silver Springs," she says, and I nod.

That's an even *smaller* community just thirty minutes from Bitterroot Valley.

"You?" she asks.

"Yeah, I'm from Bitterroot Valley."

"So you went away to medical school and came back home."

"I did." The server returns, and we put our orders in. Then we're silent for a moment as we look at each other over the table. "But let's not talk about work."

She lifts a perfect eyebrow. "Okay. What would you like to talk about?"

"You."

She snorts, then raises her water glass to her lips and takes a sip. "I'm *very* boring. This will be a short conversation."

"Somehow, I doubt that. Favorite movie?"

"Like of *all time*?"

My lips tip up at the confused frown on her pretty little face. "Yes."

"Easy. *Captain America: The First Avenger*."

I blink at her. *Holy shit.* "Nice choice."

"Yours?"

"Same. Favorite kind of music?"

"Psh. Seventies rock. Hello, have you *heard* 'Dream On' by Aerosmith?"

How did my favorite song of all time just come tumbling out of her perfect mouth?

"If you could only eat one thing for the rest of your—"

"Loaded pizza *with* anchovies. But that's only if the carbs no longer count in your fictional world."

"You don't eat carbs?"

"I'm not an animal. *Of course* I eat carbs." She lays her napkin in her lap as our meals are served. "But I try to choose gluten-free as much as I can, just because it's better for inflammation. But I'm not perfect at it. I'm not allergic or anything."

I nod and dig into my own Caesar. It sounded good when she mentioned it. "My niece, Birdie—"

"The apple of your eye."

"And the love of my life," I reply with a nod, "has celiac disease. So when we get together as a family, we make sure we have plenty of safe options for her. That poor kid was so sick for such a long time, it broke my damn heart."

"Poor baby." She frowns over at me. "Can I see a picture of her?"

Not needing to be asked twice, I whip my phone out and happily share photos of my girl.

"Oh, she's precious." Harper takes my phone and smiles down at my girl. "She's a dancer."

"Yeah. My brother's girlfriend, soon-to-be fiancée, owns a dance studio in Bitterroot Valley, and Birdie couldn't wait to join. She's actually pretty good."

"And that's not just her unbiased uncle talking."

Harper passes the phone back and digs back into her food.

"Never. I'm completely impartial." I chuckle and shove my phone back in my pocket.

"What do you do when you aren't at the hospital?" she asks.

"I spend a lot of time with my family," I reply, thinking it over. "I like to hike in the summer."

That has her pretty gray eyes sparking with interest. "Yeah? Do you have favorite trails?"

"I take it you hike?"

"I love anything outside." She decides to whip her hoodie over her head, leaving her in a little T-shirt. She hooks the hoodie on the back of her chair. "I spend so much time in hospitals that I can't wait to be outside. So yeah, I hike and bike and ski. Swim. All that stuff. It was pretty cool to travel so much because I'd be out finding local trails on my off days. I've hiked the Appalachian Trail, all through the Redwoods, Olympic National Park, which is *unbelievable*."

"I've done Kilimanjaro," I inform her, watching her jaw drop and her eyes widen.

"Holy shit, Blake. That's incredible. Did you love it?"

"It was an interesting experience."

Honestly, it was fucking lonely.

"Your cool factor just increased," she admits, and I laugh as I take one last bite of salad, then push the plate away.

"Good to know. I should have led with that."

Chapter Two

HARPER

Why does he have to be so damn handsome, funny, *and* he likes to hike? Not just little hikes, either.

The man has done Kilimanjaro.

When he said that, my core tightened, and I'm pretty sure my vagina cried out with joy.

Down, girl.

I have avoided men like the plague for the past two years. No sex. No dates. No talking to men at all unless they were at work.

No. Men.

I'll be the fun aunt once Ava or one of her brothers decides to settle down and pop out kids. I take care of babies every day at work.

I do *not* need a man in my life.

In fact, life's been pretty decent the past couple of years without one.

And then I had to get on that flight.

I noticed Blake sitting in first class when I boarded. He was watching me. There was ... *something* there. A little tingle. A little hint of awareness.

And then I ignored it.

Until the passenger next to me started having what I was sure were heart attack symptoms, and I asked the flight attendant to find me a doctor.

Dr. First Class came to save the day.

And then, after we landed and got the patient safely loaded into an ambulance, he simply held his hand out for mine as if it was the easiest, most normal thing in the world, *and I took it.*

Without a second thought, I slipped my palm against his, and we stayed that way for, like, an hour.

At least, it felt like an hour.

And now, I'm sharing a hotel room with him, and I'm sitting across from him at dinner, and this is starting to feel like a damn date.

With the sexiest man I've seen in, well, *ever.*

Holy muscles, Batman.

This man has plenty to bring to the gun show, let me tell you. His biceps bulge against the sleeves of the green Henley he's wearing. I might spontaneously combust if I try to imagine what they look like in a scrub top.

And don't even get me started on the sharp jawline, the dark hair, and the brown eyes with flecks of gold.

Did I mention the muscles?

So sue me, I'm attracted to men who work out. Probably because I share that interest. I work out. I eat okay, although I have a massive addiction to sugar, so I work out a little extra, and I'm blessed with a decent metabolism. Those genetics were the only good thing my parents ever gave me.

"Can I get you some dessert?" the server asks as she's picking up our empty plates.

"Do you have pie?" I ask her. Even I can hear the desperation in my voice.

Not sorry.

"We have apple and pumpkin pie," she says with a nod.

I bite my lip and catch Blake grinning at me.

"What?"

"Nothing."

I narrow my eyes at him. "Don't judge me for loving sugar more than anything on the planet."

"More than *anything*?"

I ignore his question and turn to the server, who's watching us with a grin. "I'll have apple."

"And I'll have the other," Blake jumps in, and I sigh in relief.

"Thank God. I'll distract you and steal a bite."

"No need to distract me." He laughs.

"You two are adorable together," the server says before walking away.

I blink rapidly and stare down at my hands.

What are you doing?

No flirting with the sexiest man alive, Harper.

Bad.

Bad girl.

"Harper."

Why does his voice have to be deep and gravelly and make my nipples pucker? *Stand down, nipples.*

"Harper."

"Sorry, I was daydreaming about pie."

He smirks, but I can tell he doesn't buy it.

The server returns way faster than I expected and sets both plates of pie on the table, but I put them both in the middle, making Blake's eyebrows wing up.

"Do you hate apple pie?" I ask.

"No."

"Then we'll just share them. Because really, who can choose between these two on the day before Thanksgiving?"

I grab a clean fork and dig in, sit back, and sigh in happiness.

"Jesus," he mutters, and when I open my eyes, he's scowling.

"What?"

"You make some sexy fucking noises when you eat."

I blink at him. What am I supposed to say to that?

Rather than try to think of something, I take another bite of pie and really work at *not* moaning.

Honest, I truly try.

But I can't help it because that might be the best pumpkin pie I've ever eaten.

Blake clears his throat.

"Sorry," I mutter. "It's not my fault. The pie is delicious."

His jaw clenches. His dark eyes narrow on me.

And I clench my thighs because this look he's giving me screams *I want to fuck you right here on this table.*

It's damn satisfying.

And when we're finished with the pie, I insist on paying for dinner.

"You *promised*," I remind him when he looks like he wants to argue. "Don't be that guy, Blake."

"Which guy?"

"The one who makes empty promises."

He shakes his head and lets me slip my card into the folder with the check. Once we're all paid up, we walk back to the elevator.

He slips his hand in mine and weaves our fingers together as he hits the button for our floor.

The air is static. My heart is hammering, and I'm ... *hot.* It's been such a long time since I had sex, I don't know if I even remember how.

But something tells me *he* knows.

I bite my lip as I watch the numbers climb above the door, and then they open, and Blake leads me down the hall, my hand still firmly in his.

He unlocks the door with the card and pushes it open. I step inside with him, then walk to the middle of the living room, turn to face him, and we spend ten seconds just staring.

It's a silent conversation.

Can I touch you?
Yes.
Can I fuck you?
Please do.

It won't happen just one time, Harper.

Thank God. Please get naked.

And then he's on the move and crashes into me after three long strides. He frames my face, and his lips cover mine, and I am completely lost to him.

Lost to this intense chemistry. Because holy shit, do we have *chemistry*.

Blake Blackwell might very well ruin me for all other men.

And I'm totally okay with that.

"Fuck, you taste so damn sweet," he growls against my lips.

"It's the pie."

"No, sugar, it's *you*."

I push my stomach against his pelvis, and we both groan. He's hard and long, and *holy shit*, he's big.

That makes sense because Blake, as a whole, is *big*. Well over six feet, with broad shoulders, he's a large specimen of a man.

And for tonight, he's *all mine*.

My hands make a dive for his shirt, pulling it out of his pants and up so I can touch his warm skin and brush my fingers over his sculpted abs. The kind of abs that make a girl sweat.

Or maybe that's just me.

He groans low in his throat as he follows suit, yanking my shirt over my head and tossing it aside, and then he flicks my bra open, and that goes sliding down my arms to the floor.

"Christ, you're beautiful," he mutters as he kisses

down to my jawline. His hands skim over my breasts, down my sides, and then he's cupping my ass, and I'm airborne with my legs wrapped around his waist, and he's heading right for the bedroom. "If you don't want this, say so now, Harper. You're in control here."

"Do. Not." I bite his neck. "Stop."

Chapter Three
BLAKE

Her hands are in my hair, her legs are around my waist, and I can't even make it to the bed.

I brace her against the wall so I can devour her, kissing the fuck out of her. She tastes like sugar and smells like fucking sunshine.

"Fuck, you're perfect," I mutter against her lips.

"Too many clothes," she says before nipping at the corner of my mouth. "Strip, Blake."

It's hot as fuck that she's as revved as I am about losing the clothes, then losing ourselves in each other.

I let her down to her feet, and then we both peel out of the rest of our clothes. Shoes, socks, and pants are all shed, and when she's standing in front of me in just her simple blue panties, I feel like I'm going to fucking explode.

"Jesus," I breathe.

"I don't have protection with me," she rasps.

"I do." I kiss her hard. "Stay. Right. Here."

I run to my bag, open it, and fish around for the few condoms I threw in *just in case*, then rush back to her.

She hasn't moved a muscle, and that makes me smile.

Without a word, she jumps in my arms, and I carry her to the bed. I toss the condoms on the bedside table, pull the covers back, then gently lay her in the middle of the king mattress.

She starts to wiggle into a sitting position, but I press my hand on her sternum.

"Stay down."

"You're bossy."

A salacious grin spreads over my face. "You have no idea." I hook my fingers into the elastic of her underwear and tug them down her legs, over her feet, and bring them to my nose.

"*Blake.*" She looks scandalized.

"You smell better than fucking pie."

She bites that lip, and I spread her wide, and suddenly, she throws her arm over her face and stops watching me.

Oh, hell no.

"Don't you dare hide from me." I push up and over her, gently move her arm aside, and brush my lips over hers. "Look at me, Harper."

She cracks one eye.

"All the way. Look at me, beautiful."

She sighs and opens those gorgeous gray eyes, and I see the hesitation. The embarrassment. And that's fucking unacceptable.

"There you are. You're beautiful. Every inch of you.

I'm going to feast on your pretty pink pussy until you pass out."

She goes to cover her face again, but I hold her wrist and kiss her hand.

"No hiding."

"I'm ... *not*."

"And no lying."

"Blake." She licks her lips. "I haven't shaved *down there* in—"

"Don't fucking care." I kiss her again, deeply. "I absolutely *don't care.* Honest."

She winces, takes a breath, and then sighs. "Okay."

Instead of kissing down her delectable little body the way I want to, I nibble across her shoulder and let my hand journey down her flat and toned stomach, over her pubis and the soft curls there, and right into her sopping wet pussy.

"Fuck, you're already so beautifully wet for me."

I press one finger inside her, circle her already hard bundle of nerves with my thumb, and grin against her skin when she moans and moves her hips.

"So responsive. Christ, you're squeezing the fuck out of my finger. You're so tight."

She licks her lips again and widens her legs, silently begging for more.

"What do you need, Harper?"

"You."

I hum into her neck. "I like the sound of that. I'm right here. I've got you. What else do you need?"

I pull my finger out and push two inside. She moans

long and deep, her hips lift off the bed, and I smile down into her face as I pull my fingers out and bring them up to my lips, sucking them clean.

"You taste like fucking heaven."

Then I kiss her so she can taste herself. Her hand moves down my side and over my ass, and I can't help but flex into her touch.

"Mmm," she moans against me. "More."

"I'm going to fuck you," I assure her, brushing her hair off her cheek. "But first, my face is going to be buried in your perfect pussy. You'll come on my tongue before you come on my cock. Got it?"

"Holy shit."

Her pupils dilate, and I kiss her chin before I move down her body, nudging her legs wider with my shoulders.

And when my tongue laps up her core, through all of that wet heat, Harper moans. Her hands dive into my hair, and I. Fucking. Feast.

I've wanted to do this since the moment I saw her on that plane. I want to consume her. I want to ravage her.

When I'm finished with this woman, no other man will ever exist for her. No one else will ever come close to being enough.

I settle in to take my time. I lick at her opening, drinking her juices as my fingers gently play with her lips.

And she moans.

I pull those lips into my mouth and suck with tiny pulses, making her squirm, and her hands tighten in my hair.

And then, I push my tongue deep inside her, move my nose over her clit, and she fucking explodes. Her climax is spectacular. Her legs shake, her hips pulse, and she makes a fucking *mess* of my face.

"Good girl." I pepper kisses all over her inner thighs as I reach for the condoms. After opening one, I slide it over my pulsing, angry cock. "You're fucking *amazing*, Harper."

Her glassy eyes are greedy as she watches me protect us both. I cover her once more and brace myself on my elbows on either side of her head. My cock rests in her heat, gently moving back and forth.

With my eyes on hers, I pull back and line the head of my cock up at her opening and push inside her in one steady, firm thrust. I don't stop until I'm fully seated, and we're both breathing hard.

"Fuck, you're tight. So damn incredible."

I stare down into stormy eyes and feel something shift inside me.

I *don't* do relationships.

But this girl could be a game changer.

I start to move, dragging through her tight-as-fuck pussy, pulling out to the crown and pushing back in again.

"Harder," she whispers against my lips.

I can't help but smile.

Fucking gladly.

I pick up the pace and slam into her harder, and she sighs. "Yes. *Harder*, Blake."

Pulling out, I flip her over and yank on her hips so

she's on her knees, then slam into her from behind. She cries out, her fists in the sheets.

"Yes! Oh fuck, yes."

I slap her ass and smooth my hand up her spine to her hair. With the flick of my wrist, I release the bun, and then I fist those thick strands, tug back, and *fuck her*.

The fast pace is hard and almost punishing.

And this girl fucking *loves it*.

"Blake. Fuck yes."

"You like it rough, sweetheart?"

She tries to nod, but I'm holding her hair so tight that she can hardly move.

"You want me to ruin this pussy? When I get done with you, you won't walk right for a month."

She whimpers as I reach around and pinch her nipple, then my hand glides down to her clit, and I pinch that, too.

Harper doesn't want it soft and sweet.

She wants it *rough*.

And I'm happy to fucking deliver.

She's pushing back against me, meeting me thrust for thrust. Her ass is *perfect*. Round and muscular, it fits in my hand like it was made for me.

Her pussy tightens, and I feel the ripples start. She's going to come again.

"Fuck, you're amazing," I growl against her back. "Come for me, Harper. Come all over me."

She starts to shiver, and the noises she makes are almost supernatural. I *love* it. I love that she isn't quiet or inhibited.

She's pure sensual lust.

And I know that one night with her will never be enough.

She comes long and hard, and my own climax is *right there*. I'm right on the edge.

What does Harper do?

She reaches beneath her, cups my balls, and I fucking explode, rocking into her through the orgasm that seems to rip my very soul from my body.

And when I collapse to the side of her, she grins at me, still panting hard.

"Not bad," she says.

I slap her ass, and she moans.

"Pretty good."

I bite her arm.

"Okay, you should have gold medals. Is that what you want to hear?"

I laugh and pull her against me. Kiss the fuck out of her and love the way her leg wraps up around my hip.

I'm going to fuck her all night.

And for the first time in my life, I'm going to share breakfast with a woman.

I can't fucking wait.

There's a sliver of light in the room when I open one eye.

It's not quite daybreak yet. Which is good because I plan to draw Harper a bath and then order room service.

We fucked again in the bed, then made it to the shower, where I fucked her some more.

Then we dropped dead into sleep.

I don't know if I've ever slept that good.

I roll over to see her sweet face and stop short when I discover I'm the only one in this bed. And when I touch the sheets where she was, they're cool. She's been gone for a while.

She left.

I get out of the bed and check the rest of the suite to make sure she's not simply in the bathroom, or in the living room, but her bags are gone.

She's gone.
Well, fuck.

Chapter Four

HARPER

"Are you ready for your first day?"

My head comes up in surprise, and I grin at Ava, who's standing in the kitchen, holding two to-go cups of coffee from Buzz, our favorite coffee shop in Silver Springs. Ava knows the code to the front door, and it's pretty standard for us *not* to knock when we visit.

"I'm ready." I ignore the nervous butterflies making a mess of my stomach and take one of the offered cups. Taking a sip, I sigh in happiness. "You didn't have to bring me coffee, but I'm glad you did."

"Are you kidding? I *finally* got my bestie to move back home permanently. I'm going to be kissing your ass for the foreseeable future." She eyes the few boxes I own currently sitting in the foyer of the gigantic house I'm staying in, thanks to Ava's brother, Xander. Xander is a hockey *superstar* who's rarely home. He usually just spends a month or so in the summer in Silver Springs and most holidays. Otherwise, he's living the celebrity life in Denver, where he's basically a god.

I mean, Xander's hot. And talented. I get it. And I'm grateful he bought this mountain mansion. Because when he found out that I was moving home, he called me and essentially forced me to live here.

Not that it's a hardship. This place is *huge*. Six bedrooms, eight bathrooms, and a view of the mountains that makes my heart hurt, it's so gorgeous. There's no way in hell I could ever afford this on my generous nurse's salary.

So when Xander told me to housesit for him until I figure out where I want to live, I didn't resist too hard.

"Which room did you pick?" Ava asks.

"The green room."

She wrinkles her nose. "Is it weird that I decorated every room in different colors?"

"No, it's pretty."

Ava is a highly sought-after interior decorator, so *of course* she sank her teeth into this place after her brother bought it.

"And you didn't go too crazy. I like the green rug and pillows against the white and natural wood of everything else. It's not *precious*. It's ... classy."

"Okay, good." She sighs dramatically and pushes her auburn hair over one shoulder. "Also, the green room has that excellent balcony with a view of the mountains."

"That's why I chose it," I reply, tying my sneakers. I'm already dressed in my pink scrubs. I had orientation last week, where I got my badge, signed a contract, and had a tour of Bitterroot Valley General.

My *only* hesitation at taking the job as charge nurse in the NICU in that hospital was the very real possibility of running into one Dr. Blackwell.

It's not a huge hospital.

It's very likely I'll see him.

But dammit, I'll figure it out if and when it happens because I *needed* to come home. Ava's dad was diagnosed as a diabetic, and the whole family has been turned on its head. Greg Hendrix raised me and gave me a home, so of course I came back to help. I need this family as much as they need me.

Besides, it feels good to be back. I missed the mountains and everything familiar to me. I was ready. And I refuse to stay away from my *home* simply because a man I once had the best sex of my life with also lives here.

I'm an adult. I can handle this.

"You're going to kill it."

I glance at my best friend. "What's that?"

"I think you're quiet because you're nervous, but you don't need to be. You're the *best*, Harpsichord. The best baby nurse ever. The hospital is lucky to have you."

"I love that you're so good at being a best friend." I pull her in and give her a smacking kiss on the cheek. "What do you have going on today?"

"Clients, meetings with a couple of contractors. The usual." She lifts a shoulder. "Then I'm coming over here tonight with some vodka and olives, and we're going to pour us some dirty martinis and talk about your first day."

"Deal." I grin and grab my coffee, my sack lunch and purse, and we leave Xander's house, lock the door, and head for Ava's pretty little Lexus. "Thanks for the ride, by the way. I'll buy something sooner or later."

"You could drive Xander's car," she reminds me as she fires up the engine.

"He drives a *Maserati*," I remind her. "No way. With my luck, I'll get in a fender bender that costs more to fix than I make in a year."

She smirks at that as we pull away from the house and toward the highway that leads us to Bitterroot Valley.

Silver Springs is a neighboring town, less than thirty minutes away, and Xander lives roughly halfway between the two towns, so it's extra convenient for me to live at his place. Much less of a commute this way.

And Ava's office is in Bitterroot Valley too, so I'm on her way to work.

Super handy.

"When do you start the night shift?" she asks.

"I have three days of days, three days off, then four nights on, then two days off. That repeats. I'll be a zombie, but it's fine. I don't mind the night shift. I'll do my best to have a car by then, though, because there is no world where you should have to get up at, like, five to pick me up from work."

She nods and reaches over to pat my leg. "Thank you. Not just for the car thing, but for coming home when I told you I needed you."

"You should have told me months ago. I'm your family, Aves. If you need me, I come home. That's the rule."

She lets out a gusty breath. "Well, there wasn't a position open at the hospital that you'd want."

"Are you telling me that you kept an eye on the *want ads* so you could talk me into moving home?"

"I'm not *not* telling you that." She laughs and puts on her blinker to turn into the parking lot. "What will you do if you run into Dr. Big Dick?"

I choke on the coffee I just sipped and do my best not to spill all over myself.

"Ava!"

"What? It's an honest question."

Ava's the only one in the world who knows what happened last Thanksgiving, five months ago. As soon as I walked into her condo, she started drilling me because she said I had *freshly fucked* written all over my face.

"I'll say hello. I don't know. I'm trying not to think about it. Besides, he's in the ER, and he works in his clinic. We're in separate parts of the hospital. I probably won't run into him."

"Famous last words," she mutters, then smiles sweetly. "For what it's worth, I hear the Blackwell family is nice. Tucker knows their oldest brother, Brooks."

Of course, he does.

Because this is a tiny community, and we were destined to have some overlap somewhere.

"How does your brother know his brother?"

"Brooks owns the auto shop here in Bitterroot Valley.

I guess Tuck uses that shop. And they'd probably be about the same age." She shrugs a shoulder. "Also, sidebar, there's a new bookstore in town. We need to check it out. It's all romance."

Okay, that grabs my interest.

I listen to a *lot* of audiobooks while I hike, and I always have my e-reader on me at work for when the night shift is quiet, and I'm just making sure all the sleeping babies are safe and happy.

"Yes, please," I reply as she pulls up to a stop. "On my first day off, it's happening. Okay, have a good day, dear."

"I'll pick you up when you're done," she says with a grin. "This is *so fun*."

With a shake of my head, I climb out of her car, wave, and walk inside. I head right up to the Neonatal Intensive Care Unit and set my personal things in the locker assigned to me last week, then walk out to the nurses' station, where my supervisor, Liz, grins at me.

"You're here," she says. "Welcome. You can set your water right here. This will be your computer today."

I nod and sit down, and a half hour later, I've been shown pretty much everything there is to know, along with current patients, doctors in house and on call, their numbers, and I've met my fellow nurses.

Thankfully, I already know the computer system, as I've worked with the same one several times before, so there won't be a learning curve there.

"We rotate duties," Liz says. "Some days, you'll be on grower duty, watching over the little ones who need to get bigger before they go home. On other shifts, you'll be with the sick babies. Today, I have you flexing between the two, along with any issues that come up from L&D."

I nod but internally roll my eyes. I am *not* a labor and delivery nurse. Some people are excellent at that, and I respect them, but it's just not my calling.

But I'm not officially in charge of anything for two weeks while I get my bearings. And that's okay.

"We have a baby in room 9, on the delivery floor, who will need a peek," Liz says. "I'll let you handle that. He's a couple of hours old, and we just got a call that he's breathing a little fast and doesn't want to latch onto Mom."

"On it." I nod and gather my stethoscope, loop it over my head, and head to the elevator. "See you soon."

L&D is one floor down, so it only takes me a few seconds to make my way to the room, where I see a dark-haired mom in the bed, crying, trying to figure out what to do with her tiny newborn.

And she's alone.

"Hey there," I say with a bolstering smile. "I'm Harper, and I hear you might need an extra hand."

"Oh, thank God. I don't know why I told my husband it was okay to go have breakfast with his brother," she says with a sniff. "I'm Dani."

Yep, the baby is breathing fast and laboring with it, but not *horribly*.

"Look at all of that dark hair," I say with a smile as I lean over them. "It's okay, Dani. You've only been doing this for a couple of hours."

"I can't get him to eat," she says with despair. She's

obviously exhausted and worried, and that's not helping the baby either. "He's fighting me."

"Let's figure this out. May I?" I hold my hands out for the baby, and she immediately passes him over. Directly in her line of sight, I lay the baby on the bed and unwrap him. I don't want to worry her, but I want to watch his ribs and chest while he breathes, and I put my stethoscope in my ears so I can listen to him.

"Is he okay?" she asks, brushing her tears away.

"He's just having a hard time catching his breath," I murmur as I listen. His sides are retracting, which means he's laboring. "Dani, do you mind if I take your little man to the nursery, just so I can put the monitor on his toe to check his oxygen levels? I'll bring him right back to you."

"Oh, of course." She bites her lip, and her blue eyes fill again. "Oh God."

"Don't panic." I take her hand in mine and give it a squeeze. "Honest, I'm not panicking, either. I just want to make sure he's getting all the air he needs."

"That makes sense." She nods and swallows down more tears. "Yes, let's make sure."

"I'll be right back."

I set the baby in his mobile crib, scan their wristbands, and roll him to the nursery. Once I get the pulse ox wrapped on his toe, I frown.

Ninety-three.

I don't like that. It's not *horrifying*, but it's not great.

I take his temperature, and it's just a little high at 99.2.

"Little man, you're going to make me work for this, aren't you?"

He's adorable, with all that dark hair. His coloring is good, but I don't like that quick breathing at all.

I note his pediatrician's name and put a call in to her, then wheel him back to his mom.

"Well, Dani, we're going to keep an eye on little Bryce. He's struggling just a little to breathe and has the tiniest fever."

Dani frowns.

"Honestly, the fever could be from the trauma of birth. This fella has been through a lot today."

She nods, her eyes pinned to her baby.

Thankfully, the pediatrician, Dr. Lachland, bustles in behind me.

"Well, hello there," she says, smiling at Dani. "I hear Bryce is breathing a little fast."

Dani bites her lip. "I should call my husband."

"You're more than welcome to do that," I assure her. "Go ahead if it'll make you feel better. Call anyone you need."

She nods and quickly types on her phone while Dr. Lachland goes through the same vitals I did.

"Oxygen was at ninety-three," I tell her.

"You know, Dani," Lachland says after nodding gratefully at me, "there's a chance this is nothing at all. But there's also a chance that Bryce might have aspirated some fluid when he was being delivered, and I want to make sure his lungs are okay. I'd like to do a chest X-ray, and maybe even run some labs to make sure there's no infection."

"He's *two hours old*," Dani says, shaking her head and wiping tears from her cheeks. "How can he already have an infection?"

"It's unlikely," Lachland assures her. "This is preventative."

Just then, two big men enter the room, and I step back out of the way.

"Oh, hello, Dr. Blackwell."

My head comes up at that.

There he is.

Blake Blackwell.

The man who's starred in every dream of mine for the past five months.

The man who gave me more orgasms and rocked my world in ways that have never happened before in my life.

I might be breathing harder than the baby.

He's listening intently to Dr. Lachland, his handsome face in a stern frown, his arms crossed over his chest, and then the doctor is addressing me.

"Harper, let's get Bryce's X-ray done and draw those labs for me, and we'll go from there."

"Of course." I nod and smile at Dani while every nerve in my body quakes.

He's fucking married. There's no other reason for him to be here. He's an ER doctor, not an OB/GYN.

I glance at the card on the bassinet.

Bryce Blackwell.

His last name is on the freaking bassinet.

He cheated on his very pregnant wife *with me.*

Because of course he fucking did.

Jesus Christ, what am I? Some kind of black hole for piece-of-shit men who treat women like garbage?

"He's safe with me, Dani. I promise. I'll bring him right back to you. It shouldn't take long at all. Then we can do some skin-on-skin time, okay?"

"You're so nice," Dani says with a nod as I scan her wristband, the baby's, and then the one on his bassinet card. "Thank you so much, Harper."

Silently fuming, I take the baby to get the labs and X-rays, but before I can close the elevator door, Blake comes running down the hall and slips into the elevator next to me.

Fuck me.

"You work here," he says as the doors close. It's not a question.

"Seems so." My voice is so cold, I'm surprised he doesn't have frostbite. "Congratulations, by the way. He's beautiful. And don't worry, I won't say anything to that gorgeous woman, who deserves *so much better*, you jerk."

He frowns down at me as the doors slide open.

"You should get back to your wife. The baby's safe with me."

And without a backward glance, I roll out of the elevator to get my work done.

This is *not* how I saw today going. I didn't have *run into the hottest sex of your life, who happens to be a new dad and a cheating asshole* on my bingo card for this month at all.

Yet here we are all the same.

I keep an eye on Bryce's pulse ox and am pleased that it never dips lower than ninety-three. In fact, right now, it's ninety-five, which is an improvement.

But when I listen to his lungs again, I hear some gunk in there.

"We're going to fix you up, Bryce. Let's figure this out."

Chapter Five
BLAKE

Just as I'm about to chase an extremely pissed-off Harper, my phone rings, and it's the clinic.

Shit.

Harper's *here*. She's even more gorgeous than I remember, and that's saying a lot. That one night with her has ingrained itself into my entire psyche, and aside from work and family, she's all I think about. I have so many regrets about not getting her last name or asking for her number. Of course, I didn't anticipate she'd sneak out on me. If I knew that was coming, I never would have gone to sleep.

But now she's here, in my hospital, and I have no intention of letting her slip out of my grasp again.

Of course, it would be just my goddamn luck that she thinks I'm fucking married. And we'll have to rectify that situation as soon as fucking possible.

Scowling, I accept the call from my office.

"Dr. Blackwell."

"Hey, Doc, this is Mo at reception. I'm wondering if I should continue rescheduling your day? I got your first hour of the day moved, and I can keep going if you think you'll be at the hospital longer."

I sigh and push my hand through my hair. "Give me another hour, Mo. I need to wrap a few things up here, but I'll be in by"—I check my watch—"ten."

"Got it," she says. "Thanks, see you soon."

I hang up and hurry back to the room where Dani and Bridger are waiting. I hate that Bryce is having issues this morning. After everything Bridger went through with Birdie when she was born so early and so small, this is the last thing my brother needs.

"Did you see him?" Dani asks right away as she pads out of the attached bathroom, and Bridger helps her back into bed.

"Sweetheart, all of this is preventive. They wouldn't be bringing him back to you if we thought he was in distress or failing."

Dani swallows hard and nods as Bridger kisses the top of her head.

"Aspirating fluid isn't uncommon," I continue. "And because they caught it so soon, they can get ahead of it. The antibiotics aren't a bad idea. I'm going to warn you, if they go that route, they'll want to keep him here for seventy-two hours because it'll be IV antibiotics."

"I have to go home *without him*?" Dani asks, her eyes wide in horror. She shakes her head. "Absolutely not."

"Hey, let's not get ahead of ourselves, kitten," Bridger says. "Let's see what they say, okay? Stop working yourself up."

Dani takes a deep breath. "Okay. Did you check in with your parents? How's Birdie?"

"Birdie's great, and she can't wait to meet her baby brother," I reply with a grin. "I FaceTimed them right after the birth and showed Bryce off."

"Good." Dani grins and relaxes a bit. "I don't like being away from her, either."

"You're such an amazing mama," Bridger tells her.

Dani isn't Birdie's biological mom, but she's become a mother to that little girl in every way, and they share a special bond.

"I have to go," I inform them, but then Dr. Lachlan comes back in with a smile.

"The good news is, the CBC didn't show any infection in his little body. We're growing some cultures to make sure. However, the X-ray does show a little fluid in there."

She opens her laptop, brings up the images, and shows them to us.

Sure enough, left superior lobe. *Damn.*

"Harper is suctioning him now. Don't worry, it's annoying but not painful for him at all, and it's probably all done by now. I *do* want to start an antibiotic to prevent any infection and get him started off on the right foot."

"Can he stay in here with me?" Dani asks.

"Absolutely," Dr. Lachlan says. "But we'll watch him and keep an oxygen monitor on his toe. If he doesn't want to eat because he's gasping, please don't panic. We can feed him today until his lungs calm down, and then he can start feeding regularly once his breathing evens out."

Dani sniffs, and her doctor rubs her hand up Dani's arm. "I know this isn't what you expected today, Mom, but this is minor in the grand scheme of things. Bryce is healthy, and his coloring is good. He's just breathing like he went for a jog."

"Well, if he takes after me," Dani says, wiping at her eyes, "he hates that because I don't run."

That makes us chuckle. The doctor finishes, answers questions, and promises to check on Bryce before she sends him back here.

"This sucks," Dani says as she leans against Bridger, who's just climbed on the bed with her and wrapped her in his arms.

He looks ridiculous. He's huge and half of his ass is hanging off the side.

"I'm going to head out," I inform them. "I have to get to the clinic, but I'll check in with you guys between patients. Try to get some rest, you two."

"Thanks, Blake," Dani says, reaching for my hand and giving it a squeeze. "You're the best brother-in-law ever. Don't tell the others."

I smirk, kiss her hand, and pat Bridger on the shoulder before I walk out of their room.

I want to go upstairs to the NICU to peek in on Bryce.

Okay, that's not entirely true. Yes, I want to see my nephew, but I'd also like to see his gorgeous nurse and explain to her that I am absolutely, without question, *not* that baby's dad.

And I'm not married.

And I'm not a fucking liar.

Rather than wait for the elevator, I take the stairs up one flight and walk down the hallway, but before I can reach the NICU, Harper herself comes walking through the doors, wheeling baby Bryce. He really *is* the sweetest little guy.

And I can see he's not panting nearly as much as he was earlier.

"I'm *not* married," I say in greeting, and Harper scowls.

"Okay," she replies, not meeting my gaze, "then I won't say anything to your girlfriend/life partner/fiancée/whatever the hell."

"I don't have any of that either."

She scowls at me, finally looking me in the eyes.

"Bryce is gorgeous, and I love him, but he's not mine."

Her shoulders fall just a bit, and I realize she's relieved.

Not because she was jealous but because she felt *guilty*.

Shit.

"He's Birdie's baby brother. The other guy who was

in that room with us? That's my brother Bridger. And Dani, although yes, she's beautiful and sweet, is Bridger's wife, and I'm one hundred percent sure he'd break my arms off if he thought I even *considered* laying a hand on her. Which I never would."

Harper frowns, swallows hard, and sighs.

"I'm no psychiatrist, but I assume that was a trigger for you."

Now those gray eyes—not behind glasses today—blow wide, and she stares up at me.

"Uh. Yeah. And I apologize."

I nod, and I want to touch her so fucking badly. But this is where we work, and there's more to say at another time and place.

"Apology accepted. Take care of my nephew for me."

"Of course. He's doing better already."

With a smile, I brush my fingertip down his head, over all that thick dark hair, then nod at Harper and walk away.

It feels *wrong* to walk away from her, and I hardly know her.

Hell, aside from knowing how she sounds when she comes, what she likes to eat, and the fact that she enjoys the same music as I do, I *don't* really know her.

But I'm going to.

It's been a fucking *week*.

An entire week of time at the clinic, the ER, getting Bryce home, and trying to fit in time with my family.

This is why I don't pursue relationships. Because I am married to the hospital, having a full-time affair with the clinic, and my family is my sidepiece. Every minute of every day, I've wanted to track Harper down, get her number, take her on a date and then back to my place.

And I don't want that for just one night.

I'm considering starting a ... a *something* with this woman, yet the rest of my life is the same as it's always been. It's not fair to her.

Yet I can't imagine not at least trying.

If she's willing, that is. And I'm going to do my fucking best to persuade her.

After being at the clinic all day, I just finished a twelve-hour shift at the ER. I should go home and crash for the next ten hours. I get thirty-six hours off, and then it's back in the clinic the next day.

However, I refuse to leave until I know if Harper's in the building.

It's four in the morning when I take the stairs up to the NICU floor. I'm still in scrubs and my white coat, and I need a shower.

I've looked better.

But I don't fucking care.

It's quiet, and the lights are low as I walk into the neonatal unit. There's no one at the nurses' station, and when I skim the area, I see Harper sitting in a rocking chair, feeding a baby.

She's in blue scrubs today, her hair in that messy bun, and she's smiling at the newborn as she whispers something to them that I can't hear.

Christ.

She's fucking beautiful.

She glances up as I walk toward her, but she doesn't pause in her rocking, and her face is calm as I approach.

"This is Jamison," she says, looking down at the infant. He's *tiny*. Maybe three pounds. "He had a rough day. His mom couldn't come in for his night feeding, so I'm doing it. It always makes me sad when one of the parents can't make it for the feedings, but she's a single parent with two other kids at home, so she's exhausted and overwhelmed."

She shrugs a shoulder and presses those plump lips together.

I squat in front of them. Monitors and machines make noises here and there, but for the most part, it's quiet in here tonight. I know about Jamison and his mom.

She's my patient.

But I can't tell Harper that, so I stay quiet.

"Bryce is home," I tell her softly.

"I know." She smiles, and it lights up the whole fucking room. "He bounced right back. He was the best-case scenario, and I'm *so* glad he's home and doing well. I really like Dani. And Birdie is hilarious. I got to meet her on their last day here."

I nod, watching her.

"How long have you worked here, Harper?"

Her smile slowly fades away, and I want to say something to bring it back.

But I don't.

"The day Bryce was born was my first day here. He was my first patient." She takes the bottle out of Jamison's mouth and guides him onto her shoulder to lightly pat his back. "I'm the new charge nurse."

My eyebrows lift. "Congratulations."

"Thanks."

"Traveling nurse gig over?"

She rolls her lips inward, then nods slowly. "Yeah. I think so. It was time to come home. My family needed me."

I frown, and without thinking, I reply, "I thought you said you didn't have—"

"Not biological," she says, but there's no heat there. "My best friend and her siblings. They're like siblings to me. Ava needed me. And maybe I needed to come home for me, too."

Fuck yes, you did, sweetheart.

With the feeding finished, Harper stands and puts Jamison in his isolette. She checks the monitors and makes sure he's settled and happy, then turns back to me.

"You look tired, Blake."

I huff out a chuckle.

"Thanks?"

Her lips tip up into a smile. "Bad night in the ER?"

"Just a regular night." I push my hand through my hair. "Listen, I'd like to—"

She stops me by putting her hand on my arm.

"I'm going to pass." She bites her lip and shuffles on her feet. "If I were ready for literally *anything* with *anyone*, I'd be giving you my number right now and would probably get a smidge clingy and you'd be like, *whoa*. Calm down, Harper."

Unlikely.

"But you're not."

Her smile is sad, and I want to ask her why.

"I'm just not. I have this new job, some family stuff, life stuff." She shrugs almost helplessly, and I want to pull her into me. I want to wrap my arms around her, bury my nose in her hair, and just *hold her.*

Instead, I put my hand out.

"May I please have your phone?"

She frowns but unlocks it and passes it to me, and I tap my number into it.

"There. You have *my* number. If you ever want to grab a meal, a coffee, go for a hike"—I lean into her so I can whisper in her ear—"or scream my name while my face is buried in that perfect pussy, you just call me."

Her face flushes, and she chokes out a laugh as she takes the phone back.

"In the meantime, I'll keep my distance. Good luck with the new job, Harper. You'll be great."

I wink at her and turn to walk away.

Every cell in my body screams at me not to leave. To go back and talk her into seeing me. Even if there's no sex at all, I just want to be with her.

But I could see it written all over her gorgeous face.

She's not ready.

And isn't it just fucking ironic that the one woman who's made me feel *anything* other than turned on for a very brief encounter is the one that I just can't have?

My brothers would give me such shit for this if they knew. Because that's what brothers do.

Not that I'll be telling them.

Chapter Six

HARPER

"I'm so sorry!" I climb into Tucker's truck, then lean over to kiss his cheek. "And thank you times a million."

"It's not your fault that my sister is a flake."

Now, I sock him in the shoulder, and he fakes like it hurt, making me smirk.

"She is *not* a flake, you big meanie. She's sick." I glance out the passenger window as I reach for my seat belt and notice Blake walking past on the sidewalk. He's not looking at me, so I can't wave at him, but holy shit, he looks good in those scrubs. He's not wearing his white coat, and I *knew* his biceps would fight against the sleeves. Don't even get me started on his ass.

Holy walking sex.

I haven't seen him at all since that *very* early morning last week when he came into the NICU. I've had about six million moments of regretting turning the man down. It's like he's a magnet, and I'm ... literally *anything* drawn to magnets. But I am *not* ready for a man. Even Blake.

I just don't trust.

Them *or* myself, if I'm being honest.

"I don't want to ride around in a car with a sick woman," I continue as he pulls away from the hospital. "But I know it's early as hell, so thank you for coming to pick me up."

It was my last night shift, and now I can sleep and enjoy a couple of days off.

"I'm up early as fuck anyway," the eldest Hendrix brother reminds me. "How's the new job going?"

"Great so far," I say with a sigh as I lean my head back against the seat. "The people are nice, and there haven't been any issues."

"Good. Let me know if I have to beat anyone up."

I snort and wrinkle my nose at him.

Tucker is the quintessential big brother. He will harass the hell out of Ava and me, but if anyone even looks at us sideways, he'll break their nose.

"You're funny. None of the babies need to be beaten up, tough guy."

He snickers at that.

"I really need to get a car." I sigh. "I can't depend on the Hendrix Taxi Service every single day anymore."

"I'm taking my truck in for an oil change today," Tucker says. "The owner of the shop usually has something hanging around for sale. Want me to ask him when I'm there?"

If memory serves, from what Ava said, that would be Blake's brother.

"Actually, yes, please. It doesn't have to be fancy, just reliable. I'm not the motorhead that you are."

"Well, it'll be reliable if it comes from Brooks. He's excellent. I'll see if he has something. Just shoot me a text when you wake up later."

"Awesome, I'll do that. Thanks."

Tuck pulls up in front of Xander's house, and I open the truck door.

"Thanks for the ride."

"Let me know if you need anything," he says and shoots me a grin before I slam the door shut. He waits until I have the front door unlocked before he drives away.

I don't know how I got so lucky to be folded into the Hendrix family. And it absolutely was luck.

One day, in the seventh grade, Ava and I smacked right into each other in gym at school. Fell on our asses. I got up first and offered her a hand. From then, we were inseparable. We texted when we weren't together, spent most of our free time together, and she often had me over to her house.

Mostly because my parents were junkies who didn't pay attention to, or give a shit about, what I was up to as long as I stayed out of the way. A couple of years after meeting Ava, my parents both died in a car accident, and Greg Hendrix brought me right into his family.

Greg's wife, Lita, left when Ava was quite young. I

don't really know much about her. Ava doesn't remember her.

Now I know that Greg had to have gone through a lot of work with the legal system to keep me. It was likely expensive and exhausting, but he did it. And they all claim me as theirs.

I kick off my shoes and immediately climb the stairs to my bedroom, where I strip out of my scrubs, toss them in the hamper, and take a shower.

Once I've dried off and dressed in my pajamas, I stop in the middle of the bedroom and chew my bottom lip.

I'm hungry. I *should* eat something.

But I'm also freaking exhausted.

The bed is way more enticing, so I crawl under the covers, and within minutes, I'm asleep.

It's clear that Brooks and Blake come from the same gifted gene pool. Tall, broad, muscular, dark hair and eyes. Brooks has a bit of a grumpier look about him, while Blake is quick to smile.

Both hot as hell.

"This is nice," I say as I sit in the driver's seat of a little SUV. It's not new and smells a little musty, but it's clean.

No tears or burns or raccoons living in it.

Score.

"It's perfect under the hood," Brooks says. "Runs great. It'll need better tires for snow before winter hits, but I can help you out there. The former owner just never came back to claim it."

"Are they going to hunt me down to steal it back?" I ask.

Both Brooks and Tucker laugh at me. I scowl up at both of them.

Rude.

"I'm serious!"

"No," Tuck says, shaking his head.

"I think they moved out of the area," Brooks adds. "I've taken care of the title. It's ready to be sold."

"I'm going to take it around the block."

Brooks passes me the key fob, and I start it up. The men step back as I put it in gear and pull out of the parking lot.

He's not wrong. It drives nice, and there are no weird noises. No dashboard lights on.

It seems to be a nice used car. I'll toss in an air freshener, and it'll be good to go. No, it's not fancy at all, and there's a dent in the side door. I'll definitely want new tires before the next winter, but it's only spring.

There's time to handle all of that. And I don't have to go to car lots and deal with haggling for something else.

This is easy. In my budget.

Did I mention easy?

I pull back into the spot I vacated and smile when I step out of the car.

"Sold."

"Nice," Tucker says with a nod. "I'll let you guys handle the details. Unless you need me, Harper?"

"Nah, I'm good. Thanks." I hug him, then follow Brooks into his office so we can arrange the payments, and he can sign the title to me.

The other upside to this whole arrangement? It takes less than an hour from start to finish.

I slept until early afternoon, and then Tucker came to get me to bring me into Bitterroot Valley to meet with Brooks.

Now that I have my own ride, and the freedom that goes along with it, I want to explore the adorable downtown area a bit. Aside from the hospital, I haven't really spent much time in this cute town in many years.

Driving down the main street, I see some cute restaurants, a flower shop, and a dress shop. There's a bakery that I'll have to try—still haven't kicked the sugar addiction—and there's the bookstore.

Extra score? It's right next to a coffee shop.

"This is my lucky day," I murmur to myself as I park in front of Billie's Books, cut the engine of my new-to-me vehicle, and climb out into the fresh spring air.

I love that the trees are budding and the days are getting warmer and longer. I plan to go for a hike tomorrow. I don't care in the least that it's still muddy around here.

Pushing through the door of the bookstore, I take a second to absorb it.

This is freaking amazing.

There are inviting chairs by the front windows for anyone who wants to sit and read. There's even a dog bed beside one, which makes me smile.

The table in the front of the store has stacks of new releases, along with some older titles that I recognize. One of the books has a sign saying it's this month's book club read.

Do I want to join the book club?

Maybe.

I bet Ava would do it with me. That would be awesome.

"Welcome in," a woman calls out, and I glance toward the checkout counter in the back and wave at the gorgeous brunette smiling at me. "Are you looking for anything special?"

"Just looking for right now," I reply. "And can I just say, I freaking *love* your store? This is amazing."

"Thank you," she says as she walks toward me on heels that make me swallow hard. I never mastered the art of walking on stilts.

This woman is truly stunning. Her perfect curves are dressed impeccably in what even *I* know are designer clothes. Her dark hair has that beachy wave look, and her makeup is perfect.

I would like to be her when I grow up.

"I'm Billie," she says, holding out her hand to shake. "Billie Gallagher."

"Ah, so you're the owner. Unless another Billie is hiding around here."

"That's me," she replies with a chuckle. "I'm so happy you found us."

"Me, too. I just started working at the hospital a couple of weeks ago, and I finally have time to wander around downtown."

"Oh, where did you move here from?"

"I'm originally from Silver Springs." She smiles at that. "But I lived away for about ten years. A lot has changed."

"You're not kidding. Well, if you decide that you need something specific, just ask. I'm around, and Emily is, too. She's stocking shelves on the other side of the store."

"Over here," Emily calls out, waving a hand, making me chuckle.

"Got it. I do have a question about book club."

"Oh my God, join our Spicy Girls Book Club," Billie says, getting excited. "Our next meeting isn't until next Friday, so you have time to read it. This month is *Steel* by Eva Simmons. It's a *delicious* motorcycle club romance that will make you sweat. Trust me. So good."

"I do enjoy a motorcycle club romance," I reply with a grin. "I'll buy two copies and make my bestie join with me. It won't be hard. This is totally her vibe."

"*Yes*," Billie says, just as the bell over the door dings, and a stunning redhead walks in with an enormous black dog at her side. "Skyla, this is our newest book club member. I'm sorry, I didn't catch your name."

"Harper," I say.

"Well, it's nice to meet you. This is my sidekick, Riley." Skyla shakes my hand, and I immediately fall in love with her voice. It sounds like music. "You'll love the book club. We have sweet treats from the Sugar Studio and talk about all the spice."

"This is my definition of heaven." The three of us giggle at that. "Wow, thank you. I'm so happy I found this store. I'll just browse a bit, leave with a stack the size of Texas, and get out of your hair."

"You are absolutely *not* in my hair," Billie assures me. "Take your time, friend."

I break off and start to browse, pulling books off shelves to read the back covers.

It seems I'm physically incapable of putting anything back.

"You have good taste," Billie says when I walk to the counter, and she sees my paperback haul.

"I have to stop before I buy out the whole store." I laugh. "How do you not have every single book in your house?"

"She does," Skyla informs me. "She's married to my brother, and he built her a *Beauty and the Beast* library in their house. It's alarmingly beautiful."

"Holy shit." I can feel my eyes bugging out of my head. "Good for you, girl. Hang on to that man."

"Oh, I plan to." With a laugh, Billie tosses in some stickers and a bookmark.

I leave with *eleven* books, not counting the extra book club copy I bought for Ava, and with my finds in a cute little Billie's Books tote bag on my shoulder, I wave at the two women and walk outside.

When I pulled in, I spotted a restaurant just across the street that I want to try, so I cross over without stowing my books in the car first.

I might want to read one while I eat.

Pushing inside, I feel the smile spread over my lips again. Sage & Salt is airy and beautiful. It looks like Joanna Gaines designed it with a farmhouse feel.

When I get to the back of the restaurant where you place your order, I see that the entire menu is gluten-free.

In fact, the signage states this is a *clean* kitchen, meaning it's safe for those with celiac disease and wheat sensitivities.

Holy shit, I'm in love. Can I move in here?

"Hey there," a pretty blonde says with a smile, showing me deep dimples in her cheeks. "Welcome in."

"Thank you. How long has this place been here?"

"Only a couple of months." She wipes the back of her hand over her brow as she leans against the counter. "I'm Juliet, the owner. It's been a labor of love, but we're finally open."

"Well, I'm Harper, and I'm thrilled because I try to stay as gluten-free as possible. I might be in here every day to get my fix and harass you."

"Excellent," Juliet replies with a wide grin. "I can't wait to be harassed. What are you hungry for today?"

I skim the menu and bounce on the balls of my feet in excitement. This *massive* menu has pasta dishes, sandwiches, and even Mexican food. Not to mention, I see that they have a big cooler full of grab-and-go options, which will be great when I'm working.

What? I love food. Sue me.

"I need those fajitas, please."

"Chips and salsa on the side? Guac?"

"You're speaking my love language," I inform her, and Juliet laughs.

"You got it. Anything to drink?"

"Just water is great."

"Have a seat anywhere, and I'll bring it out to you."

I pay the tab, drop some money in the tip jar, then settle at a table by the windows. I pull out the book club paperback to dig into and am fully immersed, several chapters in, when Juliet delivers my dinner.

"Is that good so far?" She gestures to my book.

"I'm loving it," I reply and pop a chip in my mouth. "I think I'm going to join the book club across the street. Are you a reader?"

"A voracious one," she confirms. "Less now that I'm here all the time, but yes. That bookstore is a gem, and the owner is just the best."

"You should join the book club."

Her smile turns kind of sad, and she lifts a shoulder. "It's complicated. But I'll scoop that one up for sure. Enjoy your dinner, Harper."

And I do. I've never been one of those people who doesn't like to go out to eat alone. It doesn't bother me at all.

Besides, I'm not alone. I have a whole motorcycle club with me.

I've been questioning why I didn't move home much sooner.

My job is excellent. I found a reliable car, the cutest bookstore ever, and a fucking *fabulous* restaurant. Yesterday was a great day of exploring Bitterroot Valley.

I spent this morning catching up on laundry and a little housework. I went to the grocery store to stock up for the coming week, and I even got a little more reading in. I dropped Ava's book off to her last night from the safety of her doorway, and she's excited about it, too.

And now that all of my chores are done, I'll spend the rest of the afternoon in the woods.

There's a hike I remember as a teenager that I want to do today. The trail isn't too far from Xander's house, just outside of Bitterroot Valley. I looked it up online last night to make sure it's still there, and that it's what I remember it being.

It's *better*.

New trails have been added, and according to the photos posted on social media, it looks incredible.

I'm so excited to get outside and sweat a little on the trail.

I pull up to the trailhead and park. Although the

parking lot isn't completely packed, it's also not empty, which makes me feel better.

I don't want to hike in the woods alone.

There are animals out here. Mountain lions and bears. There are also men.

And yes, if I had to choose, I'd go with the bear.

I clip my bear spray to my backpack, change into my hiking shoes, tug my hat on my head and thread my ponytail through the back, then lock the car.

I dressed in layers because it's still a bit cool, especially in the shade. But it's spring in Montana, so it'll warm up as the day progresses, and I'll start to sweat.

I'll stow my shell in my backpack when the time comes.

I pause to read the trail map sign, double-check where I want to go, then head off in that direction. I'll gain about eight hundred feet in elevation today, but the reward of seeing the view of the lake and mountains will be so worth it.

It's been dry enough that the trail doesn't have much mud on it, and before long, I'm in the *zone*, enjoying the trees and the fresh pine-scented air. I love the way my lungs start to stretch and my muscles engage.

A family of deer crosses the path about a quarter of a mile from the trailhead, making me grin. The baby is *so tiny*, covered in white spots, and she watches me curiously. I stop and wait for them to go on by, not wanting to startle them.

I pass several couples and then a single man, who

doesn't even give me a second look as he passes by, clearly zeroed in on his workout.

It feels good to be home. Better than I even thought it would when I made the decision to come back and take care of Greg. I think I avoided moving back for so long because I was ashamed that I got into that relationship with Nathan and ended up leaving with practically nothing to my name. And he was so unpredictable, I didn't know if he'd follow me.

And if that was the case, I wasn't going to lead him *here*.

The traveling nurse position gave me the opportunity I needed to leave a bad relationship and work on myself before I was ready to come home to be with the people I love the most.

And the fact that I needed to *heal* from someone who was supposed to love me really pisses me off.

When I think back to the way he treated me. The way he would sneer at me or tell me that I was horrible at being a nurse or a friend.

That I was a miserable fuck in the bedroom.

It just makes me *rage*.

Because I didn't deserve any of that. Not one second of it. And it took me way too long to get up the gumption to leave.

Between the exercise and the anger from thinking about the jerkwad, I'm starting to get hot, so I pause at the side of the trail, take my backpack off, then unzip and remove my jacket. After I roll it up, I stuff it into the backpack and then take a drink of water.

I can hear a stream or a river. I forgot about that. Its soothing babbling smooths out my rough edges from thinking about Nathan.

With a deep breath, I turn to stow my water bottle and put the backpack back on, and then freeze.

Well, shit.

Chapter Seven
BLAKE

The trail isn't too busy today, which is good. I like to run it, and sometimes if it's too packed, people don't move out of the way. It can be annoying.

Hopefully, today will be a smooth trail run. I only have today off this week, and I want to exercise outside rather than on a treadmill in the hospital's gym.

After I've tied my shoes, I pull my hoodie off and stow it in the car. After about five minutes, I won't need it.

I do a few quick stretches, then set off up the trail. I usually do ten miles on this particular trail system. The elevation gain is perfect, and the views are great, too.

The ground is remarkably dry, and within just a few minutes, I've hit my stride and am enjoying the burn in my lungs, legs, and ass. It feels good to be in the fresh air.

I come up over a ridge and have just started to come

down the other side when I look up and come to a complete stop.

Fuck. Me.

She's not facing me and has a hat on her head, but I'd know that body anywhere. Harper's standing at the side of the trail, stuffing what looks like a light jacket into her pack.

She's in a purple strappy sports bra and black yoga pants that hug every curve of her fit body. She's not simply thin.

She's *fit*.

She has toned muscles. She's lean. Her ass is round, and her waist is small.

I love *women*. All shapes and sizes. It's not the size that matters to me at all, it's the fact that she's active, enjoys it, and I have to say, the athletic wear makes my cock twitch.

She's hotter just as she is right now than if she were in a formal dress.

Harper finishes drinking her water and turns toward me. Her eyes go wide, and she freezes for a second before she lifts the pack and stows her water away.

"I didn't want to startle you." Okay, it's a white lie. I wanted to watch her while she was unaware, and I don't mean that in a creepy way.

Her eyes take a swift tour from my face, down my body to my shoes.

I'm just in a tank and shorts, but her cheeks heat, and she seems to like what she sees. Which is both good and a colossal shit show.

Because although she may want me, she won't let herself have me.

"Good day for a hike," she says as she shoulders the pack and starts to walk, and I match her pace, walking beside her. She goes at a good clip. She doesn't meander.

"And not too crowded," I add, and she nods. "Mind if I join you?"

"I don't mind," she says, offering me a small smile. "How have you been, Blake?"

Missing you, Harper.

"It's been busy but good. And you?"

"Same. I saw you yesterday morning, but you didn't see me."

"Getting in the truck?" I ask, and she nods. "I saw you."

Yeah, sugar, I saw you get in a truck with another man, and I didn't yank you out and kiss you until you couldn't remember anyone but me.

"Ava's been driving me to and from work for the most part," she says and sidesteps a log. "But she was sick yesterday, so Tucker picked me up. He's the oldest of us, and he's usually a pain in my ass, but he was useful yesterday."

She snorts, and it makes me smile. "How was he useful?"

"Well, he found me a car to buy, so I don't have to use the Hendrix Family Taxi service anymore."

"You have my number," I remind her, but she shakes her head.

"I'm thirty, for fuck's sake. I needed a car. I just

didn't want to take the time to go to a dealership and dick around with it. That's the *worst*. I'd much rather be doing *this* on my day off. Or literally anything else, including the dentist. But Tuck gets big brother props for taking that off my plate."

"Tucker Hendrix?" I ask, and she nods and looks up at me.

"Do you know him?"

"I've met him, but Brooks knows him pretty well," I reply. "And he's joined us at the Wolf Den here and there. So Ava's a Hendrix."

"Yeah." She nods, and we start up the steepest hill on this hike, but she doesn't break her stride. "So I spent yesterday afternoon in downtown Bitterroot Valley, and it's adorable. There's a new clean-kitchen restaurant that's *to die for*."

"I know. I haven't been yet."

And it's way more complicated than I care to explore with her right now.

"Juliet is *so nice*," Harper continues. "She's the owner. Anyway, the food is great, and maybe Birdie would like it there. Dani and Bridger can take her without worrying."

I can't resist. I reach over to brush my hand down the back of her thick ponytail.

It makes my chest tight that she thought of my cupcake when she saw the clean kitchen.

"I'm sure they'd love that. What else did you see?"

"I'm in love with the bookstore. Like, I would *marry* that bookstore if I could. It's so *fun*, Blake. And so pretty, and I don't always love girly, frilly things, but it's not over the top, you know?"

My lips twitch. I'm so fucking proud of my baby sister.

"And the owner? Holy shit, she's gorgeous. Talk about pretty without being over the top. She walks in heels like I walk in these hiking shoes. It's baffling. And I'm a little jealous."

"You're jealous of her heels?"

"That she can walk in them," she clarifies, looking honestly mystified, and it's fucking adorable. Her perfect face is clean of makeup and dewy from our hike, and Christ, I want to kiss those plump lips.

I just want her.

I *crave* her.

"And then," she carries on, completely unaware that I'm dying a slow death over here, "this other woman walked in with the prettiest red hair, and her accent is *so sexy*, and I was like, what universe am I even in?"

I nod and gesture for her to keep hiking. "So you enjoyed the bookstore and made some new friends. What else?"

I love that she enjoyed Billie and Skyla so much. And I know she likes Dani.

She's basically friends with all of the women in my family, and she doesn't even know it yet.

Billie's my sister.

Skyla and Dani are with my brothers.

Yeah, you're going to fit into my family just fine.

"After I ate, I dropped Ava's book off to her because

I'm making her join the book club with me, then I went home. Nothing too wild and crazy. But it was nice to be out and about by myself without having to call for a ride."

"Did you not keep a car when you did the traveling nurse thing?"

"I did at first, but it was a pain in the ass when I'd have one assignment on the East Coast, and then the next was in, like, Texas. So I sold the car and just flew. Most of the places I was in had rideshares, but we don't have that here."

"Not yet," I reply. "Probably eventually. The bigger towns have it."

She nods, and we fall into an easy silence, walking side by side.

The conversation with this woman is always so … *easy*. The back-and-forth is comfortable as if we've known each other for years. It's effortless, and the more I get, the more I want.

How can I go back to keeping my distance after this?

It's fucking torture.

When we make it up to the lake, which still has some snow around the shoreline, Harper immediately removes her socks and shoes and puts her feet in the ice-cold water.

"Oh my God, that feels good," she moans, and it makes me want to strip her out of those leggings and fuck her.

Hard.

She grins back at me, then loses her smile when she

sees my face. "What's wrong? Hey, if you want to keep going, you can head out. I was only going to do the six miles today."

Shaking my head, I kick out of my shoes and socks and join her in the water. It just about steals the breath from my lungs because it's so fucking cold.

But I take her hand and lace my fingers through hers.

"No, I don't need to keep going."

Fuck my run. Who gives a shit?

"Okay." It's a whisper before she bites that lip, and her eyes drop to my mouth.

But before I can dip down to kiss her, she turns to look at the mountains once more and loses her balance. Her free arm flails out.

I tug her against me and wrap my arms around her to keep her from falling.

"Whoa. That could have been catastrophic." She laughs but doesn't pull away.

She leans in.

And just like that, I feel the shift.

"Thanks for saving me from a *very* wet hike back to my car."

I grin and kiss the top of her head.

"My pleasure."

Now she does pull away, but she doesn't tug her hand away from mine. Just like all those months ago, after the flight from Denver, she leaves her hand in mine, and it warms my chest.

"What's your schedule like this week?" I ask.

"Well, I have today and tomorrow off, then I go to

days for three days, then off three days." She narrows her eyes. "Yeah, that's it. Sorry, it gets confusing sometimes. It's easier to remember the day shifts from the night ones, but I have it all in the calendar on my phone. How about you? What's your schedule like?"

"I have today off," I reply and inhale deeply, wishing for the first time that I didn't take on so much. "I'm in the clinic the next few days, but no ER in the evening for a while. We finally hired a new ER doc to help."

"Oh, nice. Working double shifts is exhausting, Blake."

"You're telling me." I grin down at her, then tuck a stray piece of her hair behind her ear. "Let's take a picture."

Her eyebrow lifts. "Okay."

She pulls her phone out of her pocket, and I take it since I have longer arms and can get a better angle. We both smile for the camera with the lake and mountains in the background. She's tucked up beside me, my arm around her back, and fuck if she doesn't look good right here.

When I pass the phone back to her, I say, "Please send me that."

"Oh, sure." She taps the screen, and my phone vibrates in my pocket. "It's a good picture."

"Of course it is. You're in it."

She laughs, rolls her eyes, and heads back to the shore to put her shoes back on. First, she pulls a small towel out of her pack to wipe herself off, then offers it to me.

"You come prepared," I comment as I use the towel to dry my feet before putting my own shoes on.

"Always. I even have snacks. I knew I wouldn't *need* them since this isn't a super-long hike, but you never know."

"What kind of snacks?"

She smiles and opens the pack wider, peering inside. "Let's see. We have cashews, jerky, trail mix, a protein bar, and sour candy."

Opening the candy, she pops some in her mouth.

"What can I give you?"

You can straddle my lap and let me fuck you here in the woods, sugar.

"I'll take some jerky."

"You got it." She passes me the unopened package, pops more candy in her mouth, then zips up her pack.

When she stands, she loses her balance and ends up over a log, on her ass, scowling as her hat falls right off her head.

"You okay?" I hurry over to her and cup her face, scanning her body.

"I'm a clumsy oaf," she says.

I shake my head. "The log jumped you," I reply. "I saw it. Anything hurt?"

"Just my pride and my ass." I help her to her feet, and she brushes off her backside. I pick up the hat, but I don't give it back to her yet. "Thanks."

But I don't pull away.

I don't want to pull away.

I step into her and tip her chin up before I slant my

lips over hers. A little moan comes from her throat, and she wraps her arms around my waist. She leans into me, presses her breasts against me, and kisses me back.

And every cell in my body ignites.

I frame her face in my hands and devour her. She tastes like sugar and every dream I've had for six long, brutal months.

Christ. I've missed touching her.

When I come up for air, I rest my forehead on hers. "Should I apologize for that?"

"I hope you won't," she whispers. She hasn't opened her eyes.

"Let's head back," I say, reluctantly pulling away from her but keeping her hand in mine. "Before I strip us both naked and fuck you right here where anyone can see."

She laughs, bites her lip, and grabs her pack. "I'm not into that, Blake."

"Yeah, well, me neither, but I'm damn tempted."

Hiking back to the car takes half the time since it's mostly downhill, and we spend a good portion of it jogging. Not quite as fast as if I were doing this alone, but it's a good pace, and when we reach the parking lot, we're both panting pretty hard.

We walk around, catching our breath. She stops by an older SUV that's seen better days.

"*This* is what Tucker found for you?" I ask her, eyeing the dent in the rear door.

"Yep. This is it." She opens that dented door and

tosses her pack inside. "I have to buy an air freshener. It's a little musty."

"Is it safe?" I scowl at it and then at her. "I'm pretty sure you can do better than this, Harper."

Her eyes narrow on me. "If you think it's a heap, take it up with your brother. I bought it from him."

"You bought it from Brooks?"

"Yes. It runs great. It's not brand new or fancy like that Mercedes over there, but it's reliable, and *I didn't have to deal with it.* I cannot stress to you enough how much I hate car dealerships, Blake. It's a thing for me, okay? So no, it's not pretty, but it's what's on the inside that counts."

She laughs at her own joke, and I can't help it. I cage her in against the car and kiss her again. She's smiling against my lips, and when I pull back, I don't even pause. "I want to take you out to dinner tonight."

Her smile doesn't slip. "I could eat."

"I'll pick you up in two hours."

"Okay, I'll text you the address. Don't think I didn't catch the whole *send me that picture* so you could get my number thing you did. You didn't outsmart me, Dr. Blackwell."

I can't help but laugh at that and lean in to kiss her forehead. "Got me. Hey, it worked. Shoot me that address, and I'll see you in two fucking hours."

"I'll be ready." She smiles, and I walk to my car.

When I turn back, she's gaping. Because I'm standing by the Mercedes she pointed out before, and it makes me laugh.

"Show-off!"

I smirk. "Get in the car, Harper. I won't leave until you do."

She shakes her head, sinks into her driver's seat, and pulls out ahead of me.

Two hours later, to the minute, I pull off the highway and onto a driveway that meanders back through some trees, and then a clearing opens up to a huge log-style mansion that has me blinking in surprise.

This is where she lives?

I pull up in front of the double front door and cut the engine, then climb the stairs and ring the doorbell. A few seconds later, she opens the door, and my jaw goes slack.

She's in jeans and an oversized pink blouse that falls over one shoulder, leaving it bare.

I want to sink my teeth into her there.

"You're fucking gorgeous."

Her hair is down and wavy, and she put some makeup on. Not too much, just enough to make those gray eyes look like ... magic.

She takes in my jeans and green button-down. "You're not so bad yourself."

"Are you hungry?"

"No. I'm *hangry*. I could eat literal sawdust, and it would be amazing."

I watch as she locks her door, then I take her hand and bring it up to my lips. "No sawdust tonight. How do you feel about burgers?"

"I have a fondness for burgers," she replies. "I'm down for that."

I lead her to my car and open the door for her, and once she's settled in the seat, I close the door and circle the hood, giving the house one more curious glance.

"That's a nice house," I say as I put the car in gear and pull away.

She glances back at it. "Yeah, it is. The inside is nice, too. But it's kind of ridiculous."

I blink at her in surprise. "You think your house is ridiculous?"

"Oh, it's not *mine*." She laughs at that, as if just the thought is preposterous. "It's Xander's. He's another brother. Xander's never home because he's off being a fancy hockey player, so when I moved back, he basically insisted I housesit for him."

That's right, Xander Hendrix is the starting center for the Denver Flurry.

"Ah, I see." I nod and pull onto the highway just as Harper's phone rings. She checks the screen, and I see her frown out of the corner of my eye.

"Sorry," she says. "I have to take this."

"By all means."

She holds the phone up to her ear. "Hey, what's up? Are you okay?"

She listens for a second, then shakes her head in agitation.

"No. Absolutely not. You listen to me. You can't eat that. It'll send your sugar levels into the stratosphere, Greg. I don't care what Tucker said. He's not a medical professional, and if you eat that, I will come over there, and well, I'll do something. I'll figure that out later. Seriously, please don't do that. You'll feel like shit."

I scowl and glance her way. She has literal tears in her eyes.

What's going on?

"Promise me," she says. "Okay, I'm trusting you. I'll bake you something delicious tomorrow and bring it over. It's my day off. No, I wanted to bake anyway. Okay. You stress me out, Greg. For the love of God and all the saints. Yeah, yeah, love, blah, blah. I'll see you tomorrow."

She hangs up, blows out a breath, and shakes her head.

"Family is hard," she finally says, and I immediately reach for her hand.

"What's going on, sugar?"

She links her fingers through mine.

"Greg Hendrix raised me. My parents were shit. It's a long story. Anyway, Greg was diagnosed with type two diabetes a couple of months ago, and he's so not good at regulating it. It's the biggest reason I moved home. If you think *I* have a sweet tooth? He invented the word. And he's in good shape. The man has been a rancher his whole life, and he's still active despite Tucker doing most of the work now. Anyway, he's stubborn, he doesn't listen, and I seem to be the only one who can get through to him. Mostly, I use the guilt trip tactic."

"I take it that it's worked before?"

"Like a charm. I'll bake him something delicious tomorrow to help with the sweet tooth. If he puts himself in a goddamn diabetic coma tonight, he won't have to worry about diabetes. I'll kill him myself."

I smile over at her. "He won't. I would have been afraid of you just now, too."

She smirks and lets out another breath. "Okay, enough of that nonsense. Let's go eat."

Chapter Eight

HARPER

I've been to the Wolf Den before. Usually, whenever I came home for a couple of days to visit the family, Ava and I would end up here for a girls' night. We never really liked hanging out at the dive bars in Silver Springs. This isn't a dive bar. It's a fun sports bar with pool tables and a jukebox, and the menu is great.

Therefore, when Blake pulled up here, I got excited.

We've already placed our orders, and Blake's holding my hand from across the table. This man *loves* to touch. And I am *not* complaining. I love it when he touches me, too.

"So what's the longer version of what you told me in the car?" Blake asks as he sips his iced tea. "If you don't mind sharing, that is."

Surprisingly, I don't mind. I feel like I've been able to chat this man up from the moment I met him. It's just easy. And I never feel like he's judging me. He simply listens.

It's refreshing.

"Well, let's see. I was born on a warm July night—"

Blake laughs, and I smile over at him.

"My parents were addicts," I say, and his face clears. "So *not* good at the whole parent gig. My mom would try to get her act together about twice a year, but she loved my dad, and if your partner won't get clean with you ..."

"You're less likely to succeed," Blake finishes.

I nod and sip my water.

"Yeah. The thing is, when she tried to get sober, it was almost worse. She was withdrawing so badly that all she did was cry and couldn't function at all. If she was using, she at least had lucid moments of remembering groceries and stuff."

I shrug a shoulder, but Blake scowls, so I squeeze his hand.

"When I was in the seventh grade, I met Ava at school. I mean, I'd seen her around because we grew up in such a tiny town, but we became best friends that year, and I started spending most of my time with her family. Her dad didn't even blink an eye to having me around. Greg's the best."

Blake's eyes warm. "Where's her mom?"

"Oh, she's been gone since Ava was a toddler. Took off and left everyone behind. Ava doesn't remember her, and no one really talks about her. Greg's been a single dad for a long time. About a year or so after I started hanging with the Hendrix clan, my parents were killed in a car accident. They absolutely should not have been in the car because they were so freaking wasted, and it's a miracle they didn't kill someone else with them."

I lick my lips and drink my water.

"Greg took me in. As a kid, I didn't know or understand everything that entailed for him. I just knew that I moved in with him and never left. Ava and I shared a room, her brothers became my brothers, and that was that."

I bite my lower lip, thinking about it. "But man, that must have been hard for him."

"I'm sure it was a lot of red tape to work through," Blake agrees.

"He never voiced any concerns or frustrations or anything to me. He didn't officially adopt me, so I guess I would have probably been considered in a foster situation. But he sent me to college. I got some great scholarships and stuff, but he took care of the rest because he didn't want me to be saddled with a bunch of debt after I graduated. So yeah, if I need to move home to make sure he's taking care of himself, I'm happy to do that. He probably saved my life. He definitely gave me a family and made me feel safe and cared for. And Ava and her brothers are mine, too."

Blake pulls my hand to his lips and kisses my knuckles.

"I'm glad that's how your story turned out," he says.

"You and me both. So what about you? Tell me more about your family."

"My parents are still married and recently moved back to Bitterroot Valley from Florida, where they were trying to retire. The warmer weather was better for my mom's arthritis. But they missed home and had serious FOMO most of the time."

"I get that."

"I have three brothers and a sister. They're all still here, too."

"Montana seems to produce big families."

He laughs at that. "Seems so. Why nursing?"

Our meals are delivered, and once the server is gone, I answer his question.

"Because I like it. It's really that simple. I knew that I'd always have a job. I'm not squeamish when it comes to ... *fluids* or needles or anything really. And when I did a rotation in a NICU, I knew that was it for me. The babies are so freaking strong and amazing. *Most* parents are good. There are always the few who aren't very nice, but they're scared, and I understand that. Plus, I won't have kids, so this way, I can cuddle someone else's baby without being considered a creep."

His eyes narrow at that. I keep my face neutral, but I'm surprised I said that last part out loud. I don't know that I've ever said those words before. Not even to Nathan, and I'd agreed to *marry* that asshole.

"What do you mean you won't have kids?"

"I'm not infertile, I don't think. I simply know that it's not in the cards for me."

He takes a bite of his burger, watching me as he chews.

"Why?"

I shove some fries in my mouth and decide to add

more salt. "I don't think I'd be great at it. I'm not terribly maternal. Sure, I like to take care of my patients, and I'll dote on Greg, but I'm not warm and fuzzy."

"You don't have to be warm and fuzzy to be a good parent."

I tip my head side to side as if I'm considering that. "Maybe not. I don't know. It's always been a gut feeling that I won't be a mom for as long as I can remember."

He watches me for a minute, then nods slowly. "I understand. I love kids, but it's never been in my plan to have a family, either. I'm very career-driven. I'm married to my job."

"You know, I think that's okay." I take another bite of fries. They're extra crispy tonight, just the way I like them. "Not everyone has to have a life goal of marriage and two-point-six kids. Or, around here, five kids."

I shudder at that, and he laughs at me.

"Sometimes, it's okay to want the career, the friends, the *community*. I'm not an island. I have people, and I like myself this way. It took a while to get there."

"I like you, too," he replies with a half smile. And before he can say more, his phone rings, making him scowl. "Shit, that's the hospital."

He sets his mostly eaten burger down and answers.

"This is Dr. Blackwell." His jaw firms, and he pulls his hand down his face. "I'm not on call this evening."

Sounds like our date is ending early.

"ETA is fifteen minutes." His voice is hard, and it's clear he's not happy about this as he hangs up and stares at me. "You've got to be fucking kidding me."

"Married to the job, remember?"

"Harper, I—"

"Hey, it's okay. Go."

"There was a big accident, and they—"

"You'd better hurry," I tell him. "Take that burger with you."

"I'll flag down the server and—"

"I've got this." I grab a few napkins, wrap up his burger and hand it to him, then stand with him.

"I have cash for the bill. And I'll call someone to give you a ride—"

"No. *I* will handle all of this. You go save some lives, Dr. Blackwell."

"I'm so sorry."

"You have nothing to apologize for."

He grabs my face in his hands and kisses me hard. "I'll make it up to you."

"I'm honestly fine. No bullshit. Go."

Blake's eyes are full of torment, but he kisses me again, grabs the burger off the table, and then he's off. I sit down once more and steal his fries.

Chapter Nine
BLAKE

Fuck.

Chapter Ten

HARPER

Five minutes later, Bridger walks into the pub and skims the room, then walks my way when he sees me.

"I just got a call from Blake," he says as he takes a seat across from me. "He asked me to drive you home."

"He didn't have to do that, but I appreciate it."

Bridger watches me as I finish my meal.

"Do you want some fries?" I ask him, but he shakes his head.

"You don't look mad. I mean, Blake said you weren't, but you *really* don't look irritated about the abrupt change in plans tonight."

I tilt my head to the side. "It's not his fault there was an accident, and he has to go save lives at the hospital."

"No, but a lot of women wouldn't like having their date fucked up."

I nod at that, and when the server brings the check, I reach for it, but Bridger snatches it up out of my fingers.

"I'm taking care of this," he says.

"No. You're not." I pluck it out of *his* fingers, shaking my head. "I appreciate the sentiment."

"Blake would have paid."

"You're not Blake."

"He's my brother, and I'm doing him a solid."

"He's my friend and same." I smile at him and set my card down with the bill. "It's okay, Bridger. I don't know what kind of women Blake dates, but—"

"He doesn't."

That surprises me into shutting my mouth.

"He *doesn't* date. That's what I'm telling you. He's not a Tibetan monk or anything, but he doesn't pursue women because of the job. So when he called me, all worked up because he had to suddenly leave you here and was on the verge of an anxiety attack, I came with the intention of talking everyone off the ledge."

"I think Blake's the only one on the ledge," I inform him. "And I'll make sure he knows it's fine."

In fact, I pull my phone out right now, and see that he's already left me a text.

> Blake: I'm so, so sorry, sugar.
> Bridger's coming to give you a ride home. I feel like a dick.

With a grin, I type out a reply.

> Me: Stop. I told you, I'm honestly fine. I understand, Blake! Bridger will take me home, and I'll talk to you tomorrow.

I set the phone aside as the server picks up my card.

"You're very calm about this," Bridger says, and I can't help but laugh.

"The man has a job. It's not like I think he had someone *fake* call him to get him out of here, leave me with the check, and high and dry on a ride home." I eyeball him. "Wait, he didn't, did he?"

Bridger scowls, and I laugh.

"I'm kidding. How's Bryce, by the way?"

That has Bridger's face softening sweetly. "He's great. No issues at all. And I want to thank you for everything you did for us in the hospital. Dani, in particular. She trusted you and felt at ease with you, even when she was terrified."

"It was honestly my pleasure. I'm so glad he's healthy. You have a beautiful family, Chief."

His eyebrow kicks up.

"As if anyone doesn't know who the fire chief is around here."

He laughs. Once I've signed the credit card slip, we walk out of the pub to his truck.

I arrived with one Blackwell brother, and I'm leaving with another. It's been a fascinating evening.

Bridger chats about the kids and his gorgeous wife on the way to my place, and after thanking him for the lift, I walk inside, set my stuff down, and sigh.

I'm wide awake, and it's still relatively early, so I walk to the kitchen and decide to do the week's meal prep and some baking tonight.

I turn on some music and link my phone to the speaker system and dive in.

I shared a lot with Blake tonight. More than I normally would, if I'm being honest. He's easy to talk to and doesn't make me feel awkward. His face showed no pity when I told him about my parents.

I don't need or want anyone's pity. I have an awesome family.

Suddenly, I hear the front door open, and then Xander and Easton, the third Hendrix brother, come walking in.

"Holy shit, you're home!" I run over to Xander and jump in his arms, hugging him tight. Aside from Ava, I've always been closest to Xander. Maybe because he's only two years older than us. "I've missed the fuck out of you!"

"Hey, baby sis," he says, which is what he's always called me. I'm only three months younger than Ava, but that makes me the baby. "I missed you, too."

"What am I, chopped liver?" Easton asks, and I grin at him.

"I see you all the time," I remind him. Easton is a police officer in Silver Springs. He helped me move all of my stuff into this house.

"What are you making?" Xander asks as he moves into the kitchen with Easton right behind us.

"I'm baking a berry crisp for Greg," I tell them, "and some molasses cookies. Sugar-free, of course. And I'm meal prepping for myself. Those are breakfast burritos."

Xander picks one up and starts to eat it.

"It's not *breakfast*, genius."

"Hungry," he says around a big bite, and all I do is grin at him because *he's home*.

Xander boosts himself up on the counter, feet dangling, and eats the burrito in about four bites.

Those burritos are *big*.

Easton steals a cookie that I pull out of the oven.

I don't mind at all. I adore them. I'll make them whatever they want.

"I'm sorry that you didn't make it past the second round of playoffs," I say to Xander, who's now standing in front of the fridge, taking in the contents. He pulls out some strawberries that I've already washed and digs in.

"It is what it is." He shrugs. "We'll get back at it in a couple of months."

"Are you home for the summer?" Easton asks him.

"Most of it. I want to spend some time on the ranch with Tuck," Xander confirms, then looks at me.

"Are you evicting me?" I ask.

"Fuck no. You cook like a fucking champ."

"You just love me for the food?"

"Yep." He winks at me. "How's the new job?"

"I haven't even heard this news," Easton says, getting comfortable on a stool at the island.

My date with Blake might not have gone the way I'd thought or even wanted, but I get to spend the evening with two of my favorite guys, so I'm not complaining.

It's early, but that's good because I want to get to the clinic just as it opens so I can give Blake some food before his day gets crazy.

Maybe it's silly. Perhaps he'll look at me like I'm nuts and pat me on the head with a thank you. I don't know. I just felt bad that he had to run off to work in a frenzy, and ... hell, who am I kidding? I want to see him.

I walk into Bitterroot Valley Coffee Co to get him a coffee to go along with his breakfast burrito, and when I get to the counter, I'm greeted with a friendly smile.

"Hey, what can I get you?"

"Oh crap, I don't know how he takes his coffee." I frown, then chuckle. "Sorry, thinking out loud."

"Who is it?" she asks. "I might know. I have a knack for remembering *everyone's* order."

"Blake Blackwell?"

"Ah, honey latte with oat milk," she says with a nod. "Got it. How about you? I'm Millie, by the way. I've known Blake forever and a day. His family's ranch isn't too far from *my* family's ranch."

"Small towns, right?" I grin at her. "I'm Harper. I'll take a non-fat white mocha, please. Cow's milk works."

"You bet." Millie winks at me and taps the info into her little computer. I tap my card to pay, then step aside to wait.

Ten minutes later, armed with a bag of food and Blake's coffee of choice, I walk through the clinic's door exactly one minute after they open.

"Hey," I say to the receptionist. "I know this is ... odd, but can I speak with Dr. Blackwell before he gets busy with patients? I'll only be two minutes."

She eyes the stuff in my hands, then picks up her phone to call to the back.

"Hey, this is Mo. Is Dr. Blackwell there? Can you let him know a ..." She lifts an eyebrow at me.

"Harper."

"A Harper is here to see him real quick? Thanks."

She hangs up and smiles at me. "He's on his way up here."

"Thanks."

Before the word is out of my mouth, Blake walks out from the back, and my chest pings at the sight of him.

He looks tired. But he also looks handsome as hell in those green scrubs and white jacket.

"Good morning," I say with a grin. "I won't keep you. I just brought you breakfast."

He blinks at the stuff in my hands, then looks in my eyes. "Good morning," he finally says.

"It's just a breakfast burrito that I made. Xander says they're good. Oh, he got home last night. And Millie knew your coffee order."

He's just looking at me as if I'm a mirage that will disappear at any second.

"If this is weird, I apologize. You don't have to consume any of it."

I start to back away, but then he grabs my arm and pulls me down a hallway and into an empty exam room. He closes the door, then takes the bag and cup from me and sets them aside. Then he's kissing the ever-loving *fuck* out of me, and I immediately melt into him with a little moan.

His hands frame my face, and his lips are demanding, but then he lightens the kiss, brushing his mouth over mine and giving me tingles. Finally, he bites my lower lip and pulls away.

"Jesus, you're a sight for sore eyes."

"Are you okay?" I frown up at him and rub my hand over his sternum. "Was it that bad last night?"

"It was fucking torture leaving you in that goddamn bar," he growls, shaking his head. "It was hell, and I promise it'll never happen again."

"You can't promise that." I smile up at him. "And it's okay. Do I look angry?"

"No, but you should be."

"No, I'd be an asshole if I was pissed at you, Blake. I didn't think you probably ate much this morning, although I could be wrong. So I brought you food."

He pulls me against him and hugs me. Just hugs me and kisses the top of my head. Even that makes me shiver.

Because right now, I'm pressed up against a very firm, very muscular, hot-as-hell Blake, and I know what's beneath these scrubs.

Heat pools in my core, and I clear my throat.

"I'd better let you get to work."

"Tonight," he says by my ear. "I want to see you

tonight, and I'm going to make up for the colossal dumpster fire of last night."

"It wasn't *colossal*," I say, smiling against his chest. "It was a little trash fire. Like a small bathroom-sized trash can. Nothing catastrophic."

He huffs out a laugh and tips my chin up. "Tell me I can see you tonight."

"You can see me tonight."

He kisses my nose, then my lips again. I open for him, and his tongue sweeps over mine, making my thighs clench.

"Hold that thought for later." I reach back for the door handle.

"Harper," he says, and I turn back to him. "Thank you."

"No problem." I smile, then walk out of the room and out of the clinic.

Here's hoping our second attempt at a date doesn't require a fire extinguisher.

Chapter Eleven

BLAKE

I didn't even go home after work before picking Harper up. I can't stand being away from her for even one more minute, especially after so much time was stolen from us last night.

I never resent my job, but I was there after that phone call last night, and it's something I need to think about.

But first, I'm going to spend as much time as possible with a certain brunette who tastes like sugar and makes my cock hard as fucking granite.

When I saw her at the clinic this morning, I thought for sure I was imagining things. That she was something I conjured out of my sleep-deprived mind.

But she was real.

And I'm about to see her again.

I pull in front of Xander's house and climb the steps to the massive doorway to ring the bell.

When it opens, it's not Harper who greets me.

It's Xander himself.

"I hear you want to date my sister," he says by way of greeting, and I immediately grin.

"Fuck yes, I do."

His lips twitch, but he folds his arms over his chest.

"Xander! Don't be a dick. I'm coming downstairs. I just have to grab ..." I can't hear the last part of that statement because it sounds like she's running around upstairs.

"She's not a fucking toy," he says, lifting his chin.

Xander's a big man. He's also strong as fuck, thanks to hockey.

The thing is, I'm the same height as him, and I'm just as strong. But he's her brother, so I get it.

I have a baby sister, too.

"No, she's a woman," I reply. "A beautiful, intelligent, amazing woman."

"Why are you standing like that?" Harper demands, scowling up at Xander. Christ, she's stunning in a flowy black skirt with a cropped green blouse that shows me a sliver of her tight abdomen. It makes me want to lick her there. To start. "You look like an idiot."

"I do not." He lowers his arms and frowns at Harper, making me chuckle. It seems my siblings and I aren't the only ones who give each other shit. "It's my whole job in life to make sure no one dicks with you, and I failed last time."

"No, it's your whole job to put a puck in a net." She pats his arm. "Now, get out of my way and don't wait up."

"Wait. What do you mean, don't wait up?"

Harper turns to face him. "You're *thirty-two,* X. Do I have to spell it out for you?"

"Oh my God, if you touch her, I'll skin you alive."

"Goodbye, Xander," Harper says, her voice sounding bored.

But I step up to him and hold my hand out to shake.

"I get it. I have a sister. I won't do anything she doesn't want me to do."

His eyes narrow. "That doesn't make me feel any better."

"It should."

Reluctantly, Xander shakes my hand, and I join Harper at the car, opening her door for her.

"This is like déjà vu," she says as I pull away from the house. "Maybe I should have met you there. Just in case."

"I'm taking you home with me," I reply after reaching over to take her hand and link my fingers through hers. "I'm going to cook for you, and we'll see where the night takes us."

She lifts an eyebrow. "What are you cooking?"

"Shrimp scampi. The pasta has carbs, sorry."

"Yum." She bounces in her seat. I love her enthusiasm for food. "I would have brought something had I known."

"You already fed me today." I bring her hand up to my lips and nibble on her fingertips as I drive into town. "It was delicious, by the way. Not as delicious as you, but a close second."

I hear her breath catch beside me, making me smug as hell.

Oh yeah, sugar, I'm going to nibble on your entire body tonight.

And we will not be fucking interrupted.

"So you like to cook?" she asks.

"Yes, actually, it's a hobby of mine." I turn off the highway and into my neighborhood on the edge of town. It's a quiet neighborhood of newer homes, spread apart enough so we're not on top of each other.

I pull into the garage and turn to her.

"Wait for me."

After she nods, I get out of the car and circle to open her door. When she climbs out, I cup her jaw and cheek, run my thumb over her soft skin, and kiss her. Her response is immediate. Her hands clutch my sides, and she lets out that little moan that never fails to make my cock hard.

And when I pull back, I tuck her hair behind her ear.

"I have to shower," I whisper. "And then I'll make you dinner."

"Sounds like a plan." She presses her lips together, then licks them as if she's searching for my taste. It almost makes me kiss her again.

But I really *do* need a shower.

So I grab the groceries from the back of the car, then lead her inside through the mudroom off the garage.

"This is a nice neighborhood," she says as she follows me in and kicks her shoes off by the door as if she's settling in to stay a while.

Fuck yes, get cozy, sweetheart.

"I like it," I reply, leading her into the kitchen. "Most of my neighbors are older, so it's really quiet. I don't mind kids, but it *is* nice when I have to sleep during the day, and there isn't a bunch of yelling outside in the summer."

She nods. "I get it. Xander's house is super quiet, too. Here, let me unload, and you go get in the shower."

"You sure?"

"Yes. It'll also give me time to snoop around your house."

I smirk, kiss her cheek, and wrap my arms around her chest from behind so I can hold her against me. "Snoop away, sugar. I don't have any secrets."

"I was kidding."

"I'm not." I press my lips to her head and breathe her in. "Nothing is off-limits. Open drawers, look under the bed, and check out the closets. Whatever you want. Oh, don't judge me if you find some dust bunnies."

She looks around and then cranes her neck to look up at me. "It's spotless in here, Blake."

"The housekeeper does an excellent job." I let her go and walk through the kitchen. "I'll be twenty minutes."

"Take your time."

I'd invite her to join me, but I haven't had her naked and writhing since Thanksgiving, and I want to take my time with her.

I want to fucking savor her.

Just fifteen minutes later, I walk out and find Harper

curled up at the end of my sofa, a book in her hands, chewing on the cuticle of her thumb, *crying*.

The fuck? Absolutely not.

"What's wrong?"

Her gaze jumps up to mine, startled, and she laughs and wipes her eyes. "Oh, it's fiction. Stupid books make me cry sometimes. I went to one book club meeting and got hooked. I'm reading this for the next one, and I'm a mess."

"What is it?" I ask her as I squat in front of her and wipe the tears from her soft cheek.

"It's called *Camera Shy* by Kay Cove, and it's just *so good*." She sighs, tucks the bookmark in to hold her place, and sets the book aside. "Okay, how can I help? What do you need?"

"Just the pleasure of your company." Taking her hand, I pull her to her feet and lead her to the kitchen. "Have a seat. This won't take long."

I get a pot filled with water on the stove to boil and pull ingredients out of the fridge and pantry. When I turn back, Harper's leaning on the counter, her chin in her hand.

"Who taught you to cook?" she asks.

"My mom. She's an excellent teacher, and I paid attention. Actually, all of us can hold our own in the kitchen. How about you?"

"I just figured it out with time." She shrugs. "I was pretty young when I started cooking, actually."

The reminder of how she started out in life makes me

frown. I *hate* that she had shitty parents who didn't take care of her the way she should have been.

My phone rings, and my eyes meet hers as I reach for it.

"Déjà vu," she says with half a smile.

I glance down and see that it's my sister.

Rather than answer, I shoot her a text.

> Me: Emergency?

The dots dance on the screen as she answers.

"It's my sister," I tell her. "Just making sure it's not urgent."

Harper grins.

> Billie: Nope. Just wondering if you want to come over for dinner on Sunday. Dani's comfortable bringing Bryce for everyone to meet and celebrate.

> Me: I'll be there.

With that, I power off the phone and set it on the opposite end of the kitchen, on the charger.

"Did you just turn your phone *off*?" Harper asks, her eyebrows raised in surprise.

"Yes. I refuse to be interrupted tonight. I'm not on call, and my family is fine. I want time with *you*, sugar."

She watches me for a moment, then pulls her phone out of her pocket, powers it off, and sets it next to mine on the counter, making me smile.

"Deal."

"Okay, now I'm embarrassed," Harper says after she finishes eating and pushes her plate away.

"Why?"

"Because you made me something I would get in a Michelin-rated restaurant, and I made you a *breakfast burrito*. What was I thinking?"

She covers her face with her hands, and I laugh as I take one of her hands and pull her over into my lap.

She curls her arms around my neck as she buries her face in it, too.

"No hiding," I say, nudging her chin up so I can see her. "You make a fucking *good* breakfast burrito, sugar."

She wrinkles her nose, and I kiss it.

"It's not a competition."

That makes her gray eyes sparkle. "I *like* a little competition."

I smirk and nuzzle her neck, then nibble my way over her collarbone. "You taste better than that meal."

"Not possible."

My hand slides under her cropped shirt, over the bare skin of her back, and it breaks out into goose bumps under my touch.

"Do you have any objections at all to me propping you on this table and having dessert?"

There's a little moan in the back of her throat, and she shakes her head. "No. I don't mind."

I pick her up and move down one spot where the table is empty, set her on the tabletop, and sit in the chair in front of her.

Her legs widen so I can move in close, and I scoot her skirt up her smooth legs. She lifts her ass, and when the skirt is bunched around her waist, she sits again and pushes her hands into my hair.

"Shirt off."

With her eyes on mine, she grabs the hem of the blouse and pulls it over her head, and I lean in to pepper kisses over her sternum and upper stomach.

"Your skin is so fucking soft," I murmur against her and brush my nose over one lace-covered nipple before sucking it into my mouth, making her moan. I kiss over to the other and give it the same treatment before I make my way down to her warm center.

I drag a knuckle over her wet panties, then nudge my finger under the side and tug them out of my way.

"Fucking hell, sugar. You're already so goddamn wet." I lean in and take a deep breath, and my cock is instantly rock fucking hard for this woman. Christ, I need to claim her more than I need my next breath.

"It seems to be a permanent condition when I'm around you," she replies and gasps when I brush my fingertip over her clit. "Fuuuuuck."

"For almost six months, I've thought about this," I say before planting a wet kiss on her inner thigh. "That's a long fucking time, Harper."

"Super long," she agrees.

"A few things," I say, dragging my lips down to her knee. "One, I haven't been with anyone, in any capacity, since you."

That startles her into blinking at me, her eyes wide as I continue to ghost my fingertip over her clit.

"No one?"

"I didn't want anyone else. I had you, and no one else could compare, Harper."

She gasps when I tease her entrance.

"Same." She bites her lower lip. "You're the only ... in more than two years."

I pause and stare up at her. "I'm the only man who's been inside you in more than *two fucking years*?"

"Close to two and a half."

"Tell me you're on birth control." I grip her panties in my hands and yank them down her thighs, off her feet, and toss them over my shoulder. "Tell me, Harper."

"I'm on birth control." She bites her lip and touches her left inner biceps, and I reward her with a biting kiss on her inner thigh, just an inch from her soaked pussy.

"Good. Tell me I can take you bare, sweetheart. Don't get me wrong. I'm going to sit here and eat you for as long as possible before I take you to my bed where you fucking belong and pound you into the goddamn mattress. But when that time comes—"

"Yes."

I groan and lick her bare pubis. She shaved for this date, but what I told her all those months ago is true.

I don't care.

I just want *her*.

I'll never see this dining room the same way again. Every time I walk in here, I'll see *her*, splayed open for me so fucking beautifully it hurts, and I'll be immediately rock hard for her, just the way I am now.

Every goddamn time.

I drag my nose over that place where her leg meets her core, and she whimpers.

"Blake."

"That's right. Say my fucking name when you're riding my face."

I open wide and fucking devour her. I lick my way up her seam, from entrance to clit, then back down again, so hungry for the very essence of her. For every drop, every moan, every goddamn gasp.

I want them all.

They're mine.

She doesn't know it yet, but she is fucking *mine*.

"Holy shit," she groans, her hips moving in lazy circles. She grabs the edge of the table to ground herself, and I allow it.

For now.

With my hands pressed to her strong inner thighs, I hold her firm when she instinctively tries to squeeze around my head, and my thumbs rub circles over that most tender skin, making her squirm even more.

"You're every fucking fantasy I've ever had in my life," I tell her before pulling her clit between my lips and sinking two fingers inside her. I crook them, feeling that rough G-spot, and she cries out.

"Blake! Fuck, I'm gonna—"

"Not yet." I pull my fingers out, and she growls.

Fucking growls.

It's adorable as fuck.

"I'm not ready for that quite yet, baby." I lick down and back up again, and her hand is on the back of my head, pulling me into her to give her more, and I smile against her. "You're getting greedy, sugar."

"Fuck yes, I am. I waited too, you know."

Yes, she did.

No one but me in over two motherfucking years.

I push my fingers back in and set a punishing pace with my tongue on her clit.

"Just like that. Oh God, don't stop. Don't stop."

I do *nothing* different. I hold steady and let her ride my face and fingers, let her reach for what she needs to let go.

And she lets go so fucking well.

Her hips lift, every muscle in her body tenses, and her legs start to shake as her orgasm moves through her, and she starts to fucking *gush*.

"That's my good fucking girl," I croon as she makes an absolute mess, and I love every goddamn moment of it.

"Holy shit," she pants, and then when she sees how soaked my shirt, my face, and the floor is, her face goes bright red. "Oh no. Oh God, Blake, that's never—"

"Whoa." I push up so I can kiss her lips, gently holding the back of her neck so she doesn't pull away from me. "No, don't spiral on me, sugar. This is so fucking hot. *So. Fucking. Hot.*"

"Um, I don't think I've done that before."

"Good." I sound unhinged. I sound *primal.* Because that's the way I feel right now. "I want to own that from you. Just me. Now, come on. Let's take this upstairs."

I lift her into my arms, and she squeaks.

"Wait! We have to clean all of this up. Dinner, and my, um—"

"Later." I kiss her neck, not caring at all that I'm covered in her.

Christ, if I could get away with it, I'd never wash her off me.

"I need to worship you for a while, sweetheart."

Chapter Twelve

HARPER

I've never related to women when they would make bold statements like *sex with him was a religious experience.*

I always blew it off as an exaggeration for the purposes of bragging to their friends that they had amazing sex. A dramatization, if you will.

A fun anecdote in the break room or at a party. Over text. A giggling conversation in a bar.

Fuck that.

I now believe them. And I'd like to go back in time, high-five every woman who's ever said that in my company, and buy them a drink.

Because holy shit on a cracker, it's a real thing.

And he hasn't even been inside me yet.

"You're quiet," he murmurs before kissing my forehead as he carries me back to his bedroom. The sprawling house is only one story, so no stairs. When we arrive in the bedroom, he scowls as if he's pissed that he has to set me down, but he lowers me slowly to my feet.

"Just enjoying," I reply and reach up to smooth the pad of my thumb over the line between his brows. "Would you do me a favor?"

"Literally anything. If it's mine to give, it's yours." He pushes my skirt over my hips, and it pools around my feet in a floofy heap. "Name it."

"Please get naked."

He smiles, kisses my forehead, and then we work together to strip him out of the sexy black T-shirt and blue jeans he put on after his shower. The way his shirts hug his biceps makes my core tighten and my knees weaken. But in a *black T-shirt?* Someone break out the smelling salts because I am done for.

"Better?" He holds his arms out, and heat spreads over my cheeks as I take in those fucking *incredible* abs, his chest, his arms. The way his dark eyes glint with lust and mischief as he grins at me.

Because yeah, this is so much better.

Nodding, I reach for his cock and glide my hand over the smooth, warm length, all the way to the root as I step into him. With a growl, Blake lifts me, kisses me like his life depends on it, and deposits me right in the middle of his king-sized bed, hovering over me. He kisses me, long and deep, and I can taste myself there on his lips. His hands move down my torso, down my hip and thigh, and then back up again until he's cupping my sex once more.

"So beautiful," he whispers against my lips. "I love how wet you get for me."

"Blake."

"Yeah, sugar?"

"I need you inside me ten minutes ago."

That cocky mouth tips up into the kind of grin that will knock the breath out of your lungs.

"Why are you so hot?" I ask, not at all embarrassed that the words came out of my mouth because the man should have statues made of his likeness. "Like *how*? It's unfair. It's probably illegal. You could go to *jail*, Blake."

He snorts and kisses up my jaw as he settles his hips between mine, pushing my legs up and out to the side so we can see every single thing happening down there.

"You're the sexy one," he says as he lines the crown of his cock up with my opening, dragging it up and down through my wet slit, making me squirm with every pass over my already pulsing bundle of nerves. "I can't resist you. I can't stay away from you, Harper. Please don't ask me to stay away from you anymore."

He pushes inside me, and we both moan.

"Christ, you're so fucking tight."

I gasp as he pushes in farther and grab his arms, needing to feel him. "I think—*whoa*—you're just big."

"Both can be true." He leans down to nibble the side of my mouth so sweetly, it almost brings tears to my eyes, and I am *not* going to cry while fucking this god of a man. "Breathe for me, sugar."

I do, pulling in a deep breath, and when I let it out, he pushes in farther until he's fully seated and stays there. He's balanced on his elbows, his hands in my hair, and he's staring down at me with those hot, dark eyes that seem to see right through me.

I've never felt as vulnerable as I do when I'm with this man. As open. I'd tell him anything he wants to know. But the vulnerability doesn't make me want to run away. I don't want to close him out. Because I see it reflected back to me, and it's maybe the most precious gift anyone has ever given me.

"You're incredible," he whispers. He pulls his hips back, sliding out just to the tip, and then he pushes back in.

The first time we did this, I wanted it *hard*. I don't know why, but I needed it to hurt.

But this time? I don't need the pain that comes with the pleasure he gives me.

His lips move down to my neck, and he sets a steady, leisurely pace as if we have all the time in the world to soak each other in. Lifting my hips, I clench around him, and Blake growls into my skin.

"God, keep that up, and I won't last."

I grin up at him. "I can't help it. *Ah, God.* You hit every damn button."

My toes curl as pure sensation rolls through me. My hips come off the bed, and I push on his shoulder. He reads me so well and immediately flips our position until I'm on top. I plant my hands on his chest and ride him.

"Fuck, you're stunning." His eyes sweep over my torso and up to my eyes again. His hands grip my hips so hard, I'm bound to have fingerprint bruises tomorrow, and I can't freaking wait. I want to see his marks on me.

KRISTEN PROBY

Suddenly, Blake slides his hands under my thighs and moves me up to his mouth as if I weigh nothing at all, and he's eating me once more.

"Fucking hell!" I cry out, gripping the headboard. He doesn't let me rise off him. He's holding me down on his face, and he's licking me and devouring me. Just when I swear the world is going to explode, he moves us again. "You're trying to kill me."

"Never." He slaps my ass and kisses me hard before taking me by the back of the neck and putting me on all fours. His control at this moment is intoxicating. I don't have to think, and I don't have to be in charge.

Blake is in control, and I freaking love it.

His hand slides up into my hair, and he's suddenly pounding into me from behind. With an almost punishing pace, his hips slap against my ass. "Six fucking months, you denied us both this. God-fucking-damn, it's so good. It's never been better than this, sugar. You're so." He slams into me. "Fucking." He pulls my hair back until I'm up on my knees, and his lips are pressed to my ear. "Everything. Fucking everything, Harper. Now, I want you to be my good girl and come all over my cock. I want you to make a mess of me like you did at my table."

He reaches around my front to press his fingers to my clit, and between that, his words, and his *huge,* hard cock driving in and out of me, there's no stopping the climax. I come so hard, black spots appear in my periphery, and I'm crying out his name.

"That's it," he croons, putting just a little pressure on

my throat, and I clench down even harder. "Fuck baby, yes."

And then, he's coming too, grinding into me over and over as he spills inside me until we're both a heap of heaving, sweaty, messy people.

"Shower." He pulls me off the bed, leading me on rubbery legs to the bathroom.

"Christ, we could have a party in here," I mutter, making him grin.

But then, for the first time since I met him, a thought niggles its way into my brain.

Just how many women has Blake brought home? Has he already *had* a party in here? He doesn't do relationships, but that doesn't mean he doesn't sleep with his share of women.

I let him do that to me without protection. Pregnancy is the least of my worries.

Blake starts the shower, and when he turns back to me, he frowns and immediately steps in front of me, his hands on my face.

"You're overthinking something. Talk to me, sugar."

"I think I'm being an annoying woman, and I should probably go home."

"No." His face goes hard, and his hands firm on my skin. "Talk to me. I don't care if you're being annoying. Tell me what I did to put that look on your face so I can fix it."

"Uh, there is no fixing that." I point at the bed and try to smile, to make us both laugh, but he's not working with me and just waits for me to explain. "I made the stupid comment about having a party in here."

He frowns. "Okay. It was funny. It's a big fucking bathroom."

"But maybe you've already *had* a party in here."

He blinks, then understanding moves through his eyes, and he shakes his head and sighs.

"See? Annoying. So you hop in the shower, and I'll just—"

He kisses me to shut me up, and I have to admit, it works. His hands move into my hair, holding me still so he can destroy my mouth.

"No parties in the bathroom," he says against my lips. "No women in my bedroom. In my *house*, actually. I'm no saint, Harper. Before you, yeah, I was pretty good at casual sex because I had no intention of pursuing a relationship, and I enjoy sex. A lot, actually."

"No harm in that." And I mean it. Whatever he did before me is none of my business as long as he was safe.

"No. There isn't." He pushes my hair behind my ear, and his hands never leave me. His voice is calm and low. Almost soothing. The hot shower fills the room with steam, making it feel like we're in a cocoon. "But I have no interest in anyone else and haven't since the moment I first saw you step onto that plane. So while I was promiscuous in the past, I haven't been in a while. I've been tested regularly, and I'm good to go. But no, this wasn't a fuck pad. It's my *home*. It's my safe place."

"But you brought *me* here."

He steps closer, if that's even possible, and tips my

face up so he can kiss me softly. His fingers on my chin almost scorch me, they feel so damn good.

"Yeah, I brought you here. I *want* you here, Harper. For the first time in my life, medicine isn't my only focus. It's exhilarating and exciting, and I hope you'll let me spend a lot of time with you. To get to know you, fuck you, enjoy you."

I swallow hard at his words.

Blake wants to date me.

"I know that our schedules are tough," he continues as if his words aren't devastating. "But we can figure it out. There are no other women. I promise you that. Jesus, you're all I think about, Harper. You're all I see."

And just like that, every tiny shred of doubt or jealousy is wiped away. Because how could any woman have a man say those words to her and still think that he'd fuck around on her?

Not me. And I was once with a man who *did* fuck around on me. But he never said words like that. He never made me feel like I was worthy of every bit of his energy until nothing was left over for anyone else.

"I'm sorry."

"Don't be. My brothers used to give me a lot of shit for, well, *before*. But I have no interest in that. It's not even a thought. I want *you*, here in my home and my bed, with me. This is exclusive, sugar."

I nod and reach up to drag my fingertip over his bottom lip.

"I prefer exclusive."

"Good. Me too because if another man puts his

hands on you, I won't be happy. Now, let's get cleaned up so I can mess you up again."

"Where the fuck are you going?"

I wince at the rough, growly question and look back at Blake, who's just sat up in bed. I thought I was quiet enough not to wake him. I wanted him to sleep longer.

"Nowhere without you." I snort, then crawl onto the bed with him and snuggle him. His arms wrap around me as he holds me close. I push my nose against his neck and breathe him in, remembering every blissful moment from last night.

It was perfect.

He made me feel *amazing*. Like I was the only woman in the world. Like I'm his only focus, and let me just say, having Blake's undivided attention is *the best*.

I've never really been a snuggler until this man. He held me all night as if he was terrified I'd sneak out on him again. His arms were banded around me, holding me against his chest, and I have to admit that it felt amazing. I didn't feel the need to roll away from him even once.

"I have to go home," I tell him softly and nuzzle his neck as he rolls me to the side, hugging me close. He's still under the covers, and I'm on top, but he doesn't care.

"Not happening."

I smile and cup his cheek. "I do, unfortunately. I have to work in two hours, Blake. I don't have anything here."

He sighs and brushes my hair back from my face. I freaking *love it* when he does that.

"One day, I'll get to have breakfast with you. It's on my bucket list."

I blink at him in the darkness. "Breakfast with me is on your bucket list?"

"Definitely." He kisses my nose. "I'll take you home."

"Thanks. It would be a *really* long walk." I grin at him and kiss his lips before I climb off the bed and pad into the kitchen, where I turn my phone on and wait for it to wake up.

"Do you want coffee?" Blake asks as he joins me in the kitchen. He's in the same jeans and T-shirt from last night, and he's freaking *delicious* in the morning with that disheveled dark hair and sleepy eyes that rake over me from head to toe. "Or an orgasm or three?"

I chuckle and lean over to kiss his biceps, and he pushes my hair behind my ear, sending tingles through me.

"I appreciate the sentiment, but I'll make some coffee at the house and take a rain check on the orgasms." My phone starts to light up, and I scowl. I have missed calls *and* texts, and when I check them, I simply sit on the floor. My legs no longer work as my heart starts to pound and the world spins. "No. No, no, no, no."

"Hey, what's going on?" Blake squats in front of me, also looking down at my phone.

> Greg: Hey sweetie, I don't feel great tonight. Probably should have just stuck with those treats you brought me. Gonna check my sugar.

> Greg: Pretty high. 321. Damn.

> Greg: Should I go to the hospital? Not sure.

> Tucker: Don't panic, okay? I have Dad, and we're at the ER. His levels are too high.

> Xander: Baby sis, need you to answer your phone.

I'm shaking so hard now that I can't hold the phone still, so Blake takes it from me and reads the rest of the messages to me.

"Basically, they admitted him, and he's stable now. Christ, I'm sorry, sweetheart."

"Please take me to the hospital. Right now."

"You got it." He pulls me to my feet and kisses my forehead. He grabs his own phone, my purse, and we're off.

"I shouldn't have turned my phone off," I mutter and drag my hands down my face as Blake hurries the short distance to the hospital. "But dammit, I took him all kinds of things to snack on yesterday. What in the hell did he eat?"

"We'll find out, but he didn't have to eat anything

specific, baby. Sometimes sugar levels get wacky for no reason at all," Blake says, taking my hand in his and kissing the back of it. "No more turning our phones off. We've learned that lesson."

I take a deep breath and look over at him. God, he's amazing. So calm and sure, and steady. Rock solid. I wish I could climb in his lap and cling to him like a freaking sloth on a tree.

And part of me feels so damn guilty because while I was having one of the best nights of my life, the man who raised me was headed for a diabetic coma, scared, and trying to reach me.

"Stop." Blake shakes his head. "You didn't do this, you didn't know it would happen, and you can't go back and change it now."

"I know, but he was scared and trying to find me, and—"

"You *didn't know*, Harper. I won't let you beat yourself up over this. No way."

"I came home to take care of him, not fall into bed with you. I can't just be selfish and fuck the hot doctor and forget that my father is sick and I'm the only one he listens to. I have to be there when he needs me. What am I even doing?"

Tears run unchecked down my face, and suddenly, Blake pulls into the hospital parking lot, but when he parks the car and walks to my side to open the door, he pushes his face to mine before I can get out.

"You're a human fucking being, Harper. A woman with her own needs and feelings. You're allowed to have a personal life outside of your family. No one expects you to be at their beck and call."

"Yes, they do," I reply, my voice even and hollow, even to my own ears. "And they *should*, Blake. After all they've done for me—"

"Loved you?" he demands, his eyes full of angry fire, his hands tight on my shoulders. "They love you. They expect love in return, not absolute fucking devotion, Harper."

"But they *have* absolute devotion from me, Blake. Not out of some sort of misplaced debt or gratitude but because I know what it is not to be loved by the people who are supposed to love you. And the thought of losing Greg, or any of them, is something I can't even entertain. I'm supposed to be here with them. They're *mine*, and I don't have anyone in my life as precious to me as they are. This is important."

I push my hands through my hair and lift my chin.

"I need to see him *now*." My voice is cold. I don't want to fight with Blake or try to justify why I feel the way I do.

"Fine." He backs up so I can get out of the car, but then he grabs my hand and turns me to him. "But you won't refer to us as *fucking the hot doctor* ever again, do you hear me?"

"That's what I'm doing. That's what this is."

He pushes his nose to mine. "*The fuck it is*. Let's go."

He practically drags me through the automatic doors and up the stairs to the second floor where the main admissions is. He asks the nurse where Mr. Hendrix is, and when she confirms that I'm family, she says he's in room 228.

"I'll take it from here. Thanks for the ride."

I start to walk past Blake, but he won't release my hand.

"You're not ditching me."

"Blake, this is a family situation, and you have to work—"

"I will take you over my knee right here and now if you don't stop talking to me like I'm a fucking inconvenience," he growls into my ear so I'm the only one who can hear him. "I know you're upset, but goddammit, Harper. I didn't do this either."

I can't look at him as I blink at tears and swallow hard. I love having him by my side, my hand in his. Being able to lean on him. But I don't know if it's smart to love it or to depend on it. Because I do everything myself. I always have. It's who I am.

"I don't do well with asking someone for help, and my emotions are all over the place. I'm scared."

"Clearly. Come on."

Chapter Thirteen
BLACK

She's a bundle of nerves next to me. Her face is ashen and fierce at the same time, ready to fight for the one true father she's ever known. But her hands are shaking, and she's clinging to me. Her nails dig into my arm even though she doesn't even realize it.

She *wants* me here, but I don't know if she realizes she wants me here.

My girl is struggling with guilt and fear, and I'll be goddamned if I'm going to leave her here to deal with this alone. Not until we have some answers and she's calmed down. Not even when her words try to hurt me.

They don't.

She doesn't mean them.

"I'm sorry," she whispers, holding my hand with both of hers and leaning into me, tipping her forehead against my biceps. "I don't mean to be such a jerk. I just need him to be okay."

I press my lips to her head and breathe her in.

"You're not a jerk. We'll talk about it later, sugar. Let's check on your dad."

Her lips roll in, and she bites that lower lip as she pokes her head around the doorway of Greg's room.

Xander and Easton are here, and Greg is asleep. My eyes go right to the glucose monitor and see that his numbers are stable again, but he has to be exhausted. His blood pressure and oxygen levels are perfect. He's out of the woods.

Easton immediately crosses over and hugs Harper, tugging her close.

"Hey, sweet girl," he whispers. "This one was scary."

Xander glares at me, but I hold his gaze, then gesture for everyone to talk in the hall, so we don't wake Greg.

"I don't ever want to do that again," Easton says, letting out a deep breath.

"Where are Ava and Tuck?" Harper asks.

"Tuck just took her home a few minutes ago to get some sleep," Easton replies. "We said we'd take this shift."

"Why the fuck weren't you answering your phone?" Xander asks Harper, and tears immediately spring to her eyes.

"Absolutely fucking not." My voice is low but hard as I shake my head and take Harper's hand in mine, holding on tight. "You won't speak to her like that. She doesn't deserve it."

Xander rounds on me. "Fine. Why the *fuck* wasn't she answering her goddamn phone? It's not bad enough that we were worried sick about Dad, but we had to worry about her, too?"

"X," Harper says, reaching out to rub his arm. "Stop. I'm sorry you worried, but I'm here now. What in the hell happened?"

"*You* should have answered your phone. That's what happened." Harper's body jerks in response to his harsh words.

What's up with this guy? Why is he taking this whole situation out on her? It's not her fault.

"Take a walk," Easton tells his brother before I can. "Go get some coffee. You're about to be even more of an asshole than usual, and I can't let you treat her that way."

"Fuck," Xander growls before stomping away, and Harper watches him go.

"He's not being deliberately mean." She wipes a tear off her cheek. "He gets this way when he's freaked out."

"Yeah, well, he's annoying the shit out of me," Easton replies. "Dad had spaghetti for dinner. He didn't eat anything too sugary, and he didn't realize that the carbs *are* sugar. He's still new to this, and he's learning."

Harper's eyes close, and she shakes her head as her shoulders droop.

"His numbers look good now," I tell them both. "I'm not his doctor, but his monitors look stable, and he'll rest for a good while until he gets his strength back. Is he on insulin?"

"He's bad about taking it," Harper says. "But yes. I'm going to have to go over every day to give it to him. You guys will have to rotate in when I'm working."

Easton nods in understanding.

"We'll do that," he says.

"I have to go get ready for work." My girl rubs her hand down her face and presses her fingertips into her eyes. "I'll pop in throughout the day. Did they say when he gets to go home?"

"Probably later this afternoon," Easton replies, but I turn to Harper and brush her hair over her shoulder.

"Don't go in today," I tell her. "Stay with your family. You'll feel better."

"I can't." She blows out a breath. "There are no other charge nurses to pick up my shift today. But I can pop in and out. I'll be just one floor up."

Easton nods and pulls her in for another hug.

"It's going to be okay, shortcake."

"I'm so sorry," she says, and I hear the tears in her voice.

Christ, she's breaking my heart.

"Not your fault," Easton says. "And no matter what Xander says, it's not your responsibility to keep your phone on and be at our beck and call."

Harper side-eyes me. That's exactly what *I* said.

"There are five of us," he reminds her. "We all help. Don't forget that. I'll text you if anything changes."

"I'll clock into work, get a read on how things are today, and then I'll check in on you guys," she promises him.

"Okay."

Easton nods at me, and I take Harper's hand to lead her down the hallway. When we come around the corner, we almost run right into Xander, who's still frowning.

"I'll be back in a bit to check in," Harper tells him.

"Yeah. Great."

"Whoa." I shake my head and narrow my eyes at the other man. "*She* isn't the reason that he's in that bed. This isn't Harper's fault, and you won't punish her for it. She's scared, too."

Xander sighs and sets his hands on his hips as he looks at his sister with a frown.

"You scared the piss out of me."

"I'm sorry." She pats him on the arm. "I'm fine. Greg's going to be fine."

He nods. "I love you, you know."

"Yeah, yeah, love, blah, blah." She grins at him, and he tugs on her hair. "I'll see you later."

He nods, but shoulder checks me as he walks past. I can't help but chuckle as we walk out to my car.

"Now *that*," she says after I start the vehicle and pull out of the parking lot to take her home, "is a colossal dumpster fire. In case you were wondering. For future reference."

"He's going to be okay," I tell her. "His numbers were great. He just needs to get regulated with diet and medication."

"I thought we were there," she says. "Looks like we still have some work to do."

"It's not easy. It's a lot to learn, and I have to tell you, he's doing better than a lot of my patients who don't want to listen or make lifestyle changes. At least he's trying."

She nods and nibbles on her lower lip as she reaches for my hand and weaves her fingers with mine.

"Thanks for staying with me."

"You're welcome." I kiss the back of her hand as I pull in front of Xander's house, cut the engine, and turn to her. "Are you okay, sugar?"

"Yeah. It was an alarming way to start the day, but I'm okay. I did have a good time last night."

I smile and cup her gorgeous face. "Understatement."

She meets me halfway over the center console, and I kiss her, then graze my teeth over that delicious bottom lip, and kiss her some more.

"I don't know when I'll be free," she whispers.

"We'll wing it." I tuck her hair behind her ear. "It'll be okay."

She nods and turns to open her door, but I stop her.

"Let me."

I walk around the car and open that door for her, and when she steps out, I pull her into me, hugging her close.

"You sure you're okay, sugar?"

"Better now. You give some really good hugs. You know that, right?"

Grinning, I kiss the top of her head. "It takes two to hug, baby. Have a good day. I'll be at the clinic all day, but just call if you need me."

"Thank you." She boosts up on her toes to kiss me, and then she's gone, up the stairs and into the house.

And I already miss the fuck out of her.

"So …" Bridger comes up to stand next to me, folds his arms over his chest, and we both watch as Dani, Birdie, and Bee fuss over Bryce. He's smiling at them, and they're both puddles as they make faces at the infant. "Harper."

We're at Bee and Connor's place for Sunday dinner. We usually go to Beckett's place, the house we all grew up in on the Double B Ranch, but our family is growing, and my sister's house is bigger. Connor comes to stand with Bridger and me, watching the girls.

The others haven't arrived yet.

"What about her?"

Connor raises an eyebrow. "I missed something."

"Blake's seeing a woman," Bridger says, filling him in, and Connor's green gaze turns to me.

"More than once?"

"Fuck both of you."

They laugh, and then Connor claps me on the back. "Who is she?"

"A nurse," I reply.

"Bryce's NICU nurse at the hospital," Bridger adds. "She's hot. Super nice. Dani loved her to death."

"Hot and nice," Connor repeats, nodding as he crosses his arms, mirroring Bridger's stance. "That's a good place to start."

"Who's hot and nice?"

I turn to find Skyla standing behind us, with my brother Beckett grinning at me over her head.

Clearly, Bridger's already filled him in. This family is full of a bunch of fucking gossips.

"Blake's girlfriend." This comes from Connor, who then opens his arms to hug his sister. "And how are you today, *a stór*?"

"Just fine."

Beckett proposed to the pretty ballerina at Christmastime, and they're planning for a fall wedding. I'm surprised he waited so long to ask her to marry him because it's plain as day that they're meant to be together.

"I want to know more about the pretty girlfriend," Beckett says, but I'm saved when more family comes rolling through the doors. Brooks strides in, and when he sees the baby, his whole face softens.

He's always such a grumpy ass, but he's a softy for the kids and the girls.

Skyla and Connor's parents arrive, followed closely by Skyla's best friend, Mikhail, and his husband, Benji.

By the time my parents get here, it's a full house. A chaotic one filled with noise and laughter, and it makes me grin.

"How are you, my boy?" Mom asks as she wraps her arm around my waist and leans into my side. I wrap my arm around her shoulders and hug her against me, kissing the top of her head.

"I'm great. How are you, Mom?"

"Oh, I'll feel better now that it's warming up outside."

I frown down at her. I know that my mom's rheumatoid arthritis is particularly bad in the winter for her. She doesn't do well with the cold. That's why they moved to Florida a few years ago, but they really missed the family, and with Bridger and Dani having another baby, there's no way you could keep them away.

But I worry about her.

"Are you in a flare?" I ask her, keeping my voice low.

"Coming out of one." She pats me on the chest. "I'm fine, sweet boy. Just sore and a little tired. But I want to hear about you."

"Nothing big to report."

Okay, I just flat-out lied to my mother. I'm falling in love with a gorgeous, amazing woman who has lit my world on fire.

"We'll love her," Mom murmurs and gives me a squeeze.

My gaze whips down to hers, and she just smiles.

"A mother knows these things."

"I swear you're psychic."

She wrinkles her nose. "I know my kids. Whenever you're ready, bring her around."

I nod and kiss her head. She makes a beeline for that baby, and I go in search of my brothers, who slipped away when Mom walked over to hug me.

I find them outside, near the grill.

Brooks sits by himself, a beer in his hand, listening to

the others, and I pull up a chair next to him after I grab a bottle of water out of a fancy-as-fuck cooler.

Everything in this house is bougie. And it should be. My sister married a fucking billionaire.

"Haven't seen you in a hot minute," I say before taking a sip of water.

"We've both been working," he replies.

Brooks and I have always been close. I miss spending time with him.

"How's the shop?"

"Busy as fuck. I'm hiring Jake Wild, Ryan's boy, this summer. He's about to graduate from high school, and he's interested in mechanics. He's a good kid."

I nod in agreement. Our family has been friends with the Wilds for as long as I can remember. Ryan adopted Jake a few years ago, and Brooks is right. The kid is awesome.

"He'll do well," I reply with a nod. "And how's Gabe working out?"

Gabe's our cousin and recently started working for Brooks last year. He lives in Silver Springs but makes the commute over.

"He's damn good at his job," Brooks replies. "I don't have any complaints about any of my guys right now."

"That's great. So what do you know about the Hendrix family?"

Brooks's gaze snaps over to mine, and he narrows his eyes. "Why do you ask?"

I shake my head and watch as Beckett and Bridger laugh at something Connor just said.

"It's nothing bad. I've started seeing Harper, and I know that you're friends with Tucker."

Brooks isn't often taken by surprise, but this time he is. He wings up a dark eyebrow. "The nurse?"

"Yep."

"I don't know her at all," he replies. "Sold her a car, but that's it."

"I know. It looks like a heap, Brooks. You couldn't do better than that?"

"It runs like a fucking dream. She should have gone somewhere else if she wanted something new and pretty. Is she unhappy with it?"

"No, she likes it."

He scowls, then lets out a laugh. "You're such a fucking snob."

"I am not." I shake my head, and Brooks keeps talking.

"Tucker's a solid guy. I think they're a good family. That's all I know."

I nod, and the girls come outside to join us. Birdie makes a beeline for me, climbing into my lap and wrapping her little arms around my neck in the sweetest hug.

Christ, this little girl holds my heart in her hands.

"Hi, Uncle Blake."

"Hi, cupcake. I like your braids."

She runs her hand down her long hair and preens. "Mommy did it when Daddy gave Bryce a bath this morning."

I glance over to see Dani sitting in my brother's lap, a smile on her sweet face.

Suddenly, there's commotion as Dani's brother, Holden, and his wife, Millie, come walking around the house to find us.

"You're here," Dani says, jumping up to give her brother a big hug, and Birdie pushes out of my lap to welcome them as well.

Holden was really the father figure to Dani and her three sisters in every way that counts since they were tiny. Their mother died when the youngest sister, Charlie, was a baby, and their dad was an abusive prick. Holden is the eldest and often brought the girls over to our ranch to keep them safe and let things die down at home.

He's a good friend to all of us, and I love that we're officially family through marriage.

"Hey, little mama," he says to Dani, brushing her hair off her face. "How are you feeling?"

"I'm all recovered," she says with a smile.

Holden spent a lot of time at the hospital when Bryce was in the NICU, making sure that Dani was okay.

He's just the best there is.

"Where's that baby?" Holden asks, looking around, and Skyla gently passes Bryce into Holden's arms.

"You have such a goofy grin on your face," Bridger taunts Holden with a smile.

"It's a *baby*," Holden reminds him. "It's my girl's baby. You're so handsome, aren't you? Just like your uncle Holden."

I smirk, then wink at Millie as she walks over to sit next to me.

"So."

"Not you, too."

Millie snickers into her hand, then laughs outright as if she just can't control it.

"I've watched you make your way through a lot of women in this town."

"No, you haven't." I scowl over at her. "That's a gross exaggeration."

She shrugs a shoulder. "But I like this one. She got you coffee."

Everything in me softens at that. Yeah, my girl got me coffee and brought me breakfast after I had to walk away from her in that bar.

It ranks up there as one of the single worst moments of my life, and I'll never repeat it.

And the fact that she thought to bring me food after I'd failed her like that? It absolutely stunned me.

"She brought him coffee?" Brooks asks.

"It's just a cup of coffee."

Millie scowls and smacks my shoulder, and I pretend that it hurt.

"You're a baby," she says. "And it's not *just* coffee. My drinks are masterpieces."

"Right." I decide that I need to change the fucking subject. "Hey, Billie, how's book club going?"

Billie grins over at me. "So great. We've upped it to twice a month because there's so much interest. We have a meeting later this week."

"Oh my God, the book is so good," Dani gushes. "And I'm coming to this one. I need to get out of the house and be around grown-ups."

"I'm so excited you're coming," Skyla says, clapping her hands. "Beckett and I have loved this one as well."

I raise an eyebrow at my brother, and he smiles smugly.

"You should give it a try," he says.

"What, reading romance books?" I ask.

"Yeah. They're good, man. Skyla and I read together every night."

"Dani started reading some to me, too," Bridger admits. "They're not bad."

I blink at my brothers. I have nothing at all against romantic literature. I think it's awesome. Hell, my sister has built a thriving and incredibly successful business from it, and I'm damn proud of her.

I just never expected to hear that my brothers enjoy it.

I glance over to Brooks and find a strange look on his face.

"What's wrong with you?"

He shakes his head. "They're not wrong."

My eyebrows climb into my hairline. "Are you telling me that you read smut between oil changes?"

"Don't be a dick," he says with a huff. "Jul—I've read them. *Before.* They're good for a relationship."

That's right. Juliet's a reader and got Billie started reading them when Billie was a teenager.

Before everything blew apart.

"Have you been to the new place?" I ask in a low voice, but everyone's listening in.

"No."

"Brooks."

"Give me the baby," he says, abruptly standing and crossing to Holden, who gently passes the sleeping baby over.

Brooks rocks side to side and kisses Bryce's little head.

"It's still fresh for him," Millie murmurs. "After all this time."

I nod. "Yeah. Something like that doesn't go away."

"We're having beers at the Wolf Den," Beckett informs me. "While the girls do book club."

"I happen to have that night off, so I'll join you."

"I'll be at home with my babies," Bridger says and kisses Birdie on the head.

"I'll watch them," Mom offers with a smile. "And you go out."

"Are you sure?" Dani asks her. "They're a handful."

"I had five children, darling girl," Mom reminds her. "Birdie and I will keep Bryce in line."

Chapter Fourteen

HARPER

"Baby Alice needs to be fed," my coworker tells me before she goes off shift. "She's the only one I didn't get to in time. She's only about ten minutes behind, and her mom called and said they wouldn't be able to make it to this feeding."

"Got it." I nod and start to walk toward the tiny preemie. She was born at just three pounds, and now she needs time to grow. "Have a good night."

It's my last evening on shift, and then I get a couple of days off, which I'm ready for. I love my job, but nights are particularly brutal for me.

I'm a day dweller.

But we all take turns to make it fair because babies aren't only sick during banking hours. Eventually, if I'm able to work my way up to the director of the department, I could move to day shifts all of the time, but that would mean less patient care. It's a catch-22. I love working with the little ones, so moving out of this role doesn't excite me.

Alice is eating comfortably in my arms as I rock us back and forth in the chair when my phone buzzes with a text.

The grin on my face is massive when I see it's Blake.

I miss him. I haven't seen him since that morning almost a week ago when Greg gave us all a scare. Between our jobs and families, we haven't had time to see each other, but we've sent a lot of messages back and forth, and he's called me every chance he gets.

I have no doubt in my mind that Dr. Blackwell is interested in me, and it's not all sexual. He checks in and asks how I am, if I need anything, and what he can do for me.

He's so freaking swoony.

But really, at the end of the day, the only thing I *need* is to spend time with him, and time isn't something we have to give each other right now.

It makes me wonder if pursuing something with Blake is a smart idea. But then, the thought of not having him in my life makes my heart physically hurt in my chest. I know that unless he's the one to end it, that's not an option for me right now either.

So I guess we'll simply keep going the way we are for the time being.

I open the texts and feel heat spread over my cheeks.

> Blake: So he's giving her sex lessons?
> In this book of yours?

I shift Alice onto my shoulder so I can burp her and type out a response.

> Me: Says who?

Biting my lip, I wait while the little bubbles bounce, and Blake replies to my message.

> Blake: I found your paperback on my couch where you left it the other night, and it seems I'm getting an education along with the female character.

Yeah, like Blake needs any advanced education on sex. The man could teach his own college courses on the subject. When I realized I left the book behind, I downloaded it on my reading device so I could keep going.

It's fucking *amazing*.

I snort and set my phone aside to finish up with little Alice, get her comfortable in her crib, then move on to make my rounds and check in with everyone else.

Jamison's mom is rocking him, skin to skin, and she's silently crying to herself, so I squat next to her and lay my hand on hers.

"Hey, Naomie," I say softly. "Is there something I can do?"

"No." She wipes at her tears, and I stand to get her a box of tissues, which she accepts. "No, it's just hard. I hate that I can't be up here more often with him. He deserves to have me with him all day, every day, but I have two other kids and a full-time job."

"You're doing the best you can."

She shakes her head and just looks so damn sad.

"My best isn't good enough. I'm a single mom, not by choice. And I already have so much going on at home. I think I have to give Jamison up, and it kills me, but I *know* in my heart that it's the right thing to do for him."

I blink quickly, completely blindsided by this conversation. "Naomie, this is a huge decision. I can arrange for you to speak with the hospital's counselors again and—"

"I've been through it until I'm sick to my stomach," she replies, taking a long, deep breath. "And the only time that I'm even remotely relieved or feel better is when I picture him with a family who can take care of him. We don't know what kind of medical needs he's going to have long term. I don't even have insurance. I have no idea how I'm going to pay for his hospital stay."

She starts to cry again and reaches out for my hand with her free one.

"I love him. I love him *so much*, but Harper, I think I have to love him enough to do what's right for him. And I'm not going to lie, for me, too. And for my other two kids. I don't have a big family. I don't have help. I can't do this by myself. I thought I could, but I didn't expect him to be born so early, and it's just too much. I know that makes me a bad person and a horrible mom, but—"

"Listen to me right now." I hold her hand a little tighter, and her eyes find mine, swimming with tears and despair. "You are *not* a bad person or a horrible mother. You're being realistic about what you're capable of, Naomie. You're thinking of *all* of your children and taking into consideration what their needs are. I think you're an incredibly strong woman. I also urge you to spend one more session with a counselor to make certain that this is right for you. To make sure that it's not exhaustion or fear talking. I don't want you to do something you'll regret for the rest of your life."

Jamison makes a little squeaky noise, and Naomie smiles down at him.

"I know. Thanks for letting me talk for a bit. I'll talk with the counselor and my doctor, but I think I've made up my mind, Harper."

She checks the time on her phone.

"Shit, I have to get home to put the kids to bed. My sitter has to go."

"I'll take him." Naomie transfers Jamison into my arms. She kisses his sweet head before she gathers her things and smiles at me.

"Thanks again."

"You're welcome. Will I see you tomorrow?"

She pauses and presses her lips together. She won't look at the baby now.

"Maybe."

And with that, she walks away, and I cuddle Jamison for a minute longer, then kiss his tiny cheek and lay him down.

God, that sucks.

The whole situation just tugs at my heart.

My phone buzzes in my pocket, and I remember that Blake was texting me.

> Blake: Sorry to blow up your phone, but this scene in front of the mirror? Happening. Just warning you.

A smile tugs at my lips as I shoot him a reply.

> Me: Yeah? Lucky girl. I might be jealous.

That's right, I'm a smart-ass. Not even ten seconds later, he responds.

> Blake: That's one orgasm that I'll deny you. Keep talking shit, and you won't come for a month, sugar.

I squeeze my thighs together and take a deep breath because *holy hell,* the man pushes all of my buttons.

> Me: Just wait. It gets better. I love that book. I can't believe you're reading it.

> Blake: You left it here. I was going to bring it back to you but decided you'll have to retrieve it yourself.

> Me: Not very chivalrous of you.

> Blake: I have your chivalry right here, beautiful girl.

I laugh at that and quickly reply.

> Me: I'm at work. Stop distracting me with your flirty texts.

> Blake: Do you need anything? I can bring you something to eat.

God, I'd love to see him. Hug him. I'm damn tempted to say yes.

But then I'm called down to L & D for an emergency.

> Me: Thank you so much, but I'm okay. Emergency just came in. Have to go. Sleep well, Blake. x

---

I really need tonight. It's my night off, and it's Spicy Girls Book Club time with Ava, Billie, and all the other girls I've come to know and like so much in such a short period.

This is only our second book club, but Ava and I are *hooked*.

"Wine?" Skyla asks, holding up the bottle.

"Please," I confirm with a nod. "I don't have to work tomorrow, so keep it flowing."

Skyla grins and pours me a glass, and I choose a seat next to Ava.

At least twenty-five people are here tonight. I recognize the owner of the Sugar Studio, Jackie, who just set out a spread of huckleberry lemon bars and chocolate cupcakes. Millie's here, along with Dani and two of her sisters, Alex and Charlie.

"Have you memorized everyone's names yet?" Billie asks as she joins me, a bottle of water in her hand.

"I don't know if I ever will," I reply with a laugh. "I feel like I need name tags and a chart of some kind."

Billie giggles and pats me on the shoulder. "You'll figure it out. You already know at least half of these ladies."

Before long, we dig into talking about the book and what we loved about it.

"It was sweet how he *always* reminded her that she's gorgeous. That she shouldn't be self-conscious no matter her size because he thinks she's incredible," Ava says, and there are nods all around.

"But can we talk about the hot tub?" Alex asks. "Because *holy shit*, that was hot."

"And the mirror," someone else joins in.

"And the limo," Millie adds, and we're all chuckling before long.

"I think the shower was my favorite."

Our heads turn at the sound of a man's voice, and I almost swallow my tongue when I see that it's Blake, along with Bridger and a couple of men I don't recognize.

"You know," Billie says, "I wish we could get through just *one* book club without my brothers interrupting."

I blink at her and turn back to Blake.

"He's your *brother*?" I demand.

"Those three are," Billie replies, pointing at Blake, Bridger, and another man whose name I don't know. "And that one is my husband."

"Hey, bumble. I missed you," her husband says with the same accent as Skyla, and I start to connect the dots.

"Whoa. That means that Skyla's with ..."

"Me." The one who must be Beckett speaks up and walks right to Skyla. He picks her up and sets her in his lap. "You're fucking gorgeous, Irish."

"Holy swoon," Ava says under her breath, making me huff out a laugh.

Staring at Blake, I shake my head. "Is there anyone in town who you're *not* related to?"

"A lot of people, actually," he says. "But there are a few I'm related to by marriage."

Bridger snuggles Dani, and Blake's suddenly sitting in the seat next to me. He reaches for my hand and lifts it to his lips, nibbling my knuckles.

"*That's* him?" Ava asks me in a whisper-yell that has Blake grinning. "Christ on a cracker, Harpsichord."

"Harpsichord?" Blake eyes me. "That's cute."

"Hi." Ava sticks her arm in my chest, reaching over to shake Blake's hand. "I'm Ava. Nice to finally meet you. I've heard a lot." She glances at his lap, and I want to *die*. "Like a *lot*."

"CAN WE NOT?"

"It's a pleasure," Blake replies, shaking her hand and grinning at me. "So she talks about me, huh?"

"Why is book club suddenly turning into torture Harper club?"

"It's fun," Ava replies and turns back to Blake. "She doesn't tell me enough, but she's said a couple of things, especially after Thanksgiving. *That* was a story."

"I want to die." I close my eyes and wish that I was anywhere but here. "Just a handy heart attack or a little lightning strike would work."

"I'm a doctor," Blake reminds me, kissing my hand again in front of everyone. He has mischief in his dark eyes, and I want to climb him. "I won't let you die."

"Wow, that's super hot," Ava says with an approving nod.

"Why are you talking?" I ask her, but she just rolls her eyes and keeps going.

"So you're a doctor. Does that mean you have a healthy 401k? A nice house? Do you have a shit ton of student loans to pay off? What are you doing to secure your future?"

"Oh. My. God. Ava Marie, shut your mouth!"

Everyone around us is laughing, including Blake, who looks as relaxed as can be.

"Yes, yes, no, and I could tell you, but that's a long, boring conversation." His grin turns to me. "Wanna get out of here, sugar?"

"He calls you sugar," Ava whisper-yells, and this time, I cover her mouth with my hand.

"You have *got* to shut it, or I will sew your lips closed."

"Ah, sisterly love," Dani says, winking at her own sisters. "It's so fun."

"Mmp mnnph mmb," Ava says against my hand.

"What?" I take it away, and she smiles sweetly.

"You're keeping him."

"I swear to Jesus and every single one of the disciples—"

"You're not particularly religious." Ava interrupts.

"I will smother you in your sleep."

"Before I have to bail you out of jail for homicide, let's go." Blake stands, takes my hand, and pulls me to my feet. And then, to my utter shock, he frames my face and lowers his mouth to mine, kissing me fiercely. This is *not* a safe-for-work kiss. This is the kind of kiss reserved for sexy nights at home.

"Atta girl," Ava says, and Blake smiles against my lips.

"I fucking missed you, sugar."

"Go get a room." I think that was Bridger, but I can't be sure.

"On it," Blake agrees and threads his fingers with mine. "Bye, everyone."

I wave as I grab my handbag, and I'm being led out of the bookstore, everyone laughing and smiling at us as we go.

"Did you drive?" he asks.

"No, I—"

"Excellent." He leads me to his Mercedes and pins me against the side, kissing me again. This time, his hand fists in the back of my hair, keeping my face just where he wants it as he continues to plunder my mouth. "Come home with me."

"I can do that."

"And this time, stay for fucking breakfast."

I bring my hands up to his face and soak him in. "I can do that, too. Can we swing by my place so I can grab some stuff?"

"How many days off do you have?"

"Two."

"Grab enough for two days, then. Because I'm not letting you out of my sight for the next forty-eight hours."

I blink up at him in surprise. "You don't have to work?"

"It seems I've found a reason to use my vacation days. I haven't had you in a week. That's unacceptable."

"We knew our schedules would be tough, and your job is important."

"Priorities are ... expanding." He kisses my forehead. "Come on. Let's get your stuff so I can get you home."

He opens the car for me, and within minutes, we're headed out of town toward Xander's house. Xander happens to be in the living room when we walk inside.

"You're home early—*oh*. Let me guess, you won't be staying?"

"I'm going to have wild and crazy sex with Blake for the next couple of days," I inform him. "If all goes as planned, I won't be able to walk right when it's time to go back to work."

"For fuck's sake," Xander spits out as Blake covers a laugh behind his hand. "Don't say shit like that."

"I'm a *grown-up*, Xander Hendrix. I don't know why you've suddenly forgotten that, but it's true." I shrug at him, then turn to Blake. "I'll be down in five."

"Take your time," he assures me. "There's no rush."

As I jog up the stairs, I hear Xander run his mouth. However, I'm surprised when it doesn't sound like he's giving Blake a hard time.

"Sisters are the bane of my existence," Xander says.

"I get it. I have one," Blake replies.

I don't hear anything else because I rush to my room to pack an overnight bag with enough stuff for two days of clothes, underwear, and toiletries.

When I return, the men are actually laughing.

"Whoa. Did you two sign a peace treaty or something?"

"Or something." Xander tugs on my hair. "Be safe."

"He'll wrap it before he taps it."

Blake snorts, but Xander's face turns mutinous. "For the love of God, Harps."

"I'm just teasing you." I laugh and give him a one-armed hug as Blake opens the front door and waits for me. "We don't use condoms. Have a good night!"

Xander's swearing up a blue streak as I laugh and hurry to Blake's car.

"I can't help it. He's just too much fun to harass."

Blake's still laughing when he gets in the driver's seat. "I think he's going to need therapy after that."

"He needs therapy for a lot of things. I'm happy to add topics for him. He'll get his money's worth."

Blake leans over and kisses my cheek. "Let's go home, sugar."

"Let's do it."

Chapter Fifteen
BLAKE

She sits quietly in that passenger seat, holding my hand so tightly, as if she thinks I might disappear.

Not fucking happening.

I disentangle our hands and drift my fingers up between her legs, over her soft-as-fuck skin, under her little sundress, and press the side of my hand against her wet panties. She widens her legs, giving me access to her, and my fingers tighten on her smooth skin.

"I'm fucking craving you." My voice sounds like gravel, and I smirk in satisfaction when her thighs clench, and she gasps. "I plan on being inside you every moment possible for the next few days. Do you have a problem with that?"

I glance over to see her lick her lips and shake her head.

"No problem."

"Good. Now, I want to know if you're this wet because you were talking about those filthy books you like or because of me."

She huffs out a laugh and spreads her legs a bit more, giving me more access to her warm pussy, and my cock is already hard and weeping in my jeans.

Fuck, I've missed her.

"Oh, it's because of you. Shit, all you have to do is breathe in my direction, and this happens."

I can't stop the smirk in response to her admission. "Good answer, sugar."

After pulling into my driveway, I cut the engine, but before I can get out of the car, Harper says, "Wait."

She unbuckles her belt and dives across the console, unfastens my jeans, and unleashes my cock. My girl doesn't tease. She doesn't flick her tongue around the rim or smile coyly up at me. No, she immediately sinks her mouth over me, making my head fall back against the seat.

"Fucking Christ."

"You can't do that," she says when she comes up and pumps my cock. "You can't say stuff like that, kiss me like you did back there, and expect me to be chill."

She shakes her head and sinks down again. I can't resist threading my hands in her hair and holding on.

I don't push her down at first, but her hand comes back to cover mine. She presses herself harder onto my shaft, and I take the hint.

"You want me to fuck your gorgeous face, Harper?"

She moans, deep in her throat. I thrust up into her, pressing her head down, and feel the crown slide into her throat.

She doesn't gag.

Fucking Christ, she's perfect.

"God yes, baby. Suck me just like that." She hollows her cheeks and pulls me so deep. Her nose is pressed against my skin, and I have no fucking idea how she's not gagging. "Swallow my cock, Harper. I'm going to come down your throat. Is that what you want?"

She moans, sucks harder, and cups my balls with her free hand, and I lose it. I come hard, seeing stars as I fill her throat and mouth with my cum, and this gorgeous woman cleans me right up, then sits back in the seat.

Grinning at me.

She swipes her mouth with the back of her hand and looks so damn pleased with herself. I can't resist yanking her to me so I can kiss the fuck out of her.

"I'm going to fuck you *everywhere* in this house."

"Don't threaten me with a good time." Her hands are in my hair, fisted, and Christ, I think I might lose control with this woman.

I climb out of the car and cross to her side, then take her hand and lead her inside the house. The door is barely closed behind us when I turn to her, cage her in against the door, and kiss her like I'm starved for her.

Because I am.

I boost her up, and she wraps her legs around my waist, and we cling to each other as we explore each other's mouths. She tastes like wine and heaven.

She tastes like *mine*.

"Hang on to me, baby."

She loops her arms around my neck and holds on while I walk to the kitchen, where I set her on the edge of the counter and lift her dress over her head, tossing it aside. My lips go immediately to her soft neck, nibbling up to her ear.

"You take my fucking breath away, beautiful girl."

"You're biased."

With a shake of my head, I tug on that earlobe, making her shiver. "No. I'm not. There isn't an inch on you that I don't want to fucking devour, sugar."

She sighs and reaches for the hem of my shirt, tugging it up.

I pull away long enough for her to discard the shirt and toss it away. Then her hands are on me, and it's as close to heaven as I'll ever get.

Leaning forward, she presses her sweet lips to that spot right between my collarbones and works her way down to my sternum.

"You taste good," she murmurs against my skin, making me growl.

Gripping her face in my hands, I tip her up so I can kiss her sweet lips, and her hands make a dive for my jeans.

We have two whole days to take it slow, but that's not what this is. Right now, it's been a week since I've seen her body, been inside her, *touched her*.

I'm not in the mood for soft and slow.

She works my jeans over my hips, and my already

hard cock is in her hand, pulsing into her grip. One touch, and I might embarrass myself and come.

Moving her panties to the side, I circle her opening, and she moans. I push one finger inside, and she gasps, biting that bottom lip.

"Fucking incredible," I whisper as she guides my cock to her, and without another word, I press inside, and we both groan. "Your pussy hugs my cock so damn well."

"You stretch me so damn well," she replies breathlessly. "Please, Blake."

"What do you need?"

"Please *move*."

I slide out and thrust in again, and she nods.

"Yes. More."

Her hair is like silk in my fist as I tip her head back, right where I want it, so I can plunder her mouth while I fuck her. She whimpers and holds on as my hips push harder and faster, and then we're both looking down, watching my hard length move in and out of her wet pussy.

"Rub your hot-as-fuck clit."

Her response is immediate. Her finger draws a quick circle around her hard nub, and she clenches me even tighter, making me groan.

"Just like that, beautiful." Her pussy spasms around me, and I know she's close. "Look at that. Look at how well you take this cock. Your wet cunt can't get enough, can it?"

She shakes her head, bites her lip, and falls over into a powerful orgasm that has her legs shaking.

Without pulling out of her, I lift her and carry her to the wall, where I continue to pound into her, unrelenting in my chase of another orgasm for both of us.

"Blake." Her voice catches as she clings to me. Her release soaks both of our thighs, and still, I don't let up, pounding over and over in her, driving her up this wall with every thrust. "Oh God."

"That's it, baby. That's it. You've got another one for me."

"Can't."

I grin against her lips, then bite that lower lip *hard.* "Fucking give it to me, Harper."

She whimpers, but I can already feel the quivering in her pussy.

"You're trying to kill me."

"Never." I slam into her, and that's all it takes. "Be my good girl and come all over me, baby."

She cries out as her pelvis pushes against my own, and we both come, breathing each other's air. I'm completely lost to her.

As we start to come down from the high of the climax, I push her hair off her cheek and brush my nose over hers.

"We needed that."

"A week is too long," she agrees. "It's cruel and unusual punishment."

I laugh and carry her once more toward my bedroom, loving the feel of her in my arms. "Same page, baby. It won't happen again. Now, let's go take a bath, and you can tell me about your week before I fuck you again."

She buries her nose in my neck and sighs before pressing a sweet kiss there. "That sounds really nice."

I set her on the vanity and get to work filling the tub with hot water and some Epsom salts. It's not particularly sexy, but it'll feel good because we've only just started with the sex portion of our two days together, and she'll get sore.

While the tub fills, I finish stripping us out of the last of our clothes, then step between Harper's knees, wrap my arms around her, and hug her to me.

This woman snuggles up against me and kisses my chest.

"I've never been a cuddler," she confesses softly. "But I like this."

"Good. Because if you're around, I'm a cuddler." I kiss the top of her head, then turn to check the water. "Tub's full. Let's get in."

I help her in first, and she scoots forward. I wiggle in behind her, then pull her against me.

"This feels nice," she murmurs. "I could fall asleep in here."

"Let's not," I reply with a grin. I reach for a washcloth and drag it over her skin. "Tell me about your week. How was work?"

She sighs and leans her head back against my shoulder, and I can't resist kissing her temple.

I can't keep my lips off this woman.

"It was rough, actually. I have one patient whose mom is likely going to give him up for adoption, which just makes me sad for her, but I understand where she's coming from and respect the hell out of her."

I spoke with Naomie a few days ago. My heart goes out to the woman.

"I lost a baby two days ago," she continues. "She was doing well, and then everything just went wrong all at once. It happened so fast. And her parents were right there, and *shit*, it sucked."

I kiss her head and squeeze her to me.

"I'm sorry."

"Me too." She hugs my arm against her. "But we sent five babies home, and right now, we only have one critical case and three growers, at least when I left this morning. So that's good. I really like my coworkers. There's not a lot of pettiness or bullshit."

"Always a bonus."

She nods against me. "Greg is home and back to himself. He's been better about his meds, and I make him send me his sugar levels twice a day. I know I'm annoying him, but until he's settled into a routine, I need to stay on top of it."

"I'd do the same," I reply. "He's been feeling better?"

"Yeah. At least, he tells me he is. Now it's your turn. How was *your* week?"

"Interesting. Frustrating." I shrug and drag the cloth up the outside of her thigh.

"Why interesting?"

I smile and kiss her head. "There's always a case that comes in that tests my skills. Things I need to figure out."

"Do you like that part of the job?"

"I do, yeah. I like solving puzzles, and I seem to get a new one every day."

"And why was it frustrating?"

"Because I wanted to see you, and we couldn't make it happen."

She's quiet as she takes that in. In fact, she's quiet for so long that she's starting to make me nervous.

"What's on your mind, sugar?"

"I don't know how we make this work." The words are whispered quietly as if she's afraid to speak too loudly. "I guess we just take our couple of days where we can get them."

My stomach clenches at the thought of not being able to work this out with her, and then she's turning and straddling my thighs, her arms around my neck and those gray eyes rock me to the core.

She takes my breath away. Her nipples are hard and dripping with water as my hands glide over her hips and around her back.

I want to ask her to move out of Xander's house and in with me. Then we might get more stolen moments together between shifts. I'd at least see her every day, even if only for a few minutes.

But even I know that it's too soon for that. I don't want to scare her away.

"We're going to keep doing what we're doing," I say instead and drag my hands up and down her slim back. "We're going to talk as much as possible, see each other whenever we can, and take it day by day. We're going to figure it out, Harper, because being without you isn't an option for me."

She blinks and bites her bottom lip. "I don't want to be without you either."

"Good. Then the rest will work itself out."

She leans her forehead against mine. "I hope so."

Armed with a tray full of fruit, oatmeal, bacon, and scrambled eggs, I walk into the bedroom and smile when I see my girl still asleep in my bed.

She should be in my bed every fucking night.

It's no surprise to me that she's still asleep. I kept her up most of the night, talking and fucking until we were so exhausted that we couldn't keep our eyes open.

But I was awake with the sun, and since this is the first time I get to enjoy breakfast with her, I got up to make her the meal in bed.

I set the tray aside and climb over her, peppering kisses over her warm face and neck.

Harper stirs and loops her arms around me.

"Good morning," she murmurs with a sleepy voice that has me hardening again.

I can't get enough of her.

"It's the best morning I've had in a long while," I confirm. "I made you breakfast."

She smiles. She still hasn't opened her pretty gray

eyes, and she stretches beneath me, pressing her naked breasts against my chest.

"Yum. Is there coffee?"

"Of course."

"I smell bacon."

I grin and kiss her chin. "If you opened your eyes, you'd see everything."

Slowly, she blinks them open and smiles up at me. "You're the best thing I've ever woken up to."

And just like that, here at this moment with that sleepy declaration, I've slipped right into love with this remarkable woman. There's no going back for me. She's everything I never knew I needed in my life.

"Same goes, baby." I nuzzle her cheek and then roll away before I spill all of my heart and soul at her feet. "Come on, I finally get to enjoy breakfast with you. I've waited a long time for this."

She scoots up on the bed and pulls the covers over her breasts, tucking them under her arms. I pass her a mug of coffee, and she takes a sip.

"So good," she says. "What else do we have here?"

I run through it all, and when I hold up a slice of bacon, she bites off the end and grins while she chews.

"Delicious," she says. "I didn't realize you were such a big breakfast lover."

I shake my head as I settle in next to her and take a bite of oatmeal.

"I'm not. I'm a big fan of the idea of you still being here for this meal." I offer her a spoonful of oatmeal, and she takes it. "And I have to say, I'm hooked. Breakfast should be our new thing."

"Wow, we have a thing." Sleepily, she sips her coffee. "I like that."

She pops a strawberry in her mouth.

"I want to hike with you today," I tell her, and her eyebrows climb, her eyes brightening at the idea. "If you're up for it."

"I'm always up for a hike. Where should we go?"

"There's a spot on the Wild River Ranch that's really nice, and I have permission to hike there whenever I want to. I'd love to show it to you."

"Sure, that sounds nice. Is that Millie's family?"

I nod and eat some eggs. "Yeah. Most of them live out there. The only one who doesn't is Ryan because he has his own ranch not too far away."

She nods thoughtfully. "His wife, Polly, goes to book club. She owns the dress shop in town. She's really sweet."

"They're all good friends," I reply. "What do you think of Bitterroot Valley, sugar? Now that you've been here for a while."

She chews more bacon and tips her head to the side, thinking it over. "It's really great. I mean, I can't find it in me to root for the high school football team here because they were our biggest rivals, but aside from that, I love it."

I grin and lean in to nibble her lips. "That's fair. Although we kicked your ass my senior year."

"Did you play?"

I nod and reach for a slice of peach. "I was the quarterback."

"Of course, you were." She snorts, and I narrow my eyes at her.

"What's that supposed to mean?"

"I'm just not surprised. You probably also dated a cheerleader and were prom king."

My brows pull together in a frown, and she bursts out laughing.

"I knew it."

"There's nothing wrong with any of that," I tell her.

"Nope. Not at all."

"Okay, what about you? What were you like in high school?"

Harper laughs and turns to face me, bringing her legs up toward her chest. "I was *not* popular. I was a book nerd, and I was scrawny and a little shy. Once, this idiot in my study hall decided it would be funny to shove me in a locker—"

I growl low in my throat, and she shakes her head.

"And Xander ended up shoving *him* in a locker and got suspended for it."

"I need to buy Xander a beer."

"Everyone knew that Ava and I had three older brothers who would kick their ass if they messed with us, so mostly I was a wallflower. I liked it that way. I don't like being the center of attention."

"You're the center of *my* attention," I remind her.

"For two days." She nods, but I lean in and press my lips to her ear.

"Even if I'm not physically with you, you're the fucking center of my attention. You're never far from my mind, sugar."

She bites her lip and shakes her head.

"You're too good to be true."

"What does *that* mean?"

She moves to scoot off the bed, but I keep her next to me, my hand on her arm and because it's physically impossible for me to keep my hands to myself, I tuck her hair behind her ear and drag my fingers down her jawline.

"What does that mean, Harper?"

"The other shoe is going to drop. Something has to be wrong with you. You'll be sweet like this for a while, and then when we're alone, you'll tell me I'm stupid. Or you'll sleep with someone else. Or you'll remind me that I'm a shit nurse."

"Whoa." Shaking my head, I pull her onto my lap and wrap my arms around her, keeping her against me. "None of that is going to happen. You're not stupid in the slightest, baby. You're an amazing nurse. I've seen you in action. And I already made it clear that you're the only woman I see."

"For now," she breathes and nuzzles her sweet face into my neck. Her sigh has my heart aching.

"Not for now." I pull back and hook my finger under her chin, bringing her gaze back to mine. "Who the fuck put this shit in your head? The guy you ran away from?"

She simply nods.

"You need to tell me what he did, baby. I need to

know so I understand what demons I'm navigating through here."

She sighs again and closes her eyes. "I know. Maybe we can talk while we hike?"

"That's fine." I kiss her lips and push my hand over her neck and into her hair. "No shoe is dropping. I'm not that idiot. Not even close."

"Okay," she whispers. "Let's go hike."

Chapter Sixteen

HARPER

I cannot *believe* that I spewed that shit in bed this morning. We're having a great time together, and I had to let my insecurities and the baggage from Nathan the moron rear its ugly head.

And now, Blake, who didn't deserve even one word of the comments I made, needs an explanation.

He *deserves* an explanation.

But this is so humiliating.

"This is the Wild family's ranch. It's actually the Lexingtons' as well since they combined the properties after Millie and Holden married, making it the biggest cattle ranch in Montana," Blake says. He's holding my hand as he drives down a gravel road off the highway. When the road forks, he keeps right and soon we're driving around a lake. There's a beautiful house and dock on the lake, with what looks like a large shop nearby.

"This is Chase's house," Blake continues. "He and Summer built it not long ago."

"It's a beautiful spot," I reply, taking it all in. It's truly stunning, with gorgeous views of the mountains.

"Yeah, Chase chose well when he decided to build here," Blake agrees and pulls to a stop at a little trailhead. "This is us."

I nod and step out of the car. I didn't bring my pack with me, but Blake has one we put snacks and water in, and once he has that strapped to his back, we set off through the woods.

"This is about a five-mile loop," he says. "But we can turn around anytime."

"I'll be fine," I assure him.

It's an overcast spring day, but it's not too cold, and it smells so freaking good in these trees. Pine and earth and fresh air mingle to create Mother Nature's perfume, and I absolutely love it.

"It smells good out here," I say, taking a deep breath.

Blake nods and takes my hand, links our fingers and brushes his thumb over the back of my knuckles. He's waiting. He's being patient and sweet because that's who Blake is. I *know* he's not Nathan. He's absolutely nothing like that piece of shit. So why do I get those intrusive thoughts that Blake will behave the way my ex did?

Trauma response? Maybe. It's fucking ridiculous. One more thing to be ashamed of.

"I wish I could forget him," I begin quietly. "Like, just give myself selective amnesia or something and erase those few years of my life from existence."

"I think we all have moments we would use an eraser on if we could."

I nod and lick my lips, thinking it over. Just like always when I think about that time in my life, I start to feel nauseous, but I swallow it back and lift my chin.

I can do this.

"First of all, what I'm going to tell you is stuff that I've never told anyone. Not even Ava."

"Why?"

I frown up at him, and he leans down to kiss my forehead. "What do you mean?"

"I mean, *why* didn't you tell your best friend in the world what was going on, sugar?"

"Because I'm mortified. I'm so fucking embarrassed. I don't want to tell you either, but if we're going to make a go of this, you need to know because I have bad moments sometimes, and that's not fair to do to you without giving you some context."

His hand tightens, and he stops us cold.

"Should he be in jail, Harper?"

I soften and lean in to hug him. "No. He never hit me or did anything illegal."

He relaxes a bit, kisses my head, and we start walking again.

"I met him at the hospital where I worked in Portland. He's not in health care. He was visiting his sister, who had a baby in the NICU in a situation similar to Bryce's."

Blake nods, listening. His face is calm and relaxed, and his hand is firm but not too tight in mine.

He's okay. I need Blake to be okay because, by the time I get to the end of this, I might not be.

"He seemed nice. Pretty normal. His family didn't like me, and I know now that they wouldn't like *anyone*. Nathan—never Nate. He doesn't do nicknames—was the golden boy. The perfect son, the perfect everything. So no one would ever live up to their standards for him. Anyway, he asked me out, I said yes, and we dated for a while. It was casual and normal, and I never even fucking suspected that he was a piece of shit."

"That's not uncommon," Blake reminds me, pushing a low-hanging branch out of my way.

"No, it's not. He was the *sweetest* human being. I'm not kidding. He never lost his temper, he doted on me, and he was understanding of my work schedule. It was *way* too good to be true, but I ate it up. When you have an early childhood full of neglect and being invisible, and a handsome, attentive man turns his attention to *you*, you just eat that shit up."

Blake nods and still seems okay, so I keep going.

"We'd been together for about a year when he proposed, and I said yes."

That has my man stopping short and scowling down at me, his jaw tense.

"You were going to marry him." It's not a question, and it makes me bite my lip in apprehension.

"Well, for a minute, that was the plan. But—"

He frames my face and kisses me hard as if he's claiming me and reminding me that I'm *his*. And it feels so damn good that I lean into him and hold on.

"I don't have to tell this story," I whisper when he pulls away and still looks upset.

"I'm okay." He takes a breath and kisses my forehead. "I didn't realize you'd been engaged, and, well. Turns out I'm a jealous fucker. That's new. Keep going."

We continue on the trail, and I try to gather my thoughts.

"After he proposed, things went sideways pretty fast. He'd lose his temper and snap at me for things that were just stupid. He thought it was funny to make fun of me in front of his friends or family, then cover it up and kiss me, or hug me, so it looked like I was in on the joke."

"Make fun of you how?"

"Little things, like point out that I had something in my teeth, and then laugh, or that I had a spot on my shirt. Little humiliations."

"Death by a thousand cuts," he murmurs, and I nod because that's exactly what it was.

"Very much, yes. When we looked at buying a house, he insisted that it be only in *his* name, and that I was nowhere on the mortgage. In the end, that really worked out well for me because I could leave without any ties to him."

Blake's grinding his teeth now, but I keep going.

"About six months into the engagement, after we'd moved into the house, I found out he'd been fucking his secretary." I snort at that, then laugh out loud. "What a cliché. Then because she was mad that he'd dumped her, she texted me receipts of a bunch of *other* women he'd slept with and totally ratted him out. I wish I could say that I was surprised. Before he proposed, I would have been devastated and shocked, but after? Not really. He was evasive about where he was in the evenings, and he became, well, a dick. *Not* the man I dated the year prior. And I knew, Blake. I just *knew* that it wasn't going to work for the long haul, but I didn't know how to put the pieces together to leave. So I used my job as an excuse to sleep in a different bedroom because of working nights and said I didn't want to disturb him."

"But you didn't want to be there."

"Hell no. He was never going to touch me again. I didn't know where the hell he'd been."

"Good girl." He squeezes my hand in encouragement.

"I didn't know what to do. I didn't want to tell my family because they'd already done so much for me, and to admit that I'd gotten myself into that mess and ask for help just wasn't an option for me. I *did* tell Ava that he'd cheated, but not about the mental abuse."

"Expand on that part," Blake says as we climb to the top of a hill. We pause to take in the view, and I keep talking.

"It grew into him being a jerk *all the time.* He would nitpick everything. What I wore, what I said. If I was home during the day, he'd come home on his lunch break to make sure I was where I said I was. Not because I was a liar—"

"Because *he* was," Blake guesses, and I nod.

"There were times when he'd lock me in a room for eight hours or more and lecture me. Yell at me. Remind me that I'm worthless, that I'm not fun, I'm horrible at my job, I'm a shitty friend. I'm despicable in bed."

"Fucking hell, I'm going to kill him."

I shake my head. "He did that often. Usually if I was happy about something and he needed to remind me that I suck."

"So why—" He stops talking and when he doesn't go on, I do it for him.

"Why did I stay so long?" I nod and let out a breath. "Well, that's a good question. I knew I would *not* marry him. That wasn't going to happen. But I also had to plan how to leave. I didn't have family nearby. I had a couple of work friends, but no one that I was close to, and I don't trust easily, Blake. I don't make friends quickly. I could have called Greg and the others, and they would have come right out to get me, no questions asked. But I also had a job, and—" I shrug and sigh with frustration. "I felt *stuck*. I felt like I made that choice, and it was my job to figure it the fuck out."

"Okay." Blake turns and pulls me into his arms, hugs me close and lowers his lips to my ear. "Okay, baby. I'm sorry. I just hate that you were ever made to feel anything but perfect because you *are*. But you're safe now."

"Yeah." I blink quickly, not wanting to cry. "I am."

"So what happened?"

"A miracle in the form of a bachelor party."

Blake's eyebrows wing up as we keep going on the path.

"Oh, there's going to be a *ton* of huckleberries up here in a couple of months."

He nods. "Yeah, this is a great picking spot. We can come back when they're ripe."

The fact that he hasn't already written me off is a good sign.

"I'd like that. I make a really great huckleberry lemon loaf, and I'm dying to try it gluten-free. Anyway, there was a co-ed bachelor party for one of his friends that I was expected to go to. It was in Vegas." I wrinkle my nose, and Blake snorts.

"Not a fan of Vegas?"

"Not particularly. Again, so cliché. Plus, his friends weren't super warm and welcoming. I didn't really want to go, but then one of our nurses got fired, and we were short-staffed, so I had to stay back and work. I thought he'd jump at the chance to go alone and do whatever the fuck he wanted in Vegas. I didn't really care. I'd *so* checked out of the relationship by then. But he was *livid*. Said it made him look bad to his friends, and I'm unreliable, and my job is stupid, and blah, blah, blah."

I roll my eyes, and it makes Blake laugh.

"You really didn't care what he thought."

"Not even a little. At that point, I walked on eggshells, mostly because I didn't want more lectures, and I was *so tired* of living with him. I was saving to get my own place. But he went to Vegas, and I worked, and when he got home, he stopped speaking to me altogether. Like, I got the silent treatment for *weeks*."

"He didn't speak to you for weeks?"

"Three weeks. He'd glare, and he'd still check on me on his lunch breaks, but no words were spoken. It was fucking *bliss*."

Blake snorts. "I'm sorry, it's not funny. What an asshole."

"I can laugh at a lot now because he was so ridiculous. While he gave me the silent treatment, I found the traveling nurse job. It paid well, and I could leave Oregon and put some distance between me and him. I told my family I was breaking up with him, and they were glad. Especially because Ava spilled the beans about the cheating. I think all of the brothers wanted to kick his ass."

"*I* want to kick his ass, sugar."

I laugh. "He was supposed to go on a work trip, and I was going to leave then. I know it sounds chickenshit, but he owned a gun, and he was so unstable sometimes that I didn't trust that he wouldn't hurt me when I told him it was over."

"Smart girl," Blake says, kissing my head.

"But just three days before that trip, Nathan decided the silent treatment was over."

"Shit."

"Yeah. He started in on one of his lectures, and I completely shut it down. I grabbed a few things—most of my stuff was already packed and shipped ahead to Ava—and I told him that he was never allowed to speak to me again, and I left. I've never seen him, or heard from him, since then."

We walk over a bridge where a waterfall runs through and stop to take it in.

"I already had trust issues," I say to him as he leans his back against the railing, listening to me. "And then he happened, and it really made me second-guess myself and my instincts."

"He was a lying asshole, and it took him a while to show you exactly who he is." Blake tucks a piece of my hair behind my ear. I notice he does that a lot when he wants to touch me, and I kind of love it. "But you got away, Harper. You stood up for yourself, and you ended it."

I blow out a breath, listening to the water. "Yeah. I should have done it sooner. I also need to apologize because I never should have said what I did this morning. I know that you're not the same person. That was an instinctual moment for me after what I went through with Nathan. I know, in my heart of hearts, that you're nothing like that man. You'd never intentionally hurt me, but it's a trauma response. It's been so ingrained after those two years that sometimes I just react, even if it's not what I really think."

Blake glances at the waterfall as if he's thinking, and for a heartbeat, I worry that he's about to call this whole thing off.

"We're still learning each other," he says. "Relationships aren't easy. I will tell you that I *don't* have the patience of Job. I can lose my temper now and again. Mostly when someone I love is hurting or if things don't go right at work."

"I can be a downright bitch when I'm hangry," I inform him, and he chuckles and drifts his finger down my arm. "And I don't know if you've noticed, but I'm a smart-ass."

"I might have noticed." He laughs again when I narrow my eyes at him. "I'll keep you fed, sugar. I won't *ever* disrespect you the way you have been. I'd never intentionally hurt you. Infidelity doesn't interest me. In fact, it pisses me off."

"Right? If you want to fuck someone else, that's fine, but break it off with the one you already have first. It's not hard."

He nods, a smile tickling his lips. "He's an absolute fucking idiot, Harper. I'm grateful because now you're mine, and I'll never make the mistake of fucking it up with you like that, but what a complete moron."

You're mine. Why does that make me so hot?

"Yeah." I toss my hair over my shoulder. "I *am* a catch."

I'm relieved that it's all out there and that the mood is lighter. Blake's eyes are full of tenderness and happiness as he stares down at me, and then he's taking the pack off, and I start to feel drops of rain on my face.

I look up in surprise.

"It's raining."

Blake also glances up and then smiles at me. "You might melt. You're pretty sweet."

I snort at that. "Right. So sweet."

He takes my hand and pulls me against him, wraps his arm around my waist, and presses his forehead to mine.

"You taste sweet," he murmurs just as the sky opens up and starts to *pour.*

We stare at each other in shock for a minute, and

then we start laughing. Blake kisses my wet nose and starts to dance with me. Not a little swaying slow dance, either.

He twirls me under his arm, then pushes me away and twirls me back again. If I'm not mistaken, we're doing the jitterbug here on this bridge, in the woods, in the pouring rain.

And it might be the most romantic moment of my life.

"You've got moves, Dr. Blackwell." I laugh when he dips me back and bites my neck before spinning me away from him again.

"Everyone should dance in the rain," he says, and then his arms loop around me, and he's swaying me back and forth, his lips pressed to my forehead. We're soaked to the bones, but I don't care. His lips find mine and brush back and forth before he melts into me, his tongue gliding over my lips and tongue. We both groan, pressing harder against each other.

"You're amazing," he says against my lips. "There is *nothing* about your past that scares me. You're so fucking strong, Harper. I'm proud of you. And if you need me to remind you every fucking day that I am your biggest fan, that I want to lose myself inside you and *only* you every chance I get, and that you're absolutely beautiful inside and out, I will. I have no problem with that."

I cup his cheek and close my eyes, leaning into him. "Thank you."

"It's my job to make sure you feel safe."

"You do. But I think it's my job to make *you* feel safe,

too. It goes both ways. And I feel awful that I didn't do that for you this morning."

"No more feeling awful." He hugs me to him, here in this downpour, and holds me close. "But I might have to go to Portland to kick someone's ass."

I scoff, but I see he's not kidding when I look up.

"Not worth it."

"Oh, I think it would definitely be worth it."

Shaking my head, I pull back. The rain is starting to lighten up. "I just need you here, with me, and Portland can stay in the past where it belongs."

"Deal. Come on, sugar, let's get you out of this rain before you melt away on me."

"I think we have to run back to stay warm."

He lifts an eyebrow. "Are you okay with that?"

"Psh. You forget who you're talking to."

I take off ahead of him, careful not to slip and fall in the muddy spots, and hear his footfalls behind me. I know he can run much faster than me, but he's keeping my pace. When we get back to the car, the sky opens up again, and the rain comes down in sheets.

Blake lets the backpack fall to the ground, and pins me against the side of the car, his hands cradling my face, and he's kissing me here in the rain.

"You're incredible," he says, meeting my gaze. "I don't give a shit about your past, Harper. I don't care. I want *you*, and everything that comes with you."

I cling to him. His words are a balm to my battered soul. How did I find him? How did it take me this *long* to find him?

Finally, he backs away and opens the car door, and I realize that not only are we soaked, but now we have to ride back in his fancy Mercedes.

"Get in the car," Blake yells above the noise of the rain hammering around us.

"No way. I'll ruin your fancy seat."

"I don't give a fuck about the seat. Get out of this rain, Harper."

He tosses the pack in the back, and I wince as I sit on his leather seat. Blake climbs in next to me.

"Your poor car."

"It's just a car, baby."

"No, *my* car is just a car. This is more than that."

"Nope." He takes my hand and kisses my fingers. "As long as you're okay, I don't care about this vehicle. Let's go home and get dry."

"We might just stay naked for a bit."

His eyebrow lifts. "That's a fantastic plan."

Chapter Seventeen
BLAKE

"Are you hungry?" Harper kisses my cheek and rubs her hands over my chest, over my sweatshirt. We're fresh from a hot shower, dressed, and my stomach growls, answering her question. Her eyebrow shoots up. "That's a yes."

"I could eat." I lean into where she's sitting on the bathroom vanity and kiss her delectable lips. "What do you want for dinner? I can cook, or we can go out. Whatever you want."

"I *really* want Sage and Salt." She bats her eyelashes at me and bites her lower lip, and Christ, I can't say no to her.

Here's hoping Brooks doesn't find out and kick my ass.

"Then that's where we'll go." After kissing her once more, I take her by the hips and lift her off the vanity. We grab our things and head downtown. It's still raining its ass off, and I haven't taken the time to truly process everything that Harper told me on the hike.

I want to burn her ex to the fucking ground. I don't understand how anyone could be so careless with her. So intentionally cruel. She's one of the best people I've ever met in my life. She's so fucking brave, upending her whole life to get away from a monster. She's loyal to her family and loves them all unconditionally. I have the utmost respect for her work ethic and how compassionate she is with her patients. She's so damn sweet. So kind.

"You're quiet," she says from the passenger seat, and I reach over to put my hand on her thigh.

"I'm fine, sweetheart. Hungry."

"Are *you* a bitch when you're hangry, too?" She smiles over at me, and it makes me laugh.

"Aren't we all?" I snag a parking spot, and Harper doesn't wait for me to get her door. She pushes out and meets me on the covered sidewalk. "You didn't wait."

"It's raining," she reminds me. "You don't need to get wet again."

I pull her against me and kiss her forehead. "Always wait for me."

Leading her into the restaurant, I press my hand to the small of her back and take it all in.

Way to go, Jules.

This place is beautiful. It looks like something out of a farmhouse magazine, with white shiplapped walls, hanging green plants, and black trim. The menu is a giant black chalkboard behind a counter where you place your order, and it smells fucking great.

"I *love it* here," Harper says, practically bouncing on the balls of her feet. "The fajitas are to die for."

"Good to know." When we get to the front and Juliet looks up at us, every muscle in my body stiffens.

You hurt my brother.

She hurt all of us.

"Hey," she says and blinks furiously. I'm sure this isn't easy for her either. I look a lot like my oldest brother. I haven't seen Jules in person since she moved back to Bitterroot Valley. I know that Billie and Beckett have both seen her. Juliet goes into the bookstore often, and Beck sells her all of her dairy products.

But I haven't laid eyes on her in fifteen years.

"Hey, girl," Harper says, oblivious to the turmoil raging in my gut. "This is Blake." Harper weaves her arm through mine and leans her head on my biceps. "He hasn't been in yet, but I've been singing your praises."

Jules nods and smiles at me. It's genuine.

"We know each other," I reply, nodding at Juliet. "How are you, Jules?"

Her lips fold in for a second, and she forces another smile. "I'm doing well, thanks. Welcome in."

"It's a great spot," I tell her, meaning it. "I hope you kill it."

She clears her throat, then sucks in a breath. "What can I get you?"

Harper has gone quiet, and her gaze bounces back and forth between us. Her eyes are narrowed just slightly as if she's trying to solve a puzzle.

One that I'll have to put together for her later.

Once we've ordered our meals and I've paid, Harper and I choose a table by the windows. I reach across to take her hands, but she pulls out of my reach.

"Don't fucking do that." I shake my head at her, but she licks her lips and still won't let me touch her.

"Did I just really fuck up?" Her brows are pulled together in a frown.

"Yes. You pulled away from me, and I'm not okay with that."

"The vibe back there was *thick* with awkwardness," she says, shaking her head. "Christ, Blake, you should have warned me."

"There's nothing to warn you about."

"I'd like to know if you and Juliet—"

"No." I push my hands through my hair and look Harper dead in the eyes. "No, she's Brooks's ex. And there's a *lot* of history there, but I'm not the key player in that drama."

She seems to deflate with relief. "Thank God. I mean, I know there are women out there who you *do* have a past with, but I love it here. I don't want it to be awkward because you and the owner used to bang."

I snort out a laugh at that and then wince. "God, no. She was like a sister to me at one time."

Her eyebrows climb in surprise, and she folds her arms, leaning her elbows on the table. "What happened?"

Just then, one of Juliet's employees places our meals in front of us.

"Enjoy," she says with a smile and walks away.

I take in the fajitas that I got thanks to Harper's

recommendation and feel even more pride. "This looks so damn good."

"So good," she confirms around a bite of her own dinner.

"Jules and Brooks were a couple all through high school and college. They were young, but it was serious. We all just assumed they'd end up married one day."

Harper pauses and sets her fork down, frowning at me. "What happened?" she asks again.

"A lot happened." I take a bite of my food and think about how much I should tell her. It's not my story to share, and it's something that Brooks will absolutely *not* talk about. "There was some betrayal, and I suspect some misunderstandings, although Brooks never told us everything that went down. When all was said and done, they were finished, and Juliet left town."

"She just *left*?" Harper asks, her head tilted to the side. "It must have been a *lot* of shit that went down."

"I'm sure it was, but none of us knows the whole story. Only the two of them know everything. What I do know is that Brooks was never the same. It truly broke his heart. He withdrew from us for a while until the family basically forced him to let us back in. But he refuses to speak of her, and no matter how many times we ask him to tell us what happened, he clams up and leaves. It's not open for discussion."

Harper shakes her head sadly. "That's really sad. I'm sorry to hear that. Is that why you haven't been in here before?"

I look around and notice that Juliet is watching us.

When my eyes catch hers, she turns away to wipe down a countertop.

"Yeah, that's why. I *loved* her as much as I love my own sister. She was always around. She and my brother were attached at the hip for the better part of a decade. So yeah, I've avoided this place."

"I'm sorry." My girl reaches across the table and slides her palm against mine, holding on tight. "If I'd known, we could have gone somewhere else."

"You love it here."

"Blake, you don't have to be uncomfortable just because I like the food here. I can come alone."

"I'm fine." I give her hand a squeeze. "How's your ravioli?"

"Fucking delicious. You'd never know that it's gluten-free. Here." She holds her fork up to my mouth, and I take the bite from her.

"Fuck, that's good."

"Right? So good. We can do takeout from now on if it makes you more comfortable."

"I'll be just fine, sugar. Don't worry about me."

She tips her head to the side. "I'll worry about you because I care about you. But I believe you if you say you're okay. Because I just fell head over heels for this ravioli."

And I've fallen head over heels for you.

"Yes, right there." She lifts her hips beneath me and turns her head to bite my arm as I move in and out of her at an easy, steady pace. Her pussy hugs me so fucking perfectly that I can't help but question if it's real. It's early as fuck, the sun isn't even thinking of coming up yet, but I had to have her one last time before I take her home.

Because I'll never get enough of this incredible woman.

"Your body was made for me," I whisper into her ear. It's so quiet, so dark, it's like we're in our own cocoon, wrapped up in each other. "So fucking perfect."

She moans and lifts her leg higher on my hip, opening herself up to me more, and I press my hand to the back of her thigh as I start to push faster. A little harder.

I can't help myself.

"Just like that," she whispers. "God yes, just like that."

"Come for me, baby." I lick my thumb, then press it to her clit, and she squeezes her muscles so tight, she's fucking strangling me. "Jesus, I'm going with you. Fuck, Harper."

She grips onto my ass, her nails biting, and that's all I can take. I rock into her as the orgasm works down my spine, through my balls, and I coat her pussy in my cum.

Her back bows, her muscles tighten, and with a low moan, she comes with me.

Burying my face in her neck, I breathe her in.

"Good morning," she murmurs against my shoulder and presses a sweet kiss there.

"Morning." I roll us to the side so I can hug her to me but not crush her. "I don't want our two days to be over."

She wraps her arms around me and hugs me back. "I don't either. Let's quit our jobs and stay right here."

I grin against her forehead. "Okay. I'll make some calls."

"I mean, I can survive in a tent. We could probably pitch it on your family's property and be fine."

I chuckle and roll again so she's on top of me, and with my arms wrapped around her shoulders, I hug her close. She nuzzles her face against my chest.

"We could grow food and sell it in the summer," I suggest.

"Oh, good idea. Except I have a black thumb and don't love the dirt."

"Okay, I'll grow, and you sell."

She nods. "Except I hate people. We have to think of something else."

"I hate to break it to you, sugar, but I think we have to keep our jobs."

She sighs and rubs her nose over my chest. "Okay. Well, then, I'd better get up if I'm going to get to Xander's, change, and get myself to work on time."

"We have time for a quick breakfast," I tell her. "If we hurry."

"Right. Breakfast is our thing. Let's do it."

She pushes off me, but before she can leave the bed, I snag her wrist and tug her back to me. I grip her jaw and kiss her hard and deep.

"That'll tide me over," she whispers against my lips before I let her go.

Harper has made herself at home in the kitchen, which fills me with contentment. I lean on the counter as she whips up some scrambled eggs for breakfast burritos, watching her efficiently grate some cheese to add to the eggs.

She pulled her hair back into a ponytail, and she's dressed in leggings and a T-shirt. Her face is clean of makeup.

She's mine.

Harper glances my way, then does a double take. "Why are you looking at me like that?"

"Like what?"

She finishes grating and then starts to build the burritos. "I don't know. I can't put my finger on it."

"I'm just watching you, sugar. I like having you in my kitchen."

"It's a great space. The countertops are freaking *huge*. I could make some really great sugar-free cinnamon rolls here. Greg would love those."

Move in with me, and this kitchen is all yours, sweetheart. Hell, she can have whatever the fuck she wants.

She licks her thumb, then taps her phone to light up the screen.

"No news from the family?" I ask.

"No, and no news is good news." She grins and leans over to kiss my arm. I love how physically affectionate she's become with me as if it's as natural as breathing. "I'll check in with Greg this evening. I told him I'd come to his place for dinner. I think some of the others are coming, too."

My eyes stay glued to her as she plates the burritos and passes me one.

"Cheers." She lifts her breakfast and taps it against mine before taking a massive bite. "Mmm, good."

She does make one hell of a breakfast burrito.

Before I'm ready, we're in the car headed back to Xander's house, and we're both quiet as we drive in the predawn light.

"Thank you," she murmurs, and I glance over to see her watching me. "I had a really good time."

"Me, too." I take a breath and let it out slowly. "I'll see you later today. I'll swing up on my way to the ER before my shift."

Her lips twitch. "I'd love that. I can swing through the ER on my way home from Greg's and bring you a bite to eat for dinner."

I nod, already excited to see her later. This is just how it might be for us for a while. Stealing moments here and there.

"You're on for three days?" I ask her.

"Yes, three on, then three off. What's your schedule like this week?"

I try to mentally pull up my calendar. "Half day in the clinic today, ER tonight. I have two more days in the clinic after that. I *think* I have a couple of days off once those are done."

Harper bounces in her seat, making me grin.

"The stars have aligned our schedules again."

"Thank God for the stars." I pull up to Xanders, then push out of my car and walk around to open her door. When she steps out, I tug her against me and kiss her long and slow. Her hands fist in my sweatshirt, making me groan. "If you don't go inside, I'm going to fuck you against this car."

She licks that bottom lip. "Rain check."

With a smirk, I pull her bag out of the back seat, and she takes it from me. I kiss her forehead, breathing her in one last time.

"Have a good day, Harper."

"You too." She grins at me, then she jogs up the stairs to the door, keys in the code, and disappears inside.

Rubbing my hand over my chest, I get back in the car and drive off. But when I get home, the house smells like Harper, and it's way too empty without her, so I fill a gym bag and decide to go lift some weights.

Bridger's the fire chief, and he's offered up the gym at the fire station for us siblings to use whenever we want, so I head there. It's quiet this morning. The sky has lightened to gray with the predawn light, and birds chirp as I walk inside the fire station.

No one is in the locker room, and once I've changed and shoved my stuff into a locker, I walk out to the weight room and grin.

Brooks and Bridger are at the squat rack. Brooks is lifting, and Bridger's watching, and I immediately feel good about coming here so early.

"Hey," Bridge says with a smile as I stride to them.

"Good morning." I shake my brother's hand and pull him in for a man-hug, and do the same to Brooks once he's racked the bar and stepped over.

We're all tall in our family, well into the mid-six-foot range. We're muscular and broad naturally and add in the workouts we all do, and well, we're strong.

But Brooks takes it to another level.

The man looks like he could wrestle professionally. He could give the Rock a run for his money in the size department.

"How's it going?" Brooks asks.

"It's great. I just dropped Harper off at home and thought I'd come work out for a bit. I don't have to be at the clinic until around noon."

Bridger's eyebrows climb in surprise. "You let her stay all night?"

"Don't be a dick." I shake my head and walk over to the barbells for curling. My brothers follow me over. "She's stayed a few nights now. At *my* house."

"Hold up." Brooks crosses his arms over his chest. "This is a relationship."

"Fuck yes." I set the barbells down and wipe my hand over my face. "It is. And you two can give me shit all you want, but I don't care. She's great, and I plan to spend as much time with her as possible."

They both stare at me, and Bridger sets his hand on my shoulder. "Good for you. I like her, you know that. I assume she's on the same page."

"Same page," I agree with a nod. "I'd like to murder her ex for being a general asshole and giving her some insecurity issues, but otherwise, things are great."

"Everyone has baggage," Brooks says and starts doing curls of his own. Double the amount of weight that I just lifted.

Asshole.

"If you care about her, don't give up on her."

Bridger and I share a look.

"Brooks, I have to tell you something."

"If it's about someone with a J name, no, you don't." He glares at me, and I shuffle my feet.

"Yeah, I do because I feel fucking guilty. Harper loves her restaurant and wanted to eat there yesterday, so I took her."

He blinks at me. "And?"

"And that's it."

"You feel guilty because you ate dinner at a restaurant?"

Bridger grins, and I scowl.

"That J name you won't talk about owns the fucking place, brother. And she was there, and I had to say hi, and yeah. I feel fucking guilty."

Brooks shakes his head. "It's a small town, Blake. Eat wherever the fuck you want. I don't care."

But I see the hurt in his eyes, and I hate it.

"Have you seen her since she's been back?"

The smile leaves Bridger's face.

"No."

"Maybe you should rip the bandage off."

Brooks shakes his head and walks to a leg machine, wearing a scowl on his face.

"You're going to run into her," I tell him. "Like you said, it's a small town. You're bound to see her at the grocery or the post office. Maybe her car will break down and need your shop—"

"I'm not having this goddamn conversation with you."

"Fine." I hold my hands up in surrender. "I just love you, man. And this sucks."

Bridger blows out a breath. "Did Connor call you guys about staying up at the new lodge for a few days this week?"

I frown and pull out my phone. There's no call, but I do have a text that I missed over the past couple of days when I was with Harper.

> Connor: The first phase of rebuilding the resort is almost finished, and I'd like to have the entire family up to stay for a few days to use the restaurant, the spa, everything. Bring your girl. I've also invited the Wild family, hoping to fill most of the rooms to give my staff a trial run before reservations start. It'll be fun.

He lists the dates, and I see that Harper and I will both be off work those days.

"This sounds like a good time," I say, shoving my phone back in my pocket.

"We're taking the kids up," Bridger says. "Birdie's excited about the pool. Dani not so much."

"Hell, *I'm* excited about the pool. I'll swim with Birdie," I reply. "You in, Brooks?"

"I'll go up for a bit," he confirms. "The guys at the shop claim they can handle things without me."

"They can. You're just a control freak."

A grin breaks out on my brother's face, making me blink.

Brooks never smiles like that.

"You have no idea."

Chapter Eighteen
HARPER

"Do you need an ice pack?" Ava asks as she slips a french fry in her mouth, then grins at me.

"For what?" I stab some lettuce on my salad and take a bite.

"For your vag after two straight days of sex with Dr. Big Dick."

I choke on my salad, and Ava cackles like a nutjob. I take a few sips of my water, then scowl at my best friend.

"Shut it. You can't call him that here."

"Oh stop." She waves me off and glances around the hospital cafeteria, where we're having lunch on my break. I haven't seen her in what feels like forever, and she had time to meet me today. "No one even heard me. Listen, I'm just jealous. Because he's *hot* with a capital H, and he has it so bad for you."

"You think?"

"Was I the only one at that book club meeting?"

She snorts and eats another fry. "He couldn't stop looking at you, and his eyes got all soft and gooey. I'm surprised cartoon hearts didn't float and pop over his head."

"We're not that disgusting."

"You're totally disgusting," she counters and smiles so widely, she could light up the room. "And I love it for you. You deserve someone who thinks you hung the moon, Harps. Because you fucking *did*."

I stare at her and blink slowly, feeling my eyes heat and my lower lip quiver.

"Don't make me cry at my job," I whisper.

"Okay, how about this. I met a guy," Ava says nonchalantly, trying to change the subject. "At the grocery store, actually."

"Holy shit, talk to me. I need details. Who, what, where, and when. The why is obvious."

"Why?"

"Because you're the shit."

She preens at that, making me chuckle.

"Okay, so his name is Joe."

I lift an eyebrow. "Are we sure that's his real name?"

"I mean, I didn't ask for identification. Why would he lie? Men are named Joe."

I nod and shrug. "Fair enough. What does Joe look like?"

"He's pretty cute. Taller than me, red hair, muscles. He likes to run."

We stare at each other, then both say, "Ew," before dissolving in giggles.

"You know, he's a little not toxic enough for me, but I'm enjoying him for now."

I shake my head at her. "Is that your way of saying he's a nice guy, and you're not into nice guys?"

"Kind of. Listen, I like a guy who's a little morally gray. A little mean to me sometimes."

"No, we don't want that. Trust me. No being mean." Jesus, I *really* need to tell Ava everything that went down with Nathan because I know for a fact that she does not want mean.

"Not asshole mean. I'm talking in the bedroom mean. Bite me, smack my ass, call me a whore. You know, that kind of mean. Joe is *so* vanilla. I told him to pull my hair, and he stared at me like I'd lost my mind."

I close my eyes and take a deep breath. "I can't take you out in public. We can't have these kinds of conversations *where I freaking work*."

She glances around and smiles at the doctors sitting at the next table, and my face explodes with heat.

"I apologize," I say to them, and they just shake their heads.

"All I'm saying is, he's not Mr. Forever. He's Mr. Right Now. And that's okay." Ava flashes me a grin. "Do you think Dr. Big Dick is Dr. Forever?"

"I'm going to gag you from now on."

She smirks and tosses her shiny auburn hair over her shoulder. "Kinky. No, really. How much do you like this guy, Harps?"

I blow out a breath and push my finished salad aside.

"A lot. I like him a *lot*. I can imagine a lot of things with him."

"Weddings and babies?" She blinks at me, suddenly serious.

"I don't think I want babies, you know that, but the rest?" I bite on my lower lip, thinking about Blake and how he makes me feel. "He makes me feel safe. He's *kind*. I told him all about Nathan."

"You haven't even told *me* all about that piece-of-shit fucker." She narrows her eyes, and the guilt punches me in the chest. "What did he say?"

"That my past doesn't scare him, and he wants me no matter what."

"Wow." Ava fiddles with her necklace. "Well, this is a recipe for something awesome, and I'm here for it. I love it for you. Like I said, I saw the look in his eyes, and it's not just sex for him."

"It's really good sex," I whisper behind my hand.

"I should hope so. If a man looks like him and the sex is bad, that's a sin against humanity."

I smirk at that because she's right.

"Are you going to be at Greg's tonight for dinner?" I ask her as we gather our trash and walk toward the cafeteria exit.

"Yeah, I'll be there. I think we're all going. Dad's excited."

"What's on the menu?" I ask. "Do you know?"

"Tuck's grilling some steaks and veggies. I'll bring a salad."

"Good." I nod, relieved that the menu is all appropriate for Greg. "What are you off to do now?"

"I'm going to go scandalize Joe and suggest he fuck me in the middle of the day when the sun is out and everything." She rolls her eyes and winks at me. "I'll see you tonight."

I wave at her, then take the stairs up to my unit.

It's busy today. We took in three more babies while I was away, and all three are critical patients. We have parents coming and going, asking questions and needing things.

Aside from my thirty minutes with Ava, there hasn't been time to slow down all day.

And by the time my shift is almost over, I'm wrung out. I'm standing at the nurses' station, my laptop on the high part of the counter so I can stand and type when I hear my name.

"Harper?" I turn to see what my coworker Amy needs. She's a seasoned nurse who's worked in this hospital for more than thirty years, is now part-time, and I adore her.

"Yes, ma'am, what do you need? I just need a sec to finish this note—"

Amy smiles and gestures behind her. "Dr. Blackwell is here to see you."

My heart does a little two-step in my chest when he smiles at me, and I close the laptop.

"Thanks, Amy. Hey, I'm going to take five. The patient in bay six needs a fluid change."

"I'm on it." Amy winks at me, pats my shoulder, and leans in close. "Go get him, girl."

With a laugh, I stride over to Blake, take his hand, and pull him behind me down the hall and into the stairwell, where he proceeds to press me against the wall and kiss the hell out of me.

The two-step has moved from my heart to my lady bits, and I'm not mad about it.

"Hey," I say when he pulls away. "How's your day been?"

"Not bad, actually. I hear the ER is busy, so I have to get down there, but before I do, I need to tell you about something."

"Okay." I nod, listening. "What's up?"

"Did you know the ski resort burned down about a year and a half ago?"

"Yes, I heard about that."

"Well, my brother-in-law Connor is rebuilding it. The first phase, which I guess is the main guest lodge, is ready for customers, but he wants to do a test run on it before they take reservations. He invited our whole family, the Wilds, and who knows who else to come stay for a few days during our days off."

I'm blinking at him, trying to keep up.

"Okay, I hope you have a great time."

Blake huffs out a laugh and shakes his head. "No, baby, *we're* invited. You and me."

I frown up at him. "He specifically included me?"

"Yes. He was at the book club. He saw us together."

"Oh, right." I nod, and my stomach is tied in nervous

knots. "I don't know, Blake. Maybe you should just go have fun, and I'll see you when you're back."

He frowns at me. "I don't want to go without you." He brushes his knuckles down my cheek. "I want you to spend time with the people I love. I don't know if you've figured it out yet, but you're my girlfriend."

"Wow, we're labeling this."

"Call it whatever you want." He pushes in closer to me. "You're mine, and I'm sure as fuck yours. I want you with me, and that includes when I'm with my family."

I swallow hard. "It's important to you."

"It's important to me."

I run the flat of my hand up his chest and over his neck to his face. "I'd love to go. I'm just nervous because ... *new people.*"

"If my friends start to annoy the fuck out of you, I can take you home." He grins. "But you'll like them. They're good people. You already know most of them."

"Well, that's true. I assume Billie, Skyla, and Dani will be there."

"For sure. Dani and Bridge are bringing the kids, and Birdie's excited to swim in the pool."

My eyes widen. "You should have led with the pool. I'm there."

He laughs at that and tugs me in for one of his addicting hugs. "It's all-inclusive. Billie called and told me we've been instructed to use the spa, all of the restaurants, and the coffee place. You name it, we get it."

"Wow, that's fancy." I blink up at him as the puzzle

starts to fit together. "Wait. Connor Gallagher is one of *those* Gallaghers? Like, the hotel Gallaghers?"

"He's the CEO and pretty much runs the show," Blake confirms.

"Billie's married to a billionaire."

He smirks. "Yeah. It's a good thing, too, because that girl likes fancy shit."

"Am I the only one who thinks this is ... a little weird?"

"No." He grins as he leans in to press his lips to my forehead, sending fresh tingles down my body. "Try flying in the private jet to London to watch Skyla dance at a king's coronation."

My jaw drops, and I can only stare at him, making him laugh.

"You're kidding."

"I'm definitely not kidding. That happened. Okay, so we're on for this staycation?"

"I'm in if you are."

"Great. Have you had a good day, baby?"

I nod and take a second to think just how fucking *hot* this man looks in a pair of blue scrubs and a white coat, his stethoscope around his neck.

"Harper?"

"Yeah?" My gaze jerks up to his, and he's smirking at me. "What did you say?"

"What were you thinking?"

"Stop it. You *know* you're hot in that outfit."

"It's literally my work clothes."

I swallow hard. "I know."

His eyes journey down my own pink scrubs and over the stethoscope around *my* neck, and when his hazel eyes meet mine again, those gold flecks are on fire.

"Same goes, sugar."

"We'd better get to work."

"I do believe there are cameras in these stairwells," he agrees and presses his lips to my ear. "Otherwise, you'd be boosted up against this wall right now."

"You've threatened to fuck me a lot today. Maybe someday, you can make good on that threat."

He bites his lip and shakes his head. "I'm going to spank your ass later."

"Sounds like fun." I rise on my tiptoes and kiss him on the mouth. "Have a good night. I'll swing by around eight with something for you."

"You don't have to do that."

"I know." I smile as I turn to the doorway. "I want to. See you later."

"See you."

"I brought dessert," I announce as I walk into the house I grew up in. Ava and the boys are already here, gathered in the kitchen with Greg, who's sipping water. "How is everyone?"

"Dad was just telling us about some woman he was

flirting with at the doctor's office," Tucker declares, watching Greg with humor-filled eyes.

"Who?" I demand and set the sugar-free chocolate torte in the fridge. "I want to know everything. Why are you talking about this when I'm not here yet?"

"You were slow as hell," Xander says before tugging on my hair.

"Her name is Linda," Ava says. "She's seventy."

I lift an eyebrow at Greg, who's actually blushing. "An older woman?"

"Only by two years," he reminds me. "She's a nice woman, and I'm taking her bowling this weekend."

I blink at him. I don't know how I feel about this. Greg never dated when we were kids.

At least, I don't *think* he did.

"Wait. How often do you date, Greg? Is this something you've always hidden from us?"

He shakes his head. "No. I've been busy raising you troublemakers and running the ranch. Now my babies are grown, and my boy is taking care of the business. I have time."

All five of us exchange glances, and Easton pats Greg on the back. "It's time you did something for yourself, Pops. Just be safe. We don't want any unplanned siblings."

"Oh my God!" Ava and I exclaim at the same time, making all of the boys laugh.

We settle into our normal routine of working together to make dinner and telling each other stories from work, from life.

This is home. This is what I missed for all those years I was away.

Greg walks over and sits in one of the chairs at the table, and I join him, sitting next to him. He reaches over and brushes his hand over my hair, the way he's done since I was a little girl.

"I've missed you, pumpkin."

I swear, this man will *always* call me pumpkin.

"Me too. How are you feeling?"

"Fit as a fiddle."

I narrow my eyes at him. "Tell me the truth."

"I *am* feeling better. The medicine helps, and I'm watching what I eat. I don't want you to beat me up."

I grin and lean over to give him a hug.

"You're my *dad*. You're important to me, and I need you to stick around for about forty more years."

"Only forty?"

I snort. "Maybe fifty. So you have to take care of yourself because I can't do this life without you in it."

He smiles softly and taps his fingers on the table. "I'm going to be here for a long while yet. Don't you worry. Now, I hear you're seeing a doctor."

My eyes jump across the room to where Ava's talking with Tucker, but Greg shakes his head.

"Xander mentioned it the other day."

"He's such a tattletale."

Greg chuckles. "He better be nice to you."

"Xander's a pain in my ass, but for the most part, he's fine."

Greg shakes his head. "The doctor, not your brother."

"He's nice to me." I squirm, feeling weird about talking with him about this. "He's a good person. An excellent doctor. Comes from a good family."

He nods, watching me. This man sees so much. It was why I didn't come home when things were so bad with Nathan.

"And you're already halfway in love with him."

I blink at him, and he grins.

"My kids always think I'm blind or stupid. I'm neither. The one before this was an idiot. He wasn't near good enough for you. So what makes you think this one is?"

I pause, considering the question. "He makes me feel important. Like I'm the most interesting person in the room. And when he smiles at me, it feels like my heart opens up."

I realize that the room is dead quiet, and when I look around, I find the others listening, too, and I know that I need to open up to them. I have to tell them everything that happened.

"Plus, he's handsome." I clear my throat and take a deep breath.

"The minute any of the good things stop being true, you call me," Greg says, reaching for my hand. "You won't go through anything like the last one by yourself again."

"How—"

"I'm not blind or stupid, pumpkin."

"None of us is," Easton adds, and I look around the room again.

This is my family.

"So maybe I should tell you guys what all went down. Before."

Tucker gestures for everyone to come sit at the table, and within seconds, we're all seated in the chairs that we've claimed since we were kids, and all of the attention is on me.

Xander's on my right, and he leans over to kiss my temple. "It's okay, baby sis."

"I don't really know where to start."

"Just start talking," Tucker suggests. "But I have one question first."

I lift my eyebrow.

"Do I need to kill him?"

How did I get so lucky to have all of these protective men in my life?

"No. We'll let him be miserable."

And so, with a fortifying breath, I dive in, telling them pretty much the same story I told Blake when we danced in the rain.

I don't leave anything out.

"What do you mean, he'd lock you in a room and lecture you?" Easton demands. He's leaning against the counter now because he had to stand and pace to work off the anger I could see coursing through him. His knuckles are white from gripping the edge of the countertop.

"Just that. He'd corner me somewhere, and he'd enjoy making me feel like shit."

Ava brushes a tear off her cheek. "But you know it's bullshit, right?"

"Now I do, sure." I keep talking even as Greg shakes his head. "You guys, I know I'm a good nurse, a good sister and daughter. I know that in my gut. But at that very moment, in that room, when I was told over and over again that I was worthless and not deserving of anything good, I resigned myself to that lie. And he knew he could manipulate me that way because he knew about how I grew up."

"He's going to suffer," Easton says, with a voice so calm that it makes the hair stand up on the back of my neck. "I'll find a way to make sure he never has even one day of peace. He may not know why, but I don't really give a fuck."

"I hope you got tested to make sure he didn't infect you with something," Tucker adds.

"I did. He didn't. Once I found out about the cheating, I never had sex with him again." I shudder at the thought.

"Why didn't you tell us?" Xander asks. "We would have come to Portland, loaded up your stuff, and brought you home where you belong. All you had to do was say the word, Harps."

Tears come to my eyes, and I press my lips together.

"Because it was my mess to fix." The first tear falls hot on my cheek. "And I was embarrassed."

"Never again," Greg says. His voice is deep and hard,

the way it always was when we were kids in trouble. "You'll *never* let any asshole speak to you like that again. You're *my* daughter. You're my baby. No one speaks to or treats you with anything other than respect and love ever again, or they don't get to exist anymore, pumpkin."

"Are you going to bury them somewhere on the ranch?"

He simply stares at me, and for the first time in my life, I think Greg might be a little scary.

"We've got your back," Tucker says, "just like you've got ours. You always take care of us. You always come through. You need to let us do the same for you because we love you, Harper. Always have. Always will. You're stuck with us."

My throat works as I try to keep the tears at bay. *God, I love them all so much.*

"Okay," I whisper. "But Blake is *nothing* like before."

Ava circles the table and wraps her arms around my chest from behind, kissing the top of my head. "Love you."

"You're the best of us, Harps," Easton says. "And you deserve the world."

"I also deserve not to cry anymore. Can we have dessert now?"

"Let's have dessert," Greg says with a glassy smile for me.

Chapter Nineteen
BLAKE

She's a sight for sore eyes. Christ, how does she get more beautiful every time I look at her? Those eyes get me right in the heart every single fucking time.

Harper and I have had stolen moments here and there over the past three days. I pop into her work, or she stops by mine, but those moments are fleeting because we're both so fucking busy. But now, she's rolling a small suitcase behind her as she walks out of Xander's house. She grins at me as I climb the stairs to help her.

"Thanks," she says when I take the handle from her. "Also, hold on."

She props her hands on her hips and frowns up at me.

"Really?" She looks ... I don't even know.

"What? What did I do? I haven't even seen you."

She shakes her head and points at my head, where I'm wearing a hat.

"Blake, you're in a backward baseball hat."

"Is that a crime? If so, handcuff me, sugar." I wink at her, and she presses her lips together so she doesn't burst out laughing.

"It absolutely should be illegal for you to look like that. Are you *trying* to make my ovaries explode? Because it's working. I'm pretty sure they're doing a happy dance right now."

"Your *ovaries* are dancing? That's talent."

I stow her bag in the back of the car with mine, then pull my girl into my arms and lean down to kiss her. She even smells like sugar. So sweet and tempting.

And I love that she likes what she sees when she looks at me. Because God knows that I'm obsessed with every fucking inch of this woman.

"I've missed you," I murmur against her lips. "A few minutes here and there is almost torture."

She runs her hands over my stomach, up to my chest, and that perfect smile slips over her mouth.

"I know. But we get three whole days again now, so let's make the most of them."

I open the door for her, and we're on our way up the mountain to the ski resort.

"So when the fire happened, was it a total loss?" Harper asks.

"Yeah, the arsonist set fire to every commercial structure. So the main lodge, the condos, restaurants. Even the ski rental hut. The only thing he didn't torch were the private homes. Connor had it all cleaned out and is starting fresh."

She nods, watching the scenery as I turn off the highway onto the winding road that leads up to the ski resort.

Harper fists her hands in her lap and blows out a slow breath, making me frown over at her.

"Hey, are you okay?"

She nods, but her smile is a little shaky when she looks over at me. "Yeah, sorry. I'm nervous."

"Why are you nervous?" I take one of her hands and kiss her fingers, then press the back of her hand against my chest. "Talk to me, baby."

"All of your people will be there, and it's different from book club. It's ... all of your people." She winces. "And now we're in this thing, and I'm nervous I'll screw something up. What if they don't like me? It sucks when that happens, Blake."

"You're my people, too," I remind her and set her hand on my thigh so I can use both hands on the wheel as I take a sharp turn. She starts to pull away, but I snag her hand and press it back to my leg. "Stay. Also, everyone coming is kind. Sometimes my brothers are goofy, but we're all nice people. Yes, it's our first gathering as a couple, but I'm right here. I'm right next to you. If you feel shy or unsure, tell me, and I'll help."

"I don't want to seem too needy or clingy."

"Please, cling to me, sweetheart. That's what I'm here for. Because I'm definitely needy as fuck."

That makes her snort, and her smile is relaxed.

"Okay then."

"Okay."

Twenty minutes later, I pull up in front of the entrance where a valet waits to park my car for us.

"This really *is* full service," Harper says in surprise.

"Yeah, he said it's running at full capacity, and we get to enjoy it for a few days to help work out any early kinks."

I step out of the car and hand the young man my fob, then walk to the back of the car to open the hatch and retrieve our bags. Another valet opens the door for Harper.

"We can have those delivered to your room, sir," Valet One says. "Your name?"

"Blake Blackwell," I reply and slip him a tip. "Thank you."

"Thank you," Harper echoes as we walk into the lobby. The Lodge is a log mountain retreat theme, with huge, dark logs running along the cathedral ceiling. There's a taxidermic grizzly standing nearby to greet us. The whole space looks opulent but still feels cozy and welcoming.

I grin at the sight of Connor and Billie, who come over to welcome us. "Thanks for having us," I reply as my sister gives me a big hug.

"I'm *so glad* you're here," Billie says, hugging my girl. Harper smiles shyly, but I can tell that the warm reception has calmed her nerves a little. "Usually, you would check in at the desk, but we took the liberty already so we can give you a tour."

"Is everyone else already here?" I ask.

"Aye," Connor says with a nod. "Brooks got here just

thirty minutes ago. Once you two are settled, we'll have dinner."

Harper and I weren't able to come up until we were both finished with work, but we'll be up here now for two nights and three days.

A mini vacation is just what I need with my girl.

"So this is the lobby," Billie says, gesturing to the space with a huge rock fireplace in the center, then cringes at her husband. "Sorry, I won't take over this tour."

"Go ahead, angel," Connor says with a grin and kisses my sister on the head. "I love the way you tell it."

"But it's *your* hotel," she reminds her husband.

"Last I checked, we're married," he says. "So it's ours. Tell your brother all about it."

"I'm feeling nauseous," I say, giving them both a hard time.

Billie glares at me.

"Okay, so there's a coffee shop right over there. They also serve breakfast sandwiches and pastries, and during lunchtime, they'll have grab-and-go selections from Sage and Salt."

I lift an eyebrow at Billie, and she nods.

Harper does a little dance.

"That's my new favorite," Harper tells Billie.

"It's *so good*. It's okay," Billie assures me. "It's just business."

I nod, and we're led to the far end of the lobby, where the entrance to the restaurant is.

"To the left is the bar area, where guests can order off a pub-style menu," Billie continues.

"And to the right is the formal dining room," Connor adds.

"With a *killer* view of the ski area," Harper says, gesturing to the floor-to-ceiling windows that give a spectacular view of the mountain and down to the town below. "Wow. This is a huge selling point. Even though I live thirty minutes from here, I'd come up here just to eat for that view."

Connor grins at my girl. "Aye, I agree. I'm glad you think so because that was the goal."

We're shown to the outdoor pool area, where some are already swimming, and when they catch sight of us, they wave.

"Hey, friends!" Millie yells out.

"Hey there," Harper yells back.

God, she fits in so well.

And then, as Harper takes in more of the crowd, she freezes, and her hand tightens around mine.

"Wait."

Billie grins at me. Connor shoves his hands in his pockets, giving Harper a chance to take it in.

"Is that Ava and the boys?" Harper's gaze flies up to mine and shifts to Connor. "You invited them?"

"I wanted to fill the *entire* resort," he says, smiling at her. "And they're your people. I thought it would be fun for you and make you more at ease."

Harper blinks. "You don't even know me, and you did this for me?"

"We know you." Billie tucks her hair behind her ear. "And Ava's one of the girls now. Plus, your brothers totally get along with everyone. They're already having a lot of fun."

"No one even told me!" Harper yells out at them, earning a laugh.

"Surprise, baby sis," Xander yells back, diving into the deep end of the pool.

"I want to dive," Birdie yells. Xander pops up and holds his arms up for my niece, and she jumps to him, totally trusting him.

"Thank you," Harper whispers before letting go of my hand to hug Billie tight. She pulls back and smiles at Connor. "I'd hug you, too, but you're her man, and I have a man, and that crosses a line for me."

"I can respect that," Connor replies. "And you're welcome. Now, let's show you to your suite."

"We get a *suite*?" Harper asks.

"Everyone does," Billie says. "The hotel is only suites. Because my man is bougie as hell."

"I'm not the one wearing Chanel from head to toe, bumble," Connor reminds her, and Billie just grins.

"No, you're in Armani. Don't deny being bougie, billionaire. Okay, you're on the second floor, and I love this room so much." Billie unlocks the door, and we follow her inside. I have to admit, I'm impressed.

A balcony overlooks the pool and the woods, along with one ski run. The bed is beautiful, the decor is all about bears, and the finishings are top of the line.

"This tub might be bigger than yours," Harper says

as she climbs inside the copper tub and sits. "Definitely is. I could swim in here."

Connor chuckles at her, and I can only stare at her because she takes my breath away.

"You have it so bad," Billie whispers to me.

"Guilty," I reply, not bothering to whisper in return. "We can be ready for dinner in thirty."

"Perfect," Connor says. "Take your time. Everyone will order off the menu, so everyone can come down as they please."

"I'm so excited," Harper says as she climbs out of the tub. "Thanks again. Also, can I call you out on something, Connor?"

My brother-in-law lifts an eyebrow. "Aye, you can."

"I don't believe for a second that you *need* us here to help you iron out any kinks. You're a master at what you do."

A slow smile spreads over his lips. "I'm proud of this property, and I wanted to share it with those I care about the most. Need? No. But I can. So I am. Welcome, Harper. Enjoy your stay."

Billie claps her hands, kisses me on the cheek, and they're gone.

"Did you know that they invited my family?" Harper asks as soon as the door is closed behind my sister and Connor.

"Yes."

She wraps her arms around me and rests her head against my chest, holding on tight.

"You didn't have to do that."

"There's room, it's nothing to Connor, and it makes you feel more at ease. I'll do whatever it takes to make you feel comfortable, sugar. Always. Plus, this way, I get to know them a little better, too."

"True." She grins up at me. "I just have to freshen up, and then we can go to dinner."

"Let's do it."

Chapter Twenty
HARPER

"It's chilly up here at night," I say as I snuggle down in the hoodie that Blake let me borrow.

He doesn't know it yet, but he's not getting this back. It smells like him, and it's so soft and warm. It's my new favorite thing.

We're sitting on Adirondack chairs on a huge patio around a firepit fueled by gas, so there's no smoke. But it lets off a good amount of heat, and it's pretty out here in the dark.

The stars are out, and I'm reminded just how brilliant they are here. There's no light noise to drown them out.

We're sitting out here with a few other couples. Some of the guys went inside to play pool in the pub. Others took their kids up to bed. We're truly spread out all over this resort, breaking it in.

"I think I just saw a shooting star," Millie says. She's

sitting in her husband's lap, her head back on his shoulder, looking up. "Ry, was it a shooting star?"

Ryan is her brother, and he's sitting to her right. Even I've heard of Ryan Wild. It's unbelievable that I'm just casually hanging out with a couple of billionaires over the next few days.

Whose life is this?

"I didn't see it," he replies. "And I'm not psychic, so I don't know."

"You're the star guy." Millie glances over at me. "He has a whole conservatory on the roof of his house. It's amazing."

"It sounds amazing."

"We'll have pool parties this summer," Polly, Ryan's wife, says with a happy sigh. "And when you come, we'll show you."

I lift an eyebrow. They're already including me in pool parties.

It's like Blake decided I'm his, and all of these people just followed suit as if it's the most normal thing in the world. It's overwhelming, but it feels good to be accepted by them. To be a part of this group of people.

Blake reaches over and brushes his hand over my hair.

"You okay, sugar?"

"I'm great. It's nice out here."

We've spent an hour out here by the fire, and I love that no one has been shy about asking me questions about myself. I talked about being a nurse, being from Silver Springs, and living with the Hendrix family.

They're curious about me, and Blake was right when he said that everyone is nice.

They remind me of my own family, and that makes me feel at home.

"Can you ride a horse?" Holden asks me.

"I was raised on a ranch." Holden smiles at me, and it hits me in the solar plexus. I mean, every man here is *incredible*, including my brothers, but there's something about Holden, with all of his tattoos and that cocky grin, that does something for me. He makes me nervous because he's so attractive. "Of course, I can ride a horse. I can fix fences, I can bail hay, I can do a lot. But I'm not looking for a job."

Holden laughs and shakes his head. "I was just curious. We have some rescue horses at the ranch that need the mileage, so if you want to ride, you're welcome."

All of a sudden, there's a splash at the pool and some giggling, and we all strain our necks to see who's swimming at this time of night.

"Jake! There are people over there."

Holden smirks over at Ryan. "Your boy is making the moves on his girlfriend in the pool."

Blake laughs beside me. "The kid is eighteen. I'm sure he's made quite a few moves on that girl."

"We try not to think about it." Polly cringes. "Christ, I don't want to be a grandma. I'm too young."

Ryan kisses her on the head. "He's being responsible."

"I don't want to know," Polly insists. "He's an innocent boy who loves me and would *never* touch that girl."

Now we all laugh at that.

"I come bearing midnight snacks," Ava announces, carrying a tray. Billie's right behind her with another tray. "Cookies and hot chocolate."

They pass the goodies around, and Ava collapses in a chair next to me.

"And I brought the Irish cream." Connor joins us, passing the bottle around so we can add it if we want it.

I totally want it.

Blake passes and then presses his mouth to my ear.

"Don't get drunk, Harper. You're going to be completely sober when I fuck you later."

Looks like I'll only be having one drink.

I glance over at him, and he smirks before he turns to have a conversation with Brooks, who also just joined us.

Something swoops through the air above us, and I press my lips together.

"Huh," Billie says, looking up with a frown. "I didn't know that birds fly around at night."

I look at Blake, and we both smile.

"That's not a bird, angel," Connor says, kissing her temple. "That's a bat."

Dead silence.

No one moves.

"ARE YOU FUCKING KIDDING ME?" Billie yells, making us all laugh.

"No, I'm not kidding," Connor replies. "We're in the wilderness, even if it's bougie wilderness."

"You can't exterminate everything at the top of a

mountain," Brooks reminds his sister. "Don't worry, they don't want you."

"This is legit the best thing I've ever been invited to," Ava says as she clinks her mug against mine, keeping one eye on the sky and potentially more bats.

"How are things with Joe?" I ask her, and Billie, Polly, and Millie all come to attention.

"You're holding out on me." Billie scowls at Ava. "Who's Joe? Tell us everything."

"I want to know," Millie adds, and Polly nods. Ava scowls at me.

"What?" I shrug a shoulder. "You didn't say that vanilla Joe was a secret."

"*Vanilla* Joe?" Polly asks.

"He's not terribly ... *adventurous*, if you know what I mean," I reply, and Millie snorts.

Ava stares at me in horror, and I laugh.

"What? You announced to my entire cafeteria at work that he wouldn't even pull your hair and that you prefer to be spanked. These people are our friends, not strangers."

Blake snorts next to me, and I look over at him, catching him smiling at me.

"Tell us about vanilla Joe," Polly urges Ava. "Use the dirty words."

"There's really nothing to tell." Ava sighs. "I showed up at his office the other day, during an appointment slot that I scheduled, by the way, and told him to fuck me on his desk."

Holden chokes on his cookie.

"Oh, stop," Millie tells her husband. "You've fucked me on *your* desk more times than I can count."

"I don't want to know this," Ryan says, then glares at Holden. "Keep your hands off my sister."

"She's my *wife*," Holden reminds him.

"Anyway," Ava continues. "He was so scandalized that he choked on his Fanta, and I told him we were too different to make it work. Too bad. I was hoping to corrupt him a little."

"I'm sorry." I reach over and pat my friend on the shoulder. "Someone else will pull your hair and smack your ass."

"Jesus," Brooks says. "Is this what they talk about when men aren't around?"

"Oh, this is tame," Millie says. "We haven't even started talking about positions and toys yet."

"You talk about toys?" Holden demands. He stands and picks his wife up. "Say good night, wife."

"Good night," Millie says, grinning at all of us over Holden's shoulder as he carries her inside.

"They're adorable together," Polly says with a happy sigh. "I'm so glad they finally found their way back to each other."

"Why do I think there's a story there?" I ask.

"Oh, it's a long, dramatic story," Polly confirms. "I'll tell you all about it the next time we have girls' night."

More giggling comes from the pool area, and Polly climbs off her husband's lap.

"It's time for us to go," she says. "I can't listen to my kid like that. No way."

"We're off," Ryan says and takes her hand. "Good night, everyone."

"See you tomorrow."

"I'm ready to go, too," I tell Blake around a big yawn. "I'm tired."

My man stands, takes my hand, and pulls me to my feet. After we say our goodbyes, we take the stairs to the second floor, and once we're in the room, I turn to him with a smile.

"I'm not really tired. I was just ready to have you all to myself."

The predatory smile that spreads over his face is fucking lethal.

"I want you naked, sugar. Right. Now."

Chapter Twenty-One
BLAKE

Whether she knows it or not, my girl likes being told what to do in the bedroom.

She drags her teeth over her lower lip and takes a step back from me, and I eat up the space she just created, making her eyes dance.

"But I like this sweatshirt," she says.

"And I like seeing you in my clothes, but it's coming off." I step into her and grip the hem of the sweatshirt, and she immediately grins and lifts her arms for me. Casting it aside, I tuck two fingers in the front of her jeans and pull her flush against me. "Are you having a good time, sugar?"

"Yeah, I am. You were right. Everyone's nice." Her hands dive under my shirt and up over my skin. My stomach contracts at her touch, and she grins up at me. "I like your muscles."

I lift a brow. "Is that so?"

She nods and bites that delicious lip again, and I tug

it free with my thumb before I take her T-shirt off and dispose of mine as well.

Her eyes travel down my torso, and her cheeks flush.

"I fucking love it when you blush like that, Harper."

She blinks, and her gaze finds mine again. "I can't help it. I like what I see."

My restraint is holding on by a thread as my hands roam over her skin. I unfasten her bra, and she lets it fall, and I cup her perfect tits in my palms and brush over her already hard nipples.

"I'm not taking it fast and hard tonight," I whisper next to her ear. "I'm going to savor every second. I'm going to worship every perfect inch of your body."

She swallows hard and leans into me as I drag my lips down her neck to her shoulder and nibble on that perfect, soft flesh.

"You're so damn good with your mouth," she whispers as her fingers dive into my hair.

"You're so fucking delicious. I can't get enough of you." I unfasten her jeans and work them down her legs, and she kicks out of her shoes and jeans, then makes a dive for mine.

When we're finally naked, I pick her up, and she wraps her long, toned legs around my hips. Her mouth fuses to mine, and she tastes like hot chocolate and pure fucking sin.

"I've missed you," she whispers against my lips. "So much."

"I know, baby." I lay her down in the middle of the

king bed and brace myself over her, brushing her hair off her cheeks. "We're about to make up for lost time."

She grins right before I kiss her, then bite her lower lip and pull back, letting it go. I kiss my way down her perfect neck and pause at her breasts to tease and nibble her nipples.

"Holy shit," she whispers, arching her back for more.

"Your body is every fantasy I've ever had in my life, Harps." I press wet kisses down to her navel, then farther still, spreading her legs wide, and when I see how fucking wet she is for me, my cock has gone from extremely interested to fucking ravenous. "Your pussy is weeping for me, baby."

She whimpers, lifting her hips in invitation.

Dragging one fingertip through her sopping sex, I watch her face, needing to see how her jaw drops and her eyes widen just before she closes them.

"Eyes on me."

She obeys, and I replace my finger with my tongue, licking her from her entrance to her clit and back down again, then pull her lips into my mouth and *suck*.

"Christ almighty." Her hips jerk, but I hold her steady and eat her until her nails are digging into my scalp and her legs shake.

Then I pull back.

"Blake!"

"I'm right here." I kiss her inner thighs, then her hips. When I reach her neck, I bite that tender flesh over her pulse point. "Your heart is hammering."

"God, please fuck me, Blake." She takes my face in her little hands and pulls me to her mouth. "Need you."

She sounds ... vulnerable. I don't remember hearing this tone from her before.

"Hey, I'm right here with you, and I'm not going anywhere."

Her gorgeous gray eyes close, so I bury my face in her neck and kiss her. This woman has become the center of my universe. The reason for every breath, the one person who means the most to me in this world.

I'm so in love with her that I ache with it.

"Blake." It's a whisper, and I pull up to look her in the eyes, but she has hers closed.

"Yes, baby."

"Don't break my heart, okay?" Her eyes open, and she presses her lips together in a line, and I know down to my soul that this is as vulnerable as this woman gets.

"I will never intentionally hurt you." I take her hand in mine and kiss it before I reach down and fist my cock, then line it up with her entrance.

Harper inhales in anticipation.

With a smile, I slide inside her, and when I'm balls deep, we both moan together.

"They could do medical studies on your dick."

I pause and stare down at her. "What?"

"I'm serious." She gasps when I pull back, then sink inside her again. "Because it's perfect, and I'm absolutely *sure* there's nothing else like it in the world."

"If you're talking this much, I'm not doing my job, baby."

She lifts an eyebrow. "I guess you'd better get to work."

"I fucking love your sassy mouth." I bite that lower lip, then soothe it with my tongue as I start to move faster and just a little harder. This isn't a fast fuck at all, but I needed to increase the speed just a little.

I boost up to my knees and grip her hips, pulling her onto me with every thrust.

And then, I press my hand to her lower abdomen, and feel every inch of my cock as it moves inside her.

"Christ, you're so goddamn beautiful."

Her legs tense around me, and I can feel her walls start to flutter. Nothing in the world feels this good.

"That's it, Harper. Come for me. You take my cock so well. I want you to come all over it."

She arches her back, and I watch as her pussy clenches around my cock, and the orgasm moves through her. I don't stop moving. I want to prolong this orgasm for as long as fucking possible.

"Blake! Oh, fuck me."

"I am, baby." I grin down at her as she smiles at that, and then my girl reaches up for me, and I lower myself over her again, licking inside her mouth, and my orgasm pulses through me.

"Fuuuck," I groan as I come, splashing inside her, moving through the orgasm until we're both heaving and messy, and I'm pretty sure we need to hydrate.

I press my lips to her shoulder, trying to catch my breath, and her hands dance up and down my back, over my ribs and spine.

"I love you so much, Harper."

Her hands still. Her entire body tightens.

And I don't like that at all.

"Relax, I'm not proposing," I tell her, but that doesn't help her. "Okay, talk to me, sugar."

"I don't know what to say." Her voice shakes, and I push up onto my elbows so I can see her. "Because I *do* care about you more than anyone else in my life."

She swallows hard and looks like she might cry.

"Whoa, baby. Take a breath." I inhale, and she follows suit. "That wasn't supposed to give you a panic attack."

"I'm not good at words," she says softly. Her hands start to move against me once more, and I take that as a good sign. "Even when I'm on the same page. Which is so not fair to you."

She's not running away.

"You don't have to say anything at all."

"I've never said those words to anyone in my life, ever." She blinks as if she's just realizing that, and I wrap her in my arms and turn us onto our sides so we can talk.

How the fuck is that possible?

"Tell me about that."

Her eyes look so fucking sad, it shreds my heart.

"I know you have people in your life who love you, Harper. I've seen it. The Hendrix family is crazy about you."

"I know." She nods on the pillow and brushes her fingers down my pecs. "And it's not that I *don't* l-love them." I hate that she had to stutter through that word.

"I do. I'd do anything for them at the drop of a hat. It's just that I can't say it back. Whenever they tell me that, I reply with *yeah, yeah, love, blah, blah.*"

I've heard her say that before.

"My parents." She shakes her head. "I think they were kind of indifferent to me. I was told often that they never meant to have me."

My hand fists in the comforter. *Fuck them.*

"And I don't remember them ever saying those words. To me, or to each other."

She lifts a shoulder and then sighs.

"I think Nathan said it one time when he was proposing. And I never said it back. If he noticed, he never said anything, and then after that, the way he treated me ... well, that wasn't love."

"Baby, that's not your fault."

"It's definitely not my fault. I know that. But it's like it's ingrained in me that I'm not lovable. Maybe I don't deserve—"

"And that's where I'm stopping you." I press my finger to her lips. "Because you are so fucking lovable, baby. You're the best thing that's ever happened to me. You deserve everything good in this world. I'm so damn sorry that your parents were so deep into their addiction that they didn't see how unbelievable you are."

Her eyes well, and it's my undoing. I tug her to me and wrap my arms around her, needing to be closer to her. Needing to show her how amazing she is.

I hate that the little girl who Harper was went through so much life feeling unloved. That for even one minute, she felt like no one loved her. She's so damn strong all the time, putting on a brave face and walking through life with self-confidence that it's easy to forget everything that she's been through.

"I love you, Harper. And I will say those words often until you finally trust them. I'll say it enough for both of us."

She sniffs and leans her head back to look up at me.

"I didn't plan on you," she says.

"Baby, I never thought I'd even consider a long-term relationship with anyone. Ever. And now I can't imagine my life without you in it. I knew you were mine the second I saw you walk onto that plane."

She smiles and wipes a tear off her cheek. "You were so sexy."

"Oh? Tell me more."

She huffs out a laugh and drags her fingers over my cheek and down my neck. "Now I'm just inflating your ego."

"I don't even have an ego to inflate."

She laughs and kisses my chin. "I hate to break it to you, but you do. A big ego."

"Yeah? What else is big, sugar?"

She snorts, and I push against her, my cock already hard, pressing into her belly.

"You have a big heart."

I shift her up and press the crown of my dick at her entrance, then slip right inside, and she lets out the sexiest little gasp as I fill her up.

"Anything else?"

"You have a huge cock."

"Mm, that's what I wanted to hear."

She rolls over me and starts to ride me. My hands span over her waist and hips, helping her find a rhythm, and she shivers, hitting just the right spot.

"You love this huge cock, don't you?"

"Hell yes, I do."

"Christ, you're amazing." I sit up and glide my hands down to her ass, lifting her up and down on my shaft. "You're mine, Harper. Do you understand?"

She bites my lip and then nods. "And you're mine, Blake."

There is nothing more adorable than Harper waking up in the morning. She wakes *slowly.* First, her legs start to move, stretching out. Then she wiggles her fingers and toes.

She still hasn't opened her eyes.

She lets out a little squeak as she stretches her arms above her head, and then one eye slits open to take in her surroundings.

"Good morning, baby."

I kiss her cheek, and she hums. No words for my girl yet.

"Did you sleep well?"

She nods and then curls into me, clinging to me.

So I kiss her head and breathe her in.

"I'm going to run down and get us coffee."

"Mm-hmm."

Her hands find my torso, and she scowls. "Dressed."

"Yep. I can't go to the coffee shop naked, baby."

She lets out a long breath and blinks both eyes open. "Thank you."

"For what?"

"The coffee." She kisses my chin before burying herself back under the blankets.

I grab my wallet and room key, and leave our room, making sure the door is secure behind me. Not that anything could possibly hurt her here.

I hear another door open and look up to see Brooks headed my way. If I'm not mistaken, he looks like he might crack a smile.

This resort has been good for all of us.

"Coffee?" I ask him.

"Hell yes," he replies.

We walk shoulder to shoulder down the hallway to the stairs that lead to the first floor.

"I like Harper," he says.

"I do, too."

"Her family seems nice. Her brother, Xander, is a hockey player. We talked about hockey all damn night." Brooks is a big hockey fan. Always has been. "And it's good to see Tucker and Remington. Holden."

"So you're glad you came."

"Yeah. It's cool."

I smile over at him. "I think Ava's single—"

"No."

I laugh as we descend the stairs.

"She's beautiful"—I'm ticking the list off on my fingers—"has a career, comes from a good family, seems to like her hair pulled—"

"Shut up," Brooks says, shaking his head. "You're ridiculous."

With a laugh, we turn the corner to the lobby, and both stop dead in our tracks.

Because just ahead, at the coffee shop where there's a cooler for grab-and-go meals, is a woman bent over that cooler, filling it with to-go boxes.

Brooks would recognize that ass anywhere.

Juliet straightens to grab more boxes from her cart, and when her eyes shift over to us, she also stops, and tears fill her pretty blue eyes.

She clears her throat.

"Hi, guys. Um, I'm just about done here. I can go—"

"You're good at that," Brooks finally says, and I close my eyes on a sigh.

"What?" Her eyebrows pull together in a frown.

"Running away," he says. His voice is so hard and cold, and I hear the hurt in it. I fucking hate this. "You're good at that."

"Brooks, if you'd give me just two minutes to explain—"

"I don't want an explanation," he says, his hands fisting at his sides. "I don't want anything from you. Not anymore. Congratulations on the new restaurant. I'm happy for you, Jules. But you and I won't be talking. I won't be popping by for lunch. And if you need to have your car worked on, there's a garage in Silver Springs."

"Brooks," she begins, but he shakes his head.

"Don't ever say my name again."

Brooks turns and walks away, and Juliet deflates in front of me.

"I was hoping that would go better," she murmurs as she wipes a tear from her cheek. "God, he still looks amazing."

"He'll be out on the patio," I tell her. "Maybe try again."

She looks longingly toward the way that Brooks left. "It's no use."

"Maybe *you* need to be the one to pursue him. To make him feel like you need to talk to him. If you run away now, I can guarantee you there will never be another chance, Jules. Go out to the patio."

She looks at her cart.

"I've got that, and the cart will be here when you're done."

Juliet takes a deep breath and then nods. "Thanks, Blake."

"Good luck."

Once I've set the rest of her meals in the cooler, I move the cart out of the way and order our coffees. I also grab a couple of breakfast burritos and return to the room.

When I walk inside, my girl is still sleeping, and her phone is lighting up like the Fourth of July.

"I smell coffee," she mutters from under the pillow.

"Your nose is right." I sit on the side of the bed next to her hip and pass her a cup. "I got you a breakfast burrito, too."

"Because breakfast is our thing." She sips her coffee, watching me. "I love that it's our thing because coffee is life."

"Your phone is busy."

She frowns over at it and sees that she has some missed texts and calls.

"Oh shit, Greg." She snatches her phone up and opens the messages, then breathes a sigh of relief. "Ava and Billie were wondering if I want to do yoga. Which I totally do. But Jesus, if I don't respond after one text, don't blow up my phone and give me heart failure."

She's tapping fast on her screen, then sets it aside and watches me. "Why do you look perfect in the morning, and I look like a troll who's about to make you solve a riddle?"

With a laugh, I pull her onto my lap and kiss her. "You always look perfect, sugar."

"Not even a little. But damn, I slept *good* last night. What kind of beds are these? I need one."

"I'll ask Connor." We both sip our coffee. "So you're doing yoga?"

"Yeah. Wanna come? It's down by the pool in thirty minutes."

"I could do some yoga." And I can watch my girl doing some yoga. "Want to find a hiking trail later?"

"Have you even met me? Of course, I do. This is the best vacation ever."

Chapter Twenty-Two

HARPER

I'm not going to lie. I could get used to this.

We're sitting on our mats on the patio surrounding the pool, legs crossed and hands pressed together over our chests.

Every breath is full of clean, fresh mountain air. There's only a light breeze this morning, and the sun is out, so we're not too cold.

I would do this every chance I could get.

Blake is next to me, and the man *killed* yoga. It was hard to ignore him in his little black workout shorts and teal tank top. And I *know* I felt his eyes on me, especially when it was time for downward dog.

He's a man.

There have to be thirty people out here. I recognize some from book club. Billie's here with Dani and Skyla, and I know Dani's sisters, Charlie and Alex. I'm learning the Wild family, but I still feel like I need a map or a family tree.

Ava and Xander even joined us.

It's been the most relaxing morning I've had since I moved home.

Yeah, I'd do this every damn day if I could.

"Namaste," the instructor says with a smile, and we repeat it back to her before standing and rolling our mats.

I turn to Skyla, who's behind me. "Skyla, does anyone offer yoga classes in Bitterroot Valley?"

"Of course," she says. "I offer it at my studio. I'd love to have you join us. I'll text you the times."

"Thank you. I'll be there."

I glance back to look for Blake, but he's wandered away. He's talking to Brooks, who did *not* do yoga, over by the lodge entrance. It looks like an intense conversation, so I let them have space. Blake's face is somber, and then he frowns and looks down at the floor, his hands on his hips.

I hope everything's okay.

"You're *really* good at this," Dani says as she joins me, eyeing the pool. "I, on the other hand, thought I was going to die."

I laugh and pull her in for a hug. "You did great."

"I didn't die," she counters. "And it reminded me that I need to get back to Skyla's classes. It's not easy after a baby."

"Girl, you pushed a human being out of your body. Like, less than two months ago. The fact you're even here is amazing, and you need to pat yourself on the back. You're a badass, Dani."

Dani grins, then eyes the water again and takes a step away from it.

"Wanna take a swim?" I ask her. "I have time before Blake and I go hike."

She shakes her head. "Nah. I don't like water. Childhood trauma."

I nod but don't ask any more questions. It's none of my business.

"Hey, pretty girls," Billie says as she and Ava join us. "We're going to have a girls-only cocktail hour this evening before dinner. I have a signature drink planned, and I thought it would be fun. Thoughts?"

"I'm down," I reply.

"Me too," Dani says.

"Girls' cocktails?" Alex asks as she joins us. "Hell to the yes."

Suddenly, two *very* attractive men join Alex. One takes her hand and kisses it, and the other slides his arm around her shoulders and kisses her temple.

And the smug smile on Alex's face is *adorable*.

"Harper, this is Adam," she gestures to the hottie holding her hand, "and this is Gabe." The one with his arm around her shoulders grins at me. "They're mine," she adds with a grin.

"And we're stealing you away," Gabe says. "It's throuple massage time, butterfly."

"Oh my God, *yes*," Alex says. "See you later, guys."

She waves, and then they're off, and I blink after them before turning to Dani and Billie.

"They're the hottest people I've ever seen in my life," I inform them.

"I know," Billie says. "They're *so* sexy. And I'm happy for them. They've been together as long as Connor and I have."

"Well, I'm happy for them too," I reply as Blake heads my way. "Hey, handsome. Everything okay?"

"It will be." He steps behind me, wraps his arms around me, and buries his face in my neck.

"Dude, that's my sister," Xander says, scowling from a few feet away.

"I know," Blake replies and kisses me again. "Let's get out of here, sweets."

"Have a fun day," Billie says. "Be nice to her. I like her. Let's keep her, okay? I'm going to add her to the text thread."

My heart stutters. God, they're all so sweet and welcoming.

"The goal is not to chase her away," Blake says. "Now, stop being a brat. I'll see you later."

"Bye!" Billie waves, Blake takes my hand and leads me inside.

"Your family is incredible," I inform him as we take the stairs up to our floor.

"I know." He kisses my hand and leads us to our room. "And they obviously like you back."

"That's a relief." This has been nothing like family time with Nathan's family. I feel accepted and wanted here. Welcome. Like I'm one of them already.

As soon as we're inside the room, I peel off my sports

bra because it's sweaty and then do the same for my leggings. "I have to change for the hike. These are too sweaty. That girl gave us a workout this morning."

"I'm changing too," he says, but his eyes are glued to my body.

"It doesn't look like you're changing. Looks like you're staring."

"I'm appreciating," he counters and takes a step toward me.

"Blake, if you attack me right now, we'll never go on a hike." His eyes shoot up to mine, and then he cups my face.

"Okay. A hike it is. But I might fuck you in the woods."

I scrunch up my nose. "Ew. No. I don't want dirt and bugs in my lady bits, thank you very much. You're a doctor, Blake. You know better than that."

He brushes his nose over the shell of my ear. "I'll bend you over and make you lean on a tree while I rail you from behind, baby. No dirt will touch your perfect pussy."

I bite my lip when he drags his hands up my naked sides.

"Focus, Blake. We're hiking."

He backs away, and I immediately feel the loss of his touch. Maybe I was too hasty.

"Come on, sugar. The wilderness awaits."

"How many grizzly bears do you think are on this mountain?" I ask Blake as we hike along a trail that circles around the entire ski village, and would eventually end up back in Bitterroot Valley, but we're not hiking that far today.

"I have no idea."

"But if you had to guess. Are we talking two? Or thirty? Or a thousand?"

"Probably somewhere between two and ten."

"Oh, you think that's all?" I tilt my head, thinking about it.

"Baby, it doesn't matter how many there are. I can't win against *one*."

"Sure you can." I grip his biceps and squeeze. "Look at that muscle. The bear would run from you in terror."

Blake laughs and scoops his arm around my waist, then lowers his lips to mine.

"Are you afraid of bears, Harper?"

"Every single day," I confirm, nodding my head. "I have a phobia of being mauled and killed by a pissed-off mama bear."

"I won't let that happen. Besides, you hike all the time."

"I know. But most of the places I hike don't have grizzlies."

"Black bears can be just as mean," he says, and I scowl up at him.

"Well, thanks for that little nugget of wisdom. Now I'll be on edge all the damn time."

He's so handsome when he smiles at me like this. Like he's so taken with me, so smitten.

He loves me.

I about had an aneurysm when those words came out of that talented mouth last night. They were full of passion and *truth*, and for a heartbeat, I was terrified. And then a warmth I've never felt before moved through me. My heart ached but in a delicious way. In a way that told me this was a life-altering moment, and I fucked it up.

I wish I'd said it back. I wish it was easy for me to say it back. Because I *do* love him. I love everything about this man.

So why can't I tell him?

"Blake?"

"Yes, baby." He kisses the tip of my nose.

Say it. Just say it. It's only three words.

I bite my lip. He's watching me with those hazel eyes with gold flecks, and I chicken out. I move into him, press my face to his chest, and hug him close.

"I love you, too, sweetheart."

Fuck, I'm an idiot.

"Are you okay?" he asks against the top of my head.

"Yeah. Just worried about bears."

He smiles against my hair. "I'll take your mind off that." His hands roam down over my ass, making heat pool in my core. You would think that after all of the sex we've been having, I wouldn't want to do it again. But you'd be wrong. "Have I mentioned that you look fucking incredible in these yoga pants?"

"No. I was fairly sure you hated them."

He snickers and urges me back enough that he can kiss my lips. "I can't keep my hands off your stellar ass when you wear these, sugar."

"Well, you're wearing that backward hat again today, so I'd say we're even."

He pushes his hands into my leggings, urging them down my hips. "You have the softest damn skin. Remember what I said in the room?"

"You said a lot in the room."

He spanks my ass, and a sizzle moves up my spine. It looks like Ava isn't the only one who likes a good ass smack once in a while.

"Bend over and grab onto that tree."

"Blake, literally anyone could come down this trail. Your family. My family. A *bear*."

"It wasn't a question, Harper." Gently, he guides my hands to the trunk and pulls my hips back so I'm exposed to him. "Christ, you're already dripping wet. Does the idea of getting caught turn you on?"

"Not really. Mostly, *you* turn me on."

He kisses my ass right over the spot where he spanked me.

"I like seeing my handprint on your skin." He nibbles and works his way to the middle, and then his tongue is inside me, and all rational thought leaves the premises.

"Holy shit." My head hangs down as he assaults my core with his lips, teeth, and tongue. Before I know it, he pushes two fingers inside me, and I come so hard that I see black spots at the edges of my vision.

"Good fucking girl," he says, lapping me up, and then I hear rustling as I assume he pulls his shorts down. He guides the crown of his dick against my entrance, then pushes all the way inside me, and I gasp. "Am I hurting you, Harper?"

I shake my head.

"I need your words, baby."

"You're not hurting me. God, Blake."

He starts to move, one hand planted on the small of my back and the other on my shoulder as he drives into me over and over again. It's animalistic and so out of control for me, yet I fucking *love* it.

I'm having sex with the man I love in my favorite place.

Just that thought alone could make me come.

Blake grabs my hair and pulls me up so my back is against his front, and he kisses the ball of my shoulder before dragging those lips up to my ear.

"Whose pussy is this, Harper?"

"Yours." I don't even hesitate because there is no other answer.

"You're already quivering around me. Are you about to come, baby?"

"Fuck yes."

"Good. I fucking love the way your tight cunt

squeezes my cock. Give in to it, my love. Do it. Go over for me."

Christ on a cracker, his words, combined with how amazing he feels, shoot me right into the stratosphere. I don't bother to be quiet as I come apart, and Blake follows me over, groaning and rocking into me until we're both spent and panting.

He pulls out, and when his cum starts to leak out of me, he swipes his fingers through it and tucks it back inside me.

"I belong in there," he says before helping me pull my leggings back up.

"Well, that will be fun for the next five miles."

Blake finishes righting his clothes, then palms the back of my neck and pulls me to him, covers my mouth with his, and I immediately melt against him.

The mouth on this guy.

"I want you to feel me dripping out of you all day. Every time you take a step, you'll know that I'm inside you. That you're mine and *only* mine, sweetheart."

"As long as there are no dirt and bugs."

He huffs out a laugh. "Absolutely not. Trust me, baby."

I do. I trust him more than anyone.

"Where have you guys been?" Birdie asks two hours later from a balcony at the lodge as we hike back. "You were gone forever."

"Only a few hours," Blake replies with a grin. "We went for a hike. What are you doing, cupcake?"

"I'm coloring out here because the baby is sleeping, and I'm always too loud. Can I hang out with you guys?"

"We're going to get cleaned up, then we'll come get you, okay?" Birdie immediately smiles and claps her hands.

I'm about to jog up the stairs to our floor when Blake takes my hand and stops me. He pulls me to him and cups my face.

"We don't have to hang out with Birdie if you don't want to."

"I wouldn't have offered if I didn't want to. Birdie's awesome. I like her more than most people. Hey, you should text Bridger or Dani and ask them if we can take her to the pool."

He's just staring at me, still breathing a little hard from the hike and covered in sweat.

"Blake? Are you having a stroke or something? How many fingers am I holding up?"

"I fucking love you." He kisses me hard, then pulls me behind him up the stairs to our room.

"Because I like your niece?"

"Yeah, sugar. Because you like my niece. And for a million other reasons. Get in the shower, and I'll call Bridge."

I blink at him for a second, then turn for the bathroom. I can hear his deep voice talking on the phone as I start the water and shimmy out of my gross clothes. I've just started washing my hair when he joins me and takes over scrubbing my scalp.

"Oh, that's nice. It's always better when someone else washes your hair."

"Are many men washing your hair these days, Harper?"

I squint one eye open and stare at him. "No, jealous man, I have a hairdresser. Cool your jets. Only you and Miguel wash my hair. Besides me, of course."

He stares down at me, his hands pausing in my hair, and I crack a smile.

"Her name is Melanie."

"Thank you." He kisses my nose and returns to the task at hand. "I'd better check you for ticks."

"I'm almost as scared of them as I am of bears."

"You should be." He kisses my cheek and leads me back under the water. "No Lyme disease for you."

"I'd rather not. What did Bridger say?"

"He'll meet us down at the pool in thirty, and that Birdie will love hanging out with us. She's obsessed with the pool."

"Dani said that she, as in Dani, doesn't like water."

Something sad moves over Blake's eyes, and he reaches for the conditioner. "No. She doesn't like water. It's a long story, but the five Lexington siblings grew up in an extremely abusive situation. Their mom died when Charlie was just a baby. Holden was maybe ten, if I remember right. Their dad was a piece of shit who ended up dying way too painlessly. He tormented and tortured those kids all their lives. Holden would load the girls up and bring them to our ranch when things got really bad, and my parents would help take care of them."

"Why didn't the dad go to jail?"

"Because his best friend was the sheriff, and this is a small town. Twenty years ago, it was much smaller than it is now."

"Wait, you said five kids? I've only met four."

"Darby, the second oldest, is getting a degree in veterinary medicine in Colorado."

"Good for her," I reply. "That's awesome. So the dad must have done something horrible with water?"

"He chose different forms of torture for each of the girls," Blake says as he starts to clean my body. "For Dani, it was holding her under the water."

"He waterboarded his own daughter," I breathe out.

"Pretty much."

"Fucking hell." I lean my forehead on Blake's chest and feel tears come to my eyes. "Blake, that's unimaginable."

"I know. She's so strong. They all are. Dani and Bridger always had a spark, but the timing was never right. Until it was."

"And now she's safe and loved, and oh my God, I need to hug her again."

"She's okay, baby." He kisses my forehead and nuzzles my nose. "She's great."

"I *really* like her."

"I know, and I'm glad you do because I hang out

with my family often, and I want you to be around as well."

"I don't have a problem with that."

After we've finished washing and are dry, we slip on bathing suits and walk down to the pool, where Bridger and Birdie are already waiting for us.

"She will outswim you," Bridger informs me. "She thinks she's a fish."

"No, Daddy, I'm a mermaid. I'm Ariel."

"Is she your favorite princess?" I ask her.

"No, but she's the one who swims best."

"That's fair." I nod and smile at Bridger. "I won swimming competitions in high school. She's safe, Bridger."

Blake frowns down at me. "You did?"

"She took state her senior year."

We all glance over and see Tucker and Easton sitting on lounge chairs, drinking beer and relaxing with who I *think* are Chase and Brady Wild.

I really need a spreadsheet with pictures.

Tucker grins. "She can kick your ass."

"It's a good thing the swear jar doesn't count up here," Birdie says to Tucker, who laughs. The little girl takes my hand and leads me to the deep end.

"Are you sure you don't want to go in over there?" I point at the shallow end, but she shakes her head.

"No. Let's jump together."

"Okay. One, two, three!"

We hop into the water, and when we come up for air,

I keep my hands on Birdie's sides to make sure she doesn't go back under.

But she's kicking and using her arms the way she should, and she grins at me.

"We did it!"

"We sure did. Do you know how to do a back float?"

Birdie shakes her head.

"Okay, hold on to the side while I show you. Don't let go, okay?"

"I won't," she says and brushes some hair out of her eyes, watching me closely.

I lie back and float on top of the warm water for at least ten seconds. When I right myself, Birdie's already floating, her arms stretched out and a smile on her beautiful little face.

"This is really nice, and you don't have to work super hard to do it," she says.

"I agree. I'll join you."

I lie back again, but before I close my eyes, I see Blake smiling at the edge of the pool, taking a picture of us with his phone.

"I love you," he mouths to me, and I grin up at him before I bring my hands together, making a heart.

"Okay, now what are we going to do?" Birdie asks, breaking the moment.

"Whatever you want."

"Let's race!"

Chapter Twenty-Three
BLAKE

"I hear you have a girlfriend," Dad says the following week before lifting his mug of coffee to his lips and taking a sip.

How is it possible that I'm in my mid-thirties, I'm a doctor, and I've been living my own life for a damn long time, but my father can make me feel like a teenager again with only six words?

And I want to tell him that I don't simply have a *girlfriend*. I've found the love of my fucking life, and as soon as I can talk her into it, she'll be my wife.

"I do." I cross one ankle over my knee. I'm sitting at my parents' kitchen table. Mom's off for a hair appointment, and Dad asked me to come over to "help him with something."

I've been here for twenty minutes, and he still hasn't told me what he needs help with.

I suspect he just wanted to have coffee.

"What's her name?"

I lift a brow. "Billie didn't tell you her name?"

Dad smirks. We all know who the gossip in our family is. "I want to know more about her from *you*. Better yet, I'd like to meet her myself."

"I'll bring her to the next family dinner." I sip my water. I've already had too much coffee today. "Her name is Harper. She's from Silver Springs, and she's a NICU nurse."

"Works with babies."

That's an incredibly simple way to say that Harper takes care of extremely tiny, medically fragile preemies and is honestly a fucking badass for being able to do her job, but I leave it at that.

"She does. If you and Mom had come up to the resort last week, you would have spent time with her. It was fun."

"We wanted to leave that for you kids," Dad replies, shaking his head. "I'm glad you had a good time."

"Dad, you know I always love seeing you, but what did you need help with this morning?"

"Got somewhere else you need to be, son?" Dad smiles, taking any sting out of the question. He's a smart man, and he's always been a gentle one.

"I have a little time," I reply. "But you said you needed help."

"I lied." He watches me for a few seconds and blows out a breath. "I haven't seen my boy in weeks, and I miss you. I thought we could have coffee together. If I tell you I need help, you won't turn me down."

"Dad, I won't turn you down either way. Don't do the whole crying wolf thing on me."

"I don't think you've had a girlfriend since high school."

I frown at my father. "Really? You want to talk about my *love life*? Do you have a fever?"

He chuckles and shakes his head. "No fever. A burning curiosity, sure. Because you've been so focused on your goals and your work that you've never let a woman in. So what's so special about this one? I want to know what's going on with you, kiddo."

"You're as nosy as Billie." I shake my head and sip my water. "She's just different. I took one look at her, and it was like I recognized her on a molecular level. Like something inside me said *Oh, there you are.* I know that everyone gives me shit because I don't see a woman more than once, and I never get attached, but I think I was waiting for her all this time, and I didn't even know it."

I look up into eyes so much like mine. He's listening intently, and if I'm not mistaken, his eyes have gone glassy.

"You love her."

"Fuck yeah, I love her." I nod and tap the table with my fingertips. "I'm crazy about her. I'd marry her today. She's it for me."

"Good for you, buddy. I can't wait to meet her. The next time you have a Sunday off, we'll do dinner. Now, you need to leave. I have shit to do today."

I laugh and stand, then pull him in for a hug. "You seriously wanted to gossip about my girl."

"I'm sick of getting it secondhand from your sister. I wanted it from the horse's mouth. I love you, Blake. I'm glad you found your person."

My person.

Yeah, that's exactly what she is.

I have a short shift at the clinic this afternoon, and I finally get a few hours with my girl this evening. We agreed that she'd stay the night since we'll be going to work at around the same time tomorrow morning.

I have to savor the hours with her when I can.

The chaos in my work life is why I've always shied away from looking for a relationship. Add in *her* chaotic schedule, and spending much time together has been almost impossible. Since last week's few amazing days at the resort, we've been back to stealing moments here and there. Tonight will be the first night we get to spend together since last week.

And I'm getting impatient.

I need more of her. I just don't know how to make that happen.

An hour later, I'm in my office, typing notes on my first patient of the day before I go into the next exam room. My schedule is packed, but I'll be damned if I'm staying late today. I need the medical gods to shine down and not give me anyone who needs labs drawn late in the day that I'll have to stick around for.

I need smooth sailing.

And before Harper, I never had these kinds of thoughts. That's not lost on me.

She's changed everything.

And it doesn't scare me at all.

"Room 11 is ready for you, Dr. Blake," Sharon says, poking her head in my office.

"I'll be right there."

I close the laptop, loop my stethoscope around my neck, and knock twice on the door before pushing it open.

"Good afternoon, Hillary."

"Hey, Doc." She pushes her hair back behind her shoulder and bats her eyelashes.

Yeah, I fucked Hillary a few years ago *before* she was my patient, and she won't let it go. I took her off my patient list and passed her to someone else, but she's a work-in, and there was no one else to see her. I'm taking overflow this afternoon.

"What's going on today?" I ask as I open my computer and look at the vitals that Sharon got for me. "Your blood pressure is pretty low."

"I've been woozy," she says, nodding. "And I get this warm sensation that floods over me, and it's really unsettling."

"Makes sense with the blood pressure. Dizziness is common. Hop up on the table and let me hear your heart."

She does as I ask. I'm relieved that she's not touching me inappropriately today.

"Take a deep breath for me." We go through the four more breaths, and I frown. I don't like the way her heart sounds. "Have you ever been diagnosed with a heart murmur?"

"No." She shakes her head. "Not that I'm aware of."

I press my stethoscope over her heart again and close my eyes, listening.

Definitely a murmur.

"Hillary, I'd like to get an EKG and a chest X-ray before you leave. I hear a bit of a murmur in your heart, which can sometimes be associated with low blood pressure. How much water are you drinking in a day?"

"Probably not enough," she admits. "I forget."

"Keep a bottle with you and get that water in you. Do you eat foods rich in iron?"

"I eat on the run a lot. It's wedding season, Blake. I'm *always* on the go."

Hillary is a baker and is known for her wedding cakes.

"You need to eat well. That's part of your problem. Add a little salt to your water, that will help the blood pressure a bit. If you feel like you're going to pass out, sit down. You don't want to fall and hit your head."

"I've passed out a few times," she admits, and I frown.

"Let's get those tests. Don't leave until I get the results. It shouldn't take long." I open the exam room door and point to the left. "The EKG and X-ray department are just at the end of the hall. Take this paper down there, and they'll take care of you."

"Thanks. Hey, before you go, we should get a pizza sometime or something."

I stop and look her dead in the eyes. "Thank you for

the offer, but I'm in a relationship. Go get those tests, and we'll get this figured out."

Her shoulders sag, but she nods and walks down the hall for her tests.

"Heartbreaker."

I turn at her voice and pull Harper into my arms. "I wasn't expecting to see you until dinner."

"I know. It's my lunch hour, and I missed you. So I came to hug you real quick. I know you're busy."

"Best part of my day," I whisper into her ear. "Best part of every single day, sugar."

She buries her face in my neck and holds on tight before she pulls back and grins at me.

"Same, Dr. Blackwell. I'm making you dinner tonight."

"No way."

"Way."

"I'm cooking tonight, Harps. I have a plan, and I'll get home before you. Be sure to bring an overnight bag."

"Already packed," she informs me. "And I get to cook next time. Or we can cook together."

"Deal." I press a kiss to her forehead as she walks away. "Eat something before you go back on shift."

"Are those doctor's orders?"

"If that's what gets you to eat, yes."

She laughs and turns a corner to leave the clinic, and I turn to see a smiling Hillary standing outside of room 11.

"I'm happy for you."

"Thanks. Let's look at your test results."

I've just set some chips and queso on the island when Harper walks through the front door, drops her bag on the floor, her purse on top of that, and sighs.

Her hair, which just four hours ago was in a knot on top of her head, is now floppy. Her mascara is smudged. And her lower lip is quivering.

Fuck.

After flipping off the burner, I toss the towel from my shoulder to the counter and hurry to her, scooping her up in my arms as the tears come. She buries her face in my chest, clinging to me.

"Shh." I rock her back and forth, and my heart aches as she cries. "Aw, baby. I'm so sorry."

I have no idea what happened, but it's bad. And it's rocked her to the core.

I pick her up in my arms and sit on the couch, keeping her cradled against me, and let her cry it out. After pulling her hair out of the wrecked bun, I push my fingers through it and press kisses to the top of her head.

As medical professionals, we've all seen horrific things. I've had to tell parents that their children weren't coming home. I've given diagnoses that meant my patient had days, not years ahead of them. I've seen more blood and horror than any one person should.

And I know that it's the same for her. For every good

outcome, there are more that are deeply tragic. Especially when you're dealing with medically fragile babies.

"He was so tiny," she says in the smallest voice as the sobs start to slow down. "Not my smallest, but still. And we worked on him for what felt like hours. But he was just too small, Blake. And his parents conceived through IVF, and fucking hell, it was just so goddamn sad."

"I'm sorry," I whisper and kiss her temple as she lifts her head. I wipe her tears away with a tissue. "That's heartbreaking."

"It really was. Mom almost died, too. And her poor husband was just shell-shocked, standing there like *what am I supposed to do?* I felt awful that no one could talk to him because we were too busy working on Mom and baby. Baby was born at twenty-five weeks and one day. He was twelve ounces."

Fuck, that's a small baby.

"For a few minutes, I thought he was going to rally. I knew he'd have a tough road, but then everything just went to shit, and nothing we did worked."

"Hey, it's not your fault."

"Maybe if another nurse had been there—"

"No, Harper. You know as well as I do that isn't how it works. We can do everything right, down to the letter, and still lose them. It happens every day, and it's not your fault. At twenty-five weeks, that baby had very little chance, and add on to it he only had one kidney? This wasn't your fault."

She sniffs and wipes her nose and then nods. "I know. But I wish there was a different outcome."

"I do too. Mom is going to be okay?"

"Yeah. She was a bleeder, but they got her stabilized. She was so devastated that she was pretty much catatonic by the time I left. Those two are going to need some therapy."

She wraps her arms around my neck and rolls into me, holding me tightly, and I hug her just as close.

"It's going to be okay," I tell her. "What a shit day. I'm so sorry. What do you need?"

"Hugs."

"I have a lot of those." I kiss her temple. "Maybe a bath? Some wine?"

"I have to work tomorrow. No wine. I'll shower and should be fine. I just couldn't fall apart at the hospital and held it together until I got through the door."

"This is your safe place, Harper. It always will be. You can cry or yell or do whatever you have to do here."

"Thank you. It smells good in here."

"That's fajitas on the stove."

"Are they ruined?"

Probably, but I have more I can cook up.

"Not at all. Go grab your shower, and dinner will be ready."

She sighs and cups my face in her hands, and I *know* she wants to tell me she loves me. It's like when we were on the trail, and I could see it all over her face.

"I love you too, baby."

Her eyes fill with tears again, and I brush them away.

"I'm fine, my love. I feel it every day. I don't need the words. Go take your shower."

"Can I wear your T-shirt?"

I smile and brush my nose over hers. I love that my clothes bring her comfort. "You can wear whatever you want."

"I just need fifteen minutes."

"There's no rush."

She climbs off my lap and grabs her bag, then sets off for the primary suite. I take a minute to breathe.

It's true. I don't need the words. How she feels about me is written all over her.

"I'm having a heart attack."

I frown at the fifty-year-old woman sitting on the exam table in the ER. "Why do you think that?"

"My left hand is numb."

"Your arm or your hand?"

"My hand. The last three fingers. And I have pressure in my chest."

The nurses are bustling about, getting EKG leads attached to the patient. If a patient comes in thinking they're having a heart attack, we move fast. Another nurse starts an IV, and I observe the patient's heart rate and blood pressure on the monitor.

The fact that the patient isn't freaking out is interesting. She's perfectly calm in that bed as if she's ordering dinner and I'm the server. Her color is fine, her eyes are clear, and her hands are steady.

"Is it hard to breathe?" I ask her.

"No."

"Do you—"

"I already told you my symptoms." She interrupts me. "And I'm having a heart attack. Aren't you going to take me to surgery?"

One of the nurses smirks, and I tilt my head to the side.

"I'm still gathering information, Mrs. Parker. I'm not convinced that you're having a heart attack. I'd like to run some blood tests. Your EKG is normal."

"Well, you're wrong."

I blink at her. "Are you a cardiologist, Mrs. Parker?"

"No, but I've watched eighteen seasons of *Grey's Anatomy*, haven't I? I should have MD after my name. I bet you're screwing her"—she gestures to my nurse, Lexi—"in the on-call room."

Lexi and I share a look.

"Ma'am, *Grey's* is fiction. It's made for TV. You know that, right? It's not a documentary."

Mrs. Parker just rolls her eyes. "Whatever. You're going to let me die here in this bed because you haven't taken me to surgery."

"You're not dying."

"Says you."

"Yeah. And I'm the only one in this room with an *actual* MD after his name. Now, we're running those labs, and I'll let you know what they say. I can say with certainty that when those three fingers go numb, it's usually because you have nerve issues happening from your C-1 to T-1 spine, and they're pushing on your radial and ulnar nerves. That can also cause pressure on your sternum. Your heart rate and blood pressure are normal. Your EKG is normal. But we're going to check those labs and get some fluids in you while you wait."

"I'm likely dying."

I shake my head and turn for the door. "Not today, Mrs. Parker."

I close the door behind me and walk out to the small office the doctors use when we're here. It's been a quiet day, and that's something I'll never say out loud because I don't want to jinx it.

After today, Harper and I get a day off together. Well, she gets three days, but I only have tomorrow with her. I'll gladly take it.

Just as I'm about to see if those lab results are in for Mrs. Parker, Lexi pops her head around the doorway.

"I have an Amy from up in the NICU on line two for you."

"Thanks." I pick up the phone. "This is Dr. Blackwell."

"This is Amy in the NICU. Can you please come up here? It's Harper. We had—"

"I'm on my way right now."

Chapter Twenty-Four
HARPER

Being with Blake last night was exactly what I needed after yesterday's chaos here at work. Before I arrived at his house, I'd briefly considered just going back to Xander's, pulling the covers over my head, and sending Blake a message that I didn't feel well.

But I needed him. I needed him to hold me and *love* me after the trauma of losing that little one. And as soon as his arms wrapped around me, and I felt his heartbeat so strong against my cheek, I knew it was the right move. Blake is my safe place.

Not to mention, the man can *cook*. He works magic in the kitchen. Once I had taken my shower and he'd fed me some of the best fajitas I've ever had—don't tell Juliet—we curled up and watched a show before snuggling up in bed.

We didn't even have sex, and honestly, we didn't need

to. It was still an incredibly intimate evening, and I hope we get to repeat it tonight.

Except I'd like to add in the orgasms this time.

"Jamison's going home," Amy tells me at the nurses' station.

My head swings up in surprise. "Really? Oh my gosh, I have to go say goodbye."

Amy and I both walk over to Jamison's little room, and I smile as the adoptive parents cuddle him while waiting for their final discharge papers from the doctor.

"Thank you so much," Trevor, Jamison's new dad, says as he sways side to side with the baby in his arms. "For everything."

"Jamison did all the work," I reply with a smile and slide my hands in my pockets, watching them. "We just kept an eye on him."

"You've all been so wonderful," Angie, Trevor's wife, replies. They have been here around the clock since they were approved to adopt Jamison just a couple of weeks ago. "I'm almost scared to take him home. What if something happens, and I don't have you there to help me?"

"Jamison is healthy," Amy assures her. "He's strong, and yes, he has a few challenges ahead, but the doctor would never send him home with you if he didn't think that beautiful baby was ready or that you were more than capable of caring for him."

"She's right," I add, reaching out to brush my knuckle down Jamison's cheek. "You're all going to do great. And if you ever have questions, call your pediatrician."

"Can I hug you?" Angie asks with tears in her eyes, and I immediately open my arms and let her hug me close.

"You're a great mom, Angie. You've got this."

She pulls back and then hugs Amy, who also has tears in her eyes. Trevor offers me a side hug, and after we say goodbye, I leave to check on my other patients after grabbing my laptop from the nurses' station.

We have a new little girl named Amelia, who came in a few days ago. She's full-term, but she's been struggling with breathing and heart issues, so she's hanging out with us for a while.

"How's Amelia this afternoon?" I ask as I walk into her area and open my laptop to check her chart.

"Still gasping," Cindy, Amelia's mom, says. She looks exhausted. She's pale, has dark circles under her eyes, and won't look away from her daughter.

"When was the last time you slept or ate, Cindy?"

She shakes her head. "Doesn't matter. I'm not leaving her."

"Where's your husband?"

"He'll be back. He ran down to the cafeteria for lunch."

I narrow my eyes. "Is he bringing you back something so you can switch places?"

Cindy swallows and closes her eyes for a moment. "I'm not hungry."

Setting my computer aside, I rest my hand on Cindy's shoulder. "You're no good to Amelia if you're sick, Cindy. You need to eat. You just had a baby three days ago, and your body needs all the nourishment it can get, especially since you're breastfeeding that little girl. I'm going to call down for a meal for you, and I'm going to insist that you sleep in that recliner. I'm not going to ask you to leave. But you need to take care of yourself, too."

Tears fill her eyes, and she looks up at me with so much despair, my heart aches. "What if I look away for even a second, and she dies?"

"We're doing everything possible to keep that from happening. You, us, and Amelia. She's so strong, Cindy."

"Yeah, she is." Cindy smiles through her tears and watches the baby. "Okay, I'll eat something. My husband should be back soon, too."

"Great. There's a menu right in that drawer next to you. Just let me know what you want, and I'll make it happen."

"Thanks."

With Cindy reading the menu, I get to work checking on Amelia. A lot of my job is reassuring parents because they're terrified and sad, and I understand that. I would be, too.

Suddenly, behind me, I hear something bang against the floor. Someone screams, and then running feet pound on the floor.

"Harper!" Amy looks like she's seen a ghost. "Help!"

I run with her across the unit and see a man standing over one of my nurses, who's cowering on the floor.

"Call security," I tell her.

"Already on it," Amy assures me.

"I said *don't touch my son*," he yells at the nurse on the floor. "What the fuck is wrong with you people? It's your fault he's in here."

"Whoa. What's going on?"

I quickly survey the scene. Baby Oliver is safe in his bassinet, but his mother's face is white, and her hands are trembling. A medical tray of supplies is on its side, everything from the top of it scattered around the area, and the dad, who I haven't met yet, is breathing fire, his hands fisted.

Is he on something?

"Who the fuck are you?"

"I'm the nurse in charge, and I'd like to know why you're abusing my staff."

His eyes narrow, his lips curl into a snarl, and I stand my ground as my nurse stands and quickly moves away.

He's just like Nathan.

"I told her to stay away from my kid."

"We can't stay away from Oliver. He's in our care. He's a sick little boy—"

"Because. Of. YOU!" he screams, getting right in my face. "If the staff here hadn't fucked up when my girl was having him, he wouldn't be in here. I don't want any of you touching him. Am I clear?"

"You're going to need to back away from me."

His eyes travel up and down my body, and nausea rolls through me. "Is that right? Or what? You're not going to do anything. You're a piece of shit. A pitiful excuse for a nurse. Who the fuck are you saving?"

"You're a shitty nurse, Harper. I don't even know why you bother."

Blinking, I try to stay here and not go back there. Jesus, I thought I was through this.

"Back. Off. Or I'll have you kicked out of here, and you won't be allowed back in."

"You're not going to do shit to me. You're nothing. I'm taking my boy."

"No. You're not."

"Rich, they're trying to help—" the mom says, but then he rounds on her, and I glance back, relieved to see that Amy is on the phone with security. She gives me a thumbs-up, and I take a deep breath because I've started to shake. I know I'm going to have a panic attack, but I can*not* do that in front of this guy.

"You're nothing, Harper. No one wants you. That baby probably died because you didn't know what to do. Just give it up already." Nathan's lips curled up in a happy sneer when he would start in on that shit, lecturing me for hours on end, always the same things over and over again.

"You'll shut the fuck up," this guy yells at the mother of his child. "If you weren't so goddamn pathetic, we wouldn't be here. Jesus, it's just childbirth. Women do it every day without almost killing their baby—"

"Enough!" My hands are fisted, and I'm so fucking pissed off. "Stop talking to her like that. It's not her fault, and it's not our fault that Oliver needs to be here. I get that you're overwhelmed and scared, but you don't get to abuse everyone around you. You need to leave."

"I'm not going anywhere, sweetheart."

"Yes, you are," a man says from behind me. It's George from security, and two other guards flank him. "Police are on the way, too, Miss Harper. Come on, sir. You can't hurt my girls up here."

"Fuck off. That's my baby."

"Don't care," George says with a shrug. "You gotta go."

All three guards have to forcefully remove the man from my unit, and I immediately check in with Carrie, the nurse who was on the floor.

"Are you okay?" I ask.

She nods and blows out a breath. "Yeah, mostly I'm pissed. He didn't touch me. He threw the cart, and I fell when trying to avoid getting hit by it."

"Good. Are you okay to stay on shift, or do you need to go?"

"I'm fine," she says, shaking her head. "Really. Not my first asshole. I've got this, Harper."

I'm glad you *do*. I can feel the adrenaline wearing off and the panic rising, but I manage to swallow it down and turn to the mom.

"Can we call someone to come sit with you?" I ask her, and I can hear the shake in my voice. *Hold it together, Harper. Just a few more minutes.*

"I've already texted my sister," she says. "I'm not with him, by the way. We're not married. He's Oliver's father, but we're not together."

"That's none of my business," I reply. "But if you ever feel unsafe—"

"I have family, and my brother's a cop," she says, and

I can't help but think that *my* brother is also a cop, and there's no way in hell that Easton would allow a man like that anywhere in the vicinity of my hospital room. *None* of my family would. But like I said, none of my business. "We're okay. But thank you."

I nod and turn just as Amy walks up to me. She doesn't touch me, but I know she can see that I'm going to lose it. I love this woman. She exudes *calm*. Like a grandma. Or a seasoned medical professional who knows her shit.

Amy knows this job inside and out. I've already learned so much from her.

"I need a minute," I tell her in a low voice. My breaths are already coming fast. I keep seeing Nathan's sneering face in my head, and I need a fucking minute to calm down without an audience.

I can't stand the thought of breaking down where others can see me.

"Come on." She wraps her arm around my waist and leads me into the stairwell, which is perfect because not many people use the stairs.

Oh God. Why can't I get that asshole out of my head? Am I going to fall apart like this every fucking time someone mouths off to me?

"I'll be right back," Amy promises and leaves me alone.

Immediately, the panic attack sets in, and I can't stop the tears that fall over my cheeks.

"You're nothing. Christ, you're lucky you have me because no one else in the world would bother with you.

You're no fun, Harper. You're such a fucking killjoy. Do you even remember how to smile? And don't even get me started on how pathetic you are to fuck." Nathan paces in front of where I sit on the couch, my head down, listening to the lecture.

Shaking my hands out at my sides because they've gone numb, I decide to sit on the top step because my knees are rubber and rest my forehead on the wall next to me. God, I hate his voice so much. How did I listen to him for all those years?

"Go away," I whisper. "Just fucking get out of my head."

I hear a door downstairs but ignore it. I don't want anyone to see me like this, but I can't get my legs to work quite yet, so they'll just have to judge me and go about their day.

I don't care.

Footsteps fly up the stairs, then hands are on my face.

"Baby, what's wrong? Christ, Harper, what's going on?"

I blink and frown when it's Blake's face in front of me. He's brushing the tears off my cheeks, but I still can't breathe, so I just shake my head.

"Go away," I manage to get out.

God, I don't want him to see me like this.

"Not a chance in hell, sugar."

The door behind us opens, and I hear Amy's voice.

"There was a really abusive dad a few minutes ago," she says, filling Blake in. "Harper handled him like a damn boss, but when it was all over …"

"Got it," Blake says and nods at Amy over my shoulder. "Thank you."

"Here's some water for her. Harper, we have things covered. Take your time, honey."

Humiliation washes through me, and I close my eyes and tip my forehead against Blake's shoulder.

"Fuck." It's a whisper.

"Talk to me, baby. Are you hurt? Did he hit you?" His big hands rub up and down my back, soothing me, warming me up from the inside out. This man centers me, brings me back to focus on the here and now, and reminds me that Nathan is in my past, where he belongs.

"No." Finally able to pull in a full breath, I pull back and wipe my face. "I'm sorry Amy called you. You're needed in the ER—"

"I'm needed right here with my girl," he says, those hazel eyes full of concern and love. "How often do you have panic attacks, Harper?"

"I haven't since I moved home." I shake my head. "The asshole dad used the right words to trigger me. I swear to God he was Nathan in a different skin."

Blake's hands tighten, and he growls, making me blink in surprise.

"I'm okay." With a weak smile, I reach up and cup his cheek, wanting to reassure him. "Thank you for running up here, but I'm better now. It's just not a fun voice to have in my head, and when it starts up—"

"You call *me*," he says. "When it starts up, you call me, and we'll deal with it. Because whatever those words are, they're wrong, baby. You're so fucking amazing."

"That's two days in a row you had to watch me lose it." I wince. "I don't like that."

"As long as you're okay, I don't mind. What do you need, Harper?"

Leaning close, I cover his mouth with mine and kiss him softly. "I need to spend time with you tonight, naked time, and maybe we can hike tomorrow?"

"How do you feel about a cool bike ride on my favorite path around the valley?"

My eyes widen. "Yes, please. But I don't have a bike."

He brushes my hair behind my ear, watching the motion with his eyes. "Yes, you do. You'll be introduced tonight."

"You bought me a *bike*?"

"Yes, but if it doesn't work for you, we can exchange it until you get what fits best." He pulls me to my feet. "Are you okay to go back to work?"

"Yeah, I'm okay. I'm glad I didn't fall apart in front of my staff and patients. Thank you."

"I love you, baby." He kisses my forehead, and I squeeze his hand three times, making him smile. "I'll see you tonight."

He turns and jogs back down the stairs, and when the door closes behind him, I let out a long breath.

Christ, I'm so in love with him.

Chapter Twenty-Five
BLAKE

With everything that's happened at work over the past few days for my girl, we need a night out. Not just a night together but something to distract us from work.

And then I'm going to take her home and make love to her all fucking night long.

When Harper walks into my house after work, I meet her at the door, frame her gorgeous face in my hands, and kiss the fuck out of her.

"Well, hello there," she says with a grin, and it's a hit to the solar plexus every time. Christ, those eyes.

"We have roughly thirty-six hours all to ourselves." Her dark hair is down, and I tuck one side behind her ear, the soft strands moving through my fingers like silk. "And I'm taking you out for dinner."

Her eyes brighten, and she brushes her fingers through the hair at the nape of my neck, giving me goose bumps.

"Yeah? Where are we going?"

"Anywhere you want. We need a night out, sugar."

"That does sound nice. Hmm." She taps her finger on her lips, thinking about it. "The diner?"

I grin down at her. "You want to go to the diner for dinner?"

"Is it weird that I want breakfast for dinner, and they have the *best* pancakes. I'll even indulge in the gluten. And all the maple syrup in the land."

"It's not weird at all." I nuzzle her nose with mine, soaking in her sweetness. "How are you feeling?"

"I'm totally fine. I promise." She steps closer and presses her ear to my chest. "How was the rest of your day?"

"I got schooled by a woman who claims to have gotten her medical license from *Grey's Anatomy*."

Harper's head pops up, and she laughs. "Seriously?"

"Oh, she was quite serious."

"You could totally be Dr. McDreamy," she says. "I can see it."

"Stop." I laugh and kiss her forehead. "The rest of the day was pretty standard. Nothing to report."

A broken hip, an actual heart attack that led to a triple bypass surgery, two motor vehicle accidents, and a domestic violence victim.

It was a shit day.

But I'm not going to unload on my girl. She had a rough one, too.

"I need a shower first, and then I'll be ready to go."

"Take your time, baby." I kiss her lips softly, and then

she sets off for what I've come to think of as *our* bedroom, and I take a walk out to the backyard.

One of the reasons I bought this specific house was because of the view. Growing up on the Double B Ranch, we had panoramic views of the mountains, and I knew that when I bought a home, I needed to see the mountains here, too. It's a beautiful early summer day. I can smell the lilacs on the breeze, and it relaxes me.

But knowing that my girl is home safe is what really sets my soul at ease.

Loving Harper is ... *all-consuming*. She's become the most important thing in my life, even more than medicine, and that's something I never expected to find. I didn't *want* it.

But now that she's here, I can't imagine a life without her in it. Yes, priorities are shifting.

"You're thinking awfully hard out here."

I turn and find Harper standing in the doorway, her shoulder against the doorjamb, smiling at me.

"Are you ready for dinner?" she asks.

"I'm starving." *For her.* I want to sink inside her and never let her go.

"Me, too." She holds her hand out for mine, so much like I did for her that day at the airport all those months ago, and I slide my palm against hers, weave our fingers together, and bring her hand to my lips.

"Then I'd better feed you. Let's go."

"Would you like some pancakes with your syrup?" I stare, stunned, as she drowns the pancakes in the sticky syrup.

Harper smirks. "Hey, I earned these pancakes. They're the best like this."

"We should carry a glucose monitor with us."

Harper's eyes narrow on me. "Don't ruin this for me, Dr. Blackwell."

Holding my hands up in surrender, I take a bite of my eggs. "No judgment."

"Liar. You're totally judging me." She shoves a soggy bite in her mouth and sighs with joy. "Oh God. So good. Want a bite?"

I grin, enjoying the fuck out of her. "No."

"Good, more for me." She takes another bite and does a little dance in the booth.

Kay's Diner is a traditional 1950s soda fountain diner with black-and-white checked floors, white-topped tables, and red-vinyl-covered seats. The walls are covered in classic rock & roll memorabilia, and the jukebox currently plays an old Elvis song.

It's casual and sweet, and I love that this is where she wanted to come to dinner.

"Why are you looking at me like that?"

I tip up an eyebrow and munch on some bacon. *God, why is bacon so fucking good?* "Like what?"

"I don't know. Like I did something funny."

"You're just adorable, and I can't get enough of you."

She blinks at me and then stuffs another huge, soggy bite of pancakes in her mouth. "Am I funny, Dr. Blackwell?"

I chuckle, then switch to her side of the booth, crowding her so I can whisper in her ear.

"You're fucking *everything*, sugar. I didn't know that eating pancakes turned me on so much, but all I can think about is drizzling that syrup on your tits and licking it off."

"I knew you had a sweet tooth."

I nibble on her earlobe, and she sucks in a breath. "Yeah, for you. Because you're the sweetest thing I've ever tasted in my life. I want to spread you wide open and devour you."

She turns her head, and her nose bumps mine. I'm so close to her. "Let's go home, okay?"

Home.

Yeah, I fucking love the sound of that.

"Finish your pancakes, baby." I run my hand down her hair and kiss her temple. "And then we'll go home."

"I'm good." She wipes her mouth with her napkin and flags down the server. "Check, please."

"I'll bring it right over. Was everything okay?"

"Delicious," Harper confirms and rests her hand on my thigh, giving it a squeeze.

When the server leaves, I plant my lips by her ear again. "Are you that greedy for my cock, sugar?"

"It's been a week, Blake. Throw a girl a bone. Pun intended."

I bark out a laugh just as the server arrives with the check, and I pass her my card.

Within minutes, we're headed out to the car.

"Buckle in, sweetheart."

"No way. Drive. I'm going to—"

"You're going to buckle your fucking belt, Harper." I pin her in my gaze. "I had two car accidents in my ER today, and one didn't end well."

She blinks and frowns. "You didn't tell me about that when I asked earlier."

"I'm telling you now. Please, buckle your seat belt."

She follows the command, and as I pull onto the highway toward the edge of town to my neighborhood, I feel her hot gaze on me.

"Baby—"

"No, don't baby me. You watched me fall apart *twice* in the past twenty-four hours, all because of the job. I asked you specifically how your day was, and you brushed me off because otherwise, you would have told me that you had a rough day today. This isn't a one-sided relationship, Blake, where you console me, but I don't have any idea what you're dealing with. That's not fair, and it's not healthy."

"You've had a lot going on, Harper."

"Apparently, I'm not the only one."

I pull into the garage, and before I can turn to face her, Harper is out of the car and headed into the house.

My girl is good and pissed off.

Following her into the house, I hear my front door slam shut.

"Where the fuck is she going?"

No.

She's not running away from me. Not today or any other day.

Christ, my heart can't handle this.

I run out to the porch and see Harper toss her bag in her car, and I get there in time to pull it back out again.

"Put that back. I'm leaving."

"No, you're not."

She lifts her chin and glares at me. *Glares at me.* Those gray eyes shoot daggers at me. But there's hurt there, too, and that almost brings me to my knees.

She's never looked at me like this before, and I'll do whatever it takes to make sure she never looks at me like this again. My heart can't take it.

"Obviously, we're in two very different relationships, Blake, and I don't want—"

Without another word, I pick her up, push the car door closed with my foot, and carry her back inside. I set her on the kitchen island.

"We're going to talk this out."

"I'm going to yell this out."

"Great. I'm standing right here. Yell at me, but you won't fucking leave."

She swallows and pushes me away so I'm not touching her, and that's a direct arrow to the chest.

"I feel like a fucking fool," she says as she hops off the counter to pace. "I've done this before, Blake. I've been the one whose emotions are on the line, and I get nothing in return. No information. No *say*. Like I'm the *little woman* who doesn't need to know more than he's willing to give her."

"That's not what this is."

"That's what it feels like. We both have high-stress jobs. Who is better equipped to empathize at the end of the day than each other?"

She's not wrong. Not at all.

"I can share you with your job, Blake. I knew going into this that you work sixty hour weeks, and our shifts are all over the place, and there will be times when we just don't see each other. Fine. I can deal with that because we both love what we do, and it's important. And I'm fucking *proud* of you! You save lives every day. That's a big fucking deal, and I'm here for it."

She's fucking magnificent with her flushed cheeks and bright eyes, in that pink dress that molds her body perfectly.

And I've fucked up so badly.

"I tell you when I've had a hard day. You see it written all over me, and maybe that's a mistake on my part. Maybe I shouldn't show my emotions so freely—"

"Don't you dare hide from me, sugar."

"But *you're* hiding from *me*." She stops her pacing, faces me and her eyes are practically begging me to understand. "You never talk about it. You never confide when you lose a patient, or when you're excited because you found an early diagnosis and can help someone. For all I know, you sat in your office and played solitaire all day."

I cross my arms over my chest and don't bother interrupting her because she's on a roll. And she's not wrong.

"Sure, the *Grey's Anatomy* thing was funny, but that's nothing compared to losing a patient from an accident today. Christ, Blake."

She shakes her head and turns to look outside.

"I can't tell you everything that happens at work—"

She spins and pins me in another glare. "Don't do that."

I sigh and drag my hand down my face. "I *never* talk about work," I try again. "I never have. My family doesn't want to hear about a mangled knee, or a ninety-three year-old woman with a broken hip that will likely kill her. I do the job, and then I go home, Harper."

She listens, but she's no less pissed off.

"I *need* you to talk to me," she says. "Because I can't just close myself off and not talk to you about the shit that goes down at work. That's how I process, and I made the mistake of doing that before, and then it was held over my head as all of the reasons I'm bad at my job, while I didn't know *dick* about what happened at his workplace. I really didn't know him at all."

"I'm not him."

"No, you're worse. Because I care about you so fucking deeply that—"

I can't stand it. I pull her to me, boost her back up on the counter, and stand between her legs, her core pressed to my hard cock.

"I'm not him, Harper. I'm sorry that I hurt you, and I'll work on it, but don't compare me to the piece of shit who traumatized you so badly that when triggered, you have fucking panic attacks. Don't do that."

Her lower lip quivers, but she clears her throat and swallows hard.

"Don't shut me out," she whispers and rests her forehead against mine. "Just talk to me. And if you don't want to talk, say that instead. But don't *pretend* that everything is okay when it's not. Because it makes me feel like I trust you implicitly, but you don't trust me back."

Those last three words are said in a whisper, making my heart hurt.

"I trust you, baby. I didn't want to overload you." She starts to interrupt, but I place my finger over her lips. "You had your say. Now I'll have mine. You have had a rough two days, Harper. Rougher than most. I understand it was wrong not to tell you the truth when you asked, but it wasn't because I don't trust you. I just wanted to have a fun evening with you. I really *do* leave most of my work at the hospital."

Framing her face in my hands, I kiss her gently, and she grips my wrists but doesn't push me away.

"This job, being here in my hometown, is a lot of pressure. Most of the time, I love it. I thrive under it because I'm helping people I've known all my life. But it's a lot, too."

Her eyes soften, and she pushes her fingers into my hair, soothing me.

Christ, she soothes me.

"How do I tell my high school math teacher that her husband has brain cancer?"

"*Blake.*"

"How do I explain to my high school girlfriend that her husband was killed in a hunting accident, and he didn't survive the gunshot to his liver?"

A tear rolls down her cheek, and I brush it away with my thumb.

"I love what I do, but it's not anonymous. I could have gone to a city to work where I didn't have connections to the patients like I do here. But I chose to come home, and that means that many days are just fucking *heavy*, Harper."

"You don't have to carry that by yourself." Her voice is the sweetest whisper as she continues to brush her fingers through my hair. "You can always talk to me. I know you can't give me specific details, but we can talk in generalities. You need to let go of that burden."

I lean into her touch, soaking her in.

"I'll work on it." I drag my knuckles down her cheek. "If we're going to fight, I need you to stay here and fight with me, not run away."

"I was so mad that—"

"I don't care."

Her hands glide down my shoulders, and she wiggles closer to me, pressing sweet kisses to my neck, under my chin.

"Are you still mad, sugar?"

"Only a little."

"I'm going to fuck the rest of the mad out of you."

Brushing my hands up her thighs, I lift the dress up and over her head and cast it aside, then swallow hard when I take in her bare chest, her perfect puckered pink nipples ready for me to pinch and roll between my fingers.

Harper sighs and leans into my touch as she unbuckles my belt, then unfastens my jeans and lets them fall down my hips, her hands planted on my ass.

"Shirt off," she growls against my lips, and I reach over my shoulder and tug it off, then cast it aside.

"You may be pissed off, but you're not in charge here. Don't get it twisted."

She simply bites that pillow of a lip, watching me.

"I've missed this pussy," I tell her as I kiss down her torso, pausing by each delectable nipple and her navel. I finally squat so I'm level with her gorgeous, sopping-wet cunt. "Looks like fighting with me makes you wet, sweetheart."

She doesn't answer me, so I slap her pussy, right over her clit, and she inhales sharply. "Holy shit."

Wasting no time, I rip the lace off her, exposing her to me, and lean in to take a deep breath of her essence for just a split second before I *devour her.*

"Blake!" Her voice is shrill as her hips lift, and she pushes harder into my face. "Oh God, your mouth."

"Fucking delicious." I lick and suck, then drag my lips all through her wet sex, getting her good and ready for me. Just as she's about to come, I pull away entirely, standing to my full height.

"*Blake.*"

"You were going to *leave me.*" I shake my head, then

grip onto her throat and pull her lips against mine. "That fucking *tore me apart.*"

"Blake," she whimpers and then cries out when I push inside her, impaling her with one hard thrust.

"You're *mine*, Harper." My hips move fast, pounding into her tight-as-fuck pussy. "This pussy is mine."

She clings to me, panting, her eyes glassy.

"Say it," I order her.

"All of me is yours, Blake."

I pull out, lift her off the counter, and turn her around.

"Grab the counter."

She does, and I plunge back in, and she moans loudly as I slap her ass, leaving a beautiful red mark.

"*Mine*," I say again before I fist her hair and pull her up just a bit. "Tell me you won't walk out like that again."

"I probably won't."

I pause. "That's not the right answer, Harper."

Reaching around, I press my fingers to her clit, and she cries out.

"Please, Blake."

"What do you need?"

"I need to see you."

That's not what I was expecting.

Pulling out, I turn her around once more and reach down to grip her ass and lift her easily. She wraps her legs around my waist, and I press her up against the wall, notch my crown at her opening, and push in once more.

"God, your cock does things to me."

I rut into her, unable to slow down, unable to be gentle, and she holds on, with me for every thrust as wave after wave of love and frustration battle their way through me.

"Yes, yes, *yes*," she chants. Her mouth opens on a silent scream, and her pussy clenches around my cock like a fucking vise.

"That's it. Fuck, Harper."

My spine tingles, and I can't hold back the climax that works its way through me, shooting inside my girl, claiming her with every rock of my hips. I manage to keep her in my arms as we both try to catch our breaths.

"Move in here with me." Her eyes widen in surprise, and she brings her hands to my face. "I need you here, baby."

I've never thought those words before she came into my life.

"At least, if I haven't seen or held you in a couple of days, I'll smell you on the sheets. I'll see your coffee mug in the sink and your stuff in the bathroom. Your books lying around the house. You'll be here, even when you're *not* here. No more overnight bags."

She pushes her fingers through my hair, using her nails on my scalp in that way that makes me want to fucking purr.

"Are you sure?" she asks, her voice quiet.

"I've never been more sure of anything in my life."

"Looks like we have plans for our day off tomorrow after the bike ride."

Thank God.

I rest my forehead to hers, still holding her against the wall. "Let's move you in tonight."

She frames my face and smiles at me. "*Tonight?*"

"Do you have much to pack?"

"No, just a couple of suitcases—"

"Then yes. Tonight. The faster you're here, in our house, the better."

She blinks up at me. "*Our* house."

"Yeah, baby. Our house. Unless you don't like it and want to buy something else."

She exhales with a surprised laugh, then wraps those arms around my shoulders and buries her face in my neck. "I love this house."

Tell me you love me, too.

I almost say the words out loud, but I hold them back.

She'll say them when she's ready, and it's not fair of me to demand them.

But fuck, do I need to hear it.

"Blake."

"Yes, baby."

She pauses, then says, "You're the best thing that ever happened to me."

I grin and kiss her cheek. "Same here, my love. Same here."

Chapter Twenty-Six
HARPER

"That's the last of it."

Holy shit. I'm really doing this. I'm moving in with Blake Blackwell.

I get to see him every day, even if it's only for a few minutes between our crazy schedules, and part of me is so relieved. I need him every day.

With my few suitcases and a couple of totes in the back of his vehicle, Blake reaches up to close his SUV just as Xander comes driving up in his fancy-as-fuck car and parks behind us.

"What are you guys up to?" my brother asks as he climbs out of his sports car and pulls his sunglasses off.

"Oh good, I don't have to text you. I'm moving all of my things over to Blake's place."

The smile falls from Xander's lips, and his gaze bounces between Blake and me.

"Say that again." Xander crosses his arms over his chest and glares at Blake, and I let out a sigh.

"Stop looking at him like that." I prop my hands on my hips. "Thank you for giving me a place to live, X. I appreciate you, and I have loved having some time with you since it feels like I never get to see you. But Blake and I hardly see each other as it is with our schedules, and I'm going to be living with him."

"You move fast," Xander says, still staring at Blake, and I close my eyes and shake my head.

"God save me from overprotective men. Xander, chill out."

"It's my whole job not to chill out when one of my sisters decides to shack up with some dude," he reminds me, then turns back to Blake. "Look, I like you. I like your family. I don't have beef with you, but she's my sister, and she's already been through it. So if you hurt her, if you even hurt her *feelings*, I'll hurt you tenfold."

I walk right over to him and wrap my arms around him, hugging him close.

"He won't hurt me," I tell him, meaning every single word. Sure, we might argue, and earlier, I was ready to run Blake over with my car. But when it really counts? I know that Blake won't hurt me.

"I love you, baby sis," Xander says, kissing my head.

"Yeah, yeah, love, blah, blah." I grin up at him. "Ditto, X-man. Now, stop being a bully, okay? You can pull that shit on the ice, but not with me or my man. I won't bake you any more cookies."

"You don't pull your punches." He tugs on my hair the way he always does, and I know that everything is right with him. "You'd better tell the others. And you better *not* tell Dad over text."

"I'll call him."

"We'll go see him," Blake counters and offers his hand for Xander to shake. "And we'll have you all over for dinner soon."

"Good luck with that," Xander says. "Wrangling us all together at once isn't as easy as it used to be."

"You did it for the resort," I remind him.

"No one was going to pass up that little vacation." Xander laughs and turns to go inside. "Do you need help with anything?"

"Nah, we got it. I don't have much."

"Just call if you do." Xander winks at me, nods at Blake, and disappears inside.

"That went well," Blake says as we get in his car.

"For sure. No one threw a punch." I settle back in the seat with a happy sigh. "I'll send a group text to the rest."

"We'll go over and talk to Greg tomorrow," Blake says.

I turn to look at him and smile. God, he's pretty. It should be illegal in at least twelve states to look that good. "What about *your* family?"

Blake blinks at that. "Okay, we'll go to my parents' house, too, and I'll text my siblings when we get home."

I nod, happy with that answer, and reach over to take his hand in mine. He kisses my knuckles, then sets our hands on my thigh, and I squeeze three times.

A grin spreads over his gorgeous face, and he glances my way. "I love you too, baby."

Unloading the car and getting all my clothes hung in Blake's enormous closet takes less than an hour.

I guess it's my closet now, too.

And when I sit on the couch to text the gang, I see I'm late to the party.

> Ava: Does Harps have something to share with the freaking class????
>
> Easton: What's going on? You okay, Harps?
>
> Tucker: Are you in trouble?
>
> Xander: …
>
> Easton: HARPER. What's going on?

"Why are you biting your lip like that?" Blake asks as he sits next to me on the couch, holding his own phone.

"Xander has a big fucking mouth."

Blake smirks. "It's Billie in our family."

"Are you texting them?" I ask him.

"Already done. They all say hi, you've been invited to Sunday dinner at Beckett's place this week, and Billie will be calling you later."

I blink at him. "Wow, okay."

"How about you? How's it going?"

"Well, it looks like Xander already opened his big

mouth, so now I have to calm everyone down. Hold please."

Rather than send a text, I start the voice memo.

"Hi, family. Sounds like Xander can't keep his gossiping mouth shut. Yes, I have news. I moved in with Blake today. Ava, don't yell at me. It happened really fast. I'll tell you about it later. Before you ask, yes, I'm fine. Better than fine. I'd say don't worry, but I'd be wasting my breath. We'll have you all over for dinner or something at some point. Don't tell Greg, okay? We're going over to talk to him tomorrow. I repeat, let me tell Greg myself. Hugs and kisses and all the mushy stuff. Bye."

I set the phone on the coffee table, and I'm suddenly in Blake's lap. He's kissing down my neck, sending shivers down my body. I don't know if I'll ever get used to being this close to him. If my body won't come alive whenever he touches me.

"Welcome home, sugar."

With a grin, I snuggle against him. It's true, I really like Blake's house. *Our* house. But it's right here, sitting in his strong arms that I truly feel like I'm at home.

Because *Blake* is my home.

He nuzzles my ear, and his hand moves up between my thighs and under my dress. After we fucked in the kitchen earlier, I pulled on clean underwear, but when his fingertips ghost over my center, I know they're already wet again.

"Wet already?" he whispers in my ear before biting my earlobe. "Why are you wet, baby?"

"Because you're touching me." I gasp when his finger

pushes the panties aside and then slides between my lips, making me arch against him.

"Does that feel good?" He nips my ear, then drags his nose down my jawline, and an involuntary whimper escapes my lips. I can feel him grin against my skin. "Oh, it must feel good if you're making those little sounds that make me hard as fuck."

I can feel him, hard as steel, against my hip.

"Blake." I spread my legs wider, wanting more of him, needing him to fill me and make me come apart.

"What do you need, baby?"

I swallow hard and tip my face back, needing to see him. Needing to feel the connection to him when he looks in my eyes. "You. I just need you."

"Excellent fucking answer." His mouth covers mine, and his tongue slips between my lips, devouring me whole as his hands play me like an instrument, making me feral for him. His fingers slide through my wetness, and then he pulls them away and paints my bottom lip with my own arousal.

When I lick it off, Blake's eyes darken, and he moves us quickly, laying me on my back.

"I'm fucking obsessed with you," he growls against my neck. "Every inch of you. Inside and out. I can't fucking get enough of you."

He pulls my underwear down my legs, his fingertips dragging along my skin setting fire to every nerve ending, and discards them. He pushes my legs up to my chest and buries his face in my core. A wave of pure energy moves through me, heating my skin and stealing my breath.

"Blake."

"Say it again."

"Blake." My voice cracks that time because he sucks my clit between his lips and pulses, and I know I'm about to come.

I'm about to *explode*.

When he pushes two fingers inside me, there's no holding back. The orgasm rolls through me, and my hips lift as I cry out, pushing against him, and he growls, sending new sparks through me. He's fucking *addicting*.

As I calm down, Blake licks and nibbles around my pussy, humming, and his hands roam over my stomach and thighs.

And then he's moving over me, and he kisses me, and I can taste myself there. My hands lift to his face, and I feel more connected to this man at this moment than I ever have before, and I didn't know that was possible.

"You're the most beautiful thing I've ever seen," he whispers against my lips as he slides inside me, and we both moan with the pleasure of it. "So. Fucking. Tight."

I clench around him, and the gold flecks in his eyes shine as he starts to move.

"So. Fucking. *Mine.*" He growls the words, his forehead resting on mine as he moves, and I swear, I know on a molecular level that I'll never be the same.

Where it was fast and hard earlier, this is long, slow strokes, as if he's savoring every inch. Every gasp. As though I'm the most precious thing in the world, and he's taking it all in.

Because I *am*. I'm the most precious thing in Blake's world.

He will never hurt me like Nathan did. He'll never neglect and leave me like my parents did. *This man loves me.*

Blake loves me.

Bringing my hands to his face again, and with my lips ghosting against his, I whisper, "You're my home, Blake."

He's balls deep inside me when he stops moving. His eyes widen, and his hand cups my cheek, but he doesn't pull back. His lips still brush mine, and I can taste the love pouring out of this beautiful, intelligent, dedicated man.

He is everything I respect, everything I need.

"You're everything." Tears fill my eyes, but these tears are happy ones. "*You're* my home."

He brushes a tear away and rests his forehead against my own. "I can't ever be without you again, Harper. My life doesn't work without you in it."

"I'm right here, and I'm not going anywhere."

He starts to move again, and he presses his thumb against my clit.

"Fuck," I whisper.

"Come for me, beautiful." He tugs my lower lip between his teeth. "Come, sugar."

Every cell in my body quivers from the ecstasy of this climax. I feel myself bear down on him so fucking hard that he roars and comes with me, pulsing inside me.

And when we're a tangled, panting, sweaty mess,

Blake brushes my hair off my cheek and grins down at me.

"Shower."

"Wait. Your *legs still work*?" He laughs, but I keep talking. "How? I'm pretty sure I'm boneless at this point."

"Come on, I need to clean you up so I can get you messy again."

"You're trying to kill me."

"No, baby. I'm fucking worshipping you."

Chapter Twenty-Seven

BLAKE

The sun shines right in my face, making me too warm, so I kick off the blankets, then search for my woman so I can sink inside her and start the day right, but the bed is empty, and the sheets are cool where she should be.

I don't fucking like that.

After pulling on some sweats and doing my business, I pad out to the kitchen, the smell of coffee leading the way. There's a pot on the warmer, but no Harper.

A glance around the living room tells me she's not in there, but then I glimpse her dark hair out on the patio and move to the window.

There are moments when seeing her is a punch in the gut. When all I can do is stare because she's so fucking incredible, it steals the breath from my body, and I have no words to describe how absolutely phenomenal she is.

Harper's lying against the cushions of the swing, a

book in her hands and her mug of coffee resting on the table next to her. She's wearing an old blue med school T-shirt of mine that looks way better on her than it ever did on me and a pair of little denim shorts, leaving those long legs bare. I want those legs over my shoulders or wrapped around my waist, and I want to lose myself in her perfect body.

It doesn't look like she's eaten anything, so I make us each a quick protein shake and walk out to join her, needing to be near her.

"Good morning," she says with a smile, pulling her feet back so I can join her on the swing, her eyes dancing up and down my naked torso. A blush works its way up her cheeks, making me grin and my cock stir in my pants. "You were sleeping too peacefully for me to wake you up. Also, you're damn hot when you're shirtless, Blake. Jesus, warn a girl."

I pass her a shake, sit down, and pull her feet into my lap. The boost to my ego that she likes what she sees doesn't go unnoticed, but I want to hear all about her this morning. "How are you, baby?" I ask as I set the swing in motion and reach for her hand, linking our fingers.

"Never better." She sips her shake, licks her lips, and her eyebrows climb. "That's pretty good for being green."

"Green is good for you." I grin and gesture to her book. "What are you reading?"

She holds the book up, showing me the cover, which is what my sister Billie calls a *hot guy cover*.

"*The Knockout* by Bella Matthews. I *love* this author." She sighs and lays the book across her chest. "This is a good one. He's a hockey player, and she's a ballerina, and I'm really interested to hear what Skyla thinks of this one. If she identifies with the heroine at all because, in the book, she has a foot injury, stress fractures in her foot, and can't dance, and it's horrible for her. So it'll be fun to hear what Skyla thinks."

"I'd also be interested to hear her thoughts on that," I reply, rubbing Harper's calf, up and down, and she sighs and melts into my touch. Skyla moved here almost two years ago, leaving a ballet career in New York, along with an unhinged stalker, to settle here in Montana. Her ankle was badly injured, ending her career, but she opened her dance studio, met my brother, and the rest is history. She's one of us now, and I love her like a sister.

"I'm almost finished," she says with a happy sigh, sipping more of her smoothie. "There's a surprise baby, and the tension is high."

My eyebrows climb. "A surprise baby?"

"Yeah, she's pregnant, not on purpose, and he doesn't know yet, and *oh, the drama.*" She grins and sips her smoothie. "I'm not usually a fan of the surprise baby trope myself. Because I'm not so sure that a whoops pregnancy is particularly romantic, and definitely not sexy to me, but this book is great."

"Surprise babies." I shake my head, but I don't feel the dread or fear that would have come at the mention of an unplanned pregnancy before I met Harper. In fact, the idea of a home and children with this woman doesn't frighten me at all.

I'm changing all my rules for her.

"I had no idea that was a thing in books," I continue.

"It's a thing in real life, Blake."

I blink at her, and she giggles.

"No, not me." She shudders at the thought. "Just fiction in my world. Anyway, book club is Thursday night, and I have to finish this bad boy before then, but I'm almost there. I have a busy few days off coming up."

"What are your plans, sugar?" God, I love chatting with her in the morning. Just sitting here, sleepy, starting the day together.

The first of many.

This is what I pictured when I asked her to move in here.

"Well, you have to go back to the clinic tomorrow. Boo." She squeezes my hand. "I'm going to hike tomorrow if my legs aren't too sore after riding today. I also need to do some meal prep, and I want to make some cookies for Greg and Xander. Ava and I are going to do some shopping on Thursday and grab dinner before book club."

"I have clinic *and* ER tomorrow," I inform her, dragging my fingertips up and down the top of her bare foot. "So I won't be home until well past midnight."

"Snuggle up with me when you get here."

I grin at her. "That's a given. It's one of the reasons I wanted you to move in here, baby, so I can crawl into bed and hold you every chance I get."

"You're swoony, Dr. Blackwell."

I lift her foot and bite the end of her big toe, making her squeal.

"Ew! No toe biting."

"You have delectable little toes, sugar."

"No." She wiggles her feet, trying to get out of my grasp. "Toes aren't clean, Blake."

"You're pretty clean, Harper."

My phone pings in my pocket, and I pull it out to check it.

"My parents will be around this morning," I inform her. "We can swing by anytime."

"Greg said the same thing. Maybe we knock the parent stuff out first, then we can go for a ride."

"I like that plan, but let's sit here for a few more minutes. It's nice."

She smiles and sits up so she can kiss me, skimming her fingertips down my jaw. "It's better than nice."

One full day together wasn't enough, but at least she was there this morning, and I was able to start my day with my face between her thighs and my cum in her pussy before I had to come into the clinic for the day.

Christ, I'm addicted to her.

And I'm perfectly okay with that.

I've seen two ear infections and had three annual

exams before I walk into the next room. I come up short when I see the name on the computer.

Greg Hendrix.

I glance up and frown at the man sitting before me.

"I just saw you yesterday," I say conversationally as I sit on the rolling stool and check his vital signs.

Everything looks fine.

"I'm just here for a follow-up," he replies. "I promised my kids that I wouldn't slack when it comes to this shit, and I keep my word. Had labs drawn yesterday."

I nod, looking over the results, then smile at him. "You're doing great, Mr. Hendrix. Your numbers are excellent. I can tell that you're being smart with your diet and the medication. How are you feeling?"

"Better," he says, taking a deep breath. "It feels like it's been a shit show, but I think we're on the other side of it. I have too much to live for to dick around."

I sit back and let him talk. I enjoyed our time with him yesterday. It's evident that Greg adores Harper.

"My babies might not be babies anymore, but they still need their old man."

"Absolutely."

"And I want to spend time with my grandkids. I want to spoil them, teach them how to ride a horse. And I have a lady friend."

I lift an eyebrow, and Greg grins.

"Does Harper know?" I ask him.

"Of course. The kids might have been scandalized, but what are they going to do about it? Besides, if I can deal with the fact that you're shacking up with my girl, she can handle me going on a few dates here and there."

Smiling back at him, I close the computer. "I love your daughter, Greg."

"I know. It was written all over you yesterday. If you didn't look at her like she hung the goddamn moon, I'd have put up a fight. Because the asshole before you? He did some damage, and none of us knew it was happening until it was too fucking late."

I take a breath, nodding.

"I know. I've seen the damage. It fucking pisses me off, if I'm being honest."

"Good. It should." Greg taps his finger on his knee. "My girl deserves the best of everything life has to offer. I'm so proud of her, of the shit she's pulled herself through. If you're what's best, then I'm all for it. She seems happy."

"My one goal in life is to keep her that way," I assure him. "She's amazing."

"That she is. I'd love to take credit for it, but that's all her. Now, do I get an A on this report card?"

"You do. Well done."

Greg nods and pushes to his feet.

"Don't hesitate to call if you have questions. Call my personal cell," I tell him. "Keep doing what you're doing."

"Thanks, Doc," he says with a wink, and then he's off.

It's been four hours since I was home, and I already miss her.

I've turned into a fucking sap.

But I pull out my phone and text my girl.

> Me: How are you, sugar?

The message sits on read while I update Greg's chart, and then I see movement out of the corner of my eye. Dark hair. Perfect legs.

And when I glance over, there she is, smiling at me, holding a bag.

"I'm fine, how are you?"

Without a word, I take her hand and pull her into my office. I close the door behind us.

"I was missing you," I murmur before I brush my lips over hers.

"I hiked for a bit, then I grabbed lunch from Juliet's place and brought you some," she says, gesturing to the bag. "I hope you're hungry."

"Thanks, baby." I set the bag aside. "How was the hike?"

"Meh." She wrinkles her nose, and I turn to her, giving her my full attention. I don't like her tone or the fact she looks exhausted. "I'm not feeling all that great today, so I didn't go far."

"What do you mean, you don't feel great? What are your symptoms?"

I immediately press my fingers to her pulse point and my lips to her forehead. I don't feel a fever, and her pulse feels okay.

"I'm *fine*, Dr. Blackwell." She presses her hands to

my chest but doesn't push me away, which is good because I'm not going anywhere. "I'm just not myself today. Maybe that twenty-mile bike ride in the sunshine did me in yesterday. I got myself some lunch, too, and I'm going to go home and chill. Read a book."

Examining her eyes and feeling okay with what I find, I tug her against me and hug her close. "Are you sure? Do you need me to run a blood test, check your CBC, or something?"

"Blake. I'm tired. I have a bit of the icks today. That's it." She kisses my chest, right in the middle of my sternum.

"Take a nap." I lift her chin and tug her lip out of her teeth. "Drink lots of water."

"Yes, sir."

Her lips twitch, and my cock stirs.

"You're being sassy, so that's a good sign."

"I'm really not sick," she assures me. "I just need a lazy day."

"Okay. I'll check on you later." Leaning down, I brush my lips over hers again. "Take care of my girl."

"She's in good hands." She does a little curtsey, making me grin. "I'm a nurse. I know what to do. Don't worry about me."

"Impossible. You're mine. That means I worry."

"You're quite mushy. You know that, right?"

Shaking my head, I press my lips to her forehead. "Get used to it, sugar. Go feel better. Let me know if you need anything."

"I will. Have a good day, dear." She blows me a kiss,

and then she's gone, and before the door can close, my nurse pokes her head in.

"We have a chest pain patient who just came in through urgent care."

"I'm right behind you."

Chapter Twenty-Eight

HARPER

"But are you feeling better today?" Ava asks as we stow our purchases into the back of my car. "You seem fine."

"Yeah, I'm much better. It was the weirdest thing." My best friend and I have made our way up and down the main street in Bitterroot Valley, buying things from Pocket Full of Polly, the flower shop, and the bookstore. You name it, we probably bought it today. Now, we're headed over to Sage & Salt to grab dinner before our book club meeting. "I was hiking along, and suddenly, I was just so *tired*. I felt achy and just generally not good. But then I rested at home, and a few hours later, I was fine."

I shrug as we push into the restaurant. I love that it's already busy in here. I want Juliet's restaurant to be here for a long, long time.

"Maybe it was the bike ride," Ava says with a nod. "Too much sun and all that jazz."

"Probably." We step up to order, and my stomach growls so loudly, Juliet laughs.

"You're my kind of customer. What can I feed you, friend?"

"Apparently, I need all the food you have." I chuckle and check out the board. "Oh, I'll take that fish and chips special. That sounds good."

"Make it two," Ava says, passing over her credit card before I can. "It's on me tonight."

"Hey, thanks." I kiss her cheek, and we go find a place to sit. "I didn't realize I was so hungry until we walked in here."

"We worked off a lot of calories this afternoon," she says, leaning on her elbows. "Now, tell me everything that's going on. I know you moved in with Blake, but we haven't hung out in way too long, and I feel like I'm missing everything."

"I know. It all happened so fast." I lean back in the chair, suddenly feeling tired again. Man, I really do need some protein. "Blake and I are great. It was getting to be torture, spending so much time apart because of our work schedules, and then only catching glimpses of each other here and there."

"So naturally, the next step is to shack up," Ava says, her voice dry as sand.

"When the sex is that good?" I nod at her. "Hell yeah, that's the answer."

"There's no need to be a bitch and brag about your hot boyfriend," she says as Juliet arrives with our food.

"I have some vinegar here and some tartar sauce. Let me know if you need anything else."

"Looks amazing," Ava says, and I nod in agreement. When Juliet walks away, Ava continues right where she left off. "Is his house nice?"

"Yeah, it's great. I'll have you over. You can come home with me later if you want."

"Hell yeah, I want."

"And how's everything with you?" I ask her before biting into my fish and sighing in happiness. "Holy shit, that's good."

"So good." She nods and then sighs. "I'm working my ass off. Connor Gallagher hired me to work on the new condos at the resort that are going up next, and it's a *huge* deal, Harps. The biggest account of my life. Most of the condos are up for sale, and they want them to be designed and staged for listing. The ones that are already sold, well, he's recommending me to the owners so I can design according to their specifications."

"How many total condos are there?" I ask her.

"Forty-six." A smile spreads over her face. "That's a whole lot of work, friend. And Billie and Connor asked me to start with their super-fancy penthouse."

"Holy shit, that's incredible."

"I know. I had a nice long chat with Billie when we were all up at the resort, and I think I can do a good job for them."

"I *know* you can. And you will. You're a badass bitch, and you've got this, babe."

She grins, nodding slowly. "Yeah, I got this. I also

kind of love that our circle has widened since you moved here. The Blackwell girls are pretty fucking awesome."

"Right?"

"I guess it's good that we like them, considering they're all related to your boyfriend."

I narrow my eyes at her. "What are you saying?"

"Just that if his family was full of assholes, I might not be so excited for you to be with him."

"He has a single older brother," I remind her, but Ava shakes her head.

"Nah. I mean, Brooks is great, and let's face it, hot as shit, but there's no spark. I don't want or need a man right now. I'll be busy with this resort project for a while, and it's too good of a boost to my career to get distracted by a man."

"I can see that."

"The only romance I'll be getting is in the form of smutty books." Ava smiles at me. "But add a vibrator, and that combo works just fine."

"It's no substitute for the real thing."

She shakes her head. "Depends on what kind of *real thing* a girl's getting. If it's vanilla Joe? No thanks. You have the sexy doctor."

A slow smile spreads over my face.

Fuck yeah. I have the sexy doctor.

I think it's fair to say that aside from sexy time with Blake, Spicy Girls Book Club has become my favorite way to spend an evening.

I've always loved being in a bookstore, but Billie takes it to another level. She always has the most delicious snacks and drinks, and Jackie spoils us all with sweets from her shop. The girls actually *read* the book, so the conversation is lively and fun, and I would do this all the time if I could.

My favorite, though, is after the meeting, when most of the girls have gone home, and it's just a few of us left. Tonight, that's Billie, Ava, Dani, Skyla, and Dani's twin sister, Alex. The six of us sit in a circle, drinking wine and giggling our asses off while we finish the lemon bars Jackie brought with her.

"I didn't say this with the others here," Ava says, "and maybe I should have, but I don't love a surprise baby book."

"Oh my God, I'm glad I'm not the only one," Dani says, shaking her head. "Because that would just be *stressful*. Not sexy."

"I mean, the author made it sexy in this case," Billie reminds us. "I like it in fiction because we know we're getting an HEA and all is well. But in real life? Fuck that. Hard pass."

"So I have an idea." Ava bites her lip and opens the tote bag she brought in from my car earlier. "Just hear me out. I know, I'm a little crazy, but this could be fun. I saw this on an Instagram reel a while ago and thought it was funny."

"Oh God." I press my fingers to my eyes. "This could be literally *anything*."

"What if we all take a pregnancy test, toss the tests in a basket so we don't know whose is whose, and then we see if any of them are positive?"

We all stare at Ava in horror, but then Billie covers her mouth and laughs. "I'm down."

"Wait," Alex says, holding up a hand. "Is anyone here *knowingly* already pregnant?"

We all look at each other and shake our heads.

"I'd better *not* be pregnant again so soon," Dani says, sounding pissed off at just the thought of it. "Bridger and his superhero sperm can just calm the heck down."

"What if one of them *is* positive," Skyla asks. "And then we don't know who it is?"

"Then we all have to take it again and hang on to our tests," Ava says. "But for all we know, they'll be negative."

Mine had better be negative. There's no way I'm pregnant. My birth control method is almost flawless. I don't have any symptoms.

There's no way.

"Let's do it," Dani says, standing and holding her hand out for the test. "I'll go first. And if the chief got me pregnant again already, he's sleeping on the couch tonight."

"Oh, like you'd let him sleep anywhere but with you," Skyla says, shaking her head and laughing.

"Fair, but he'll get a stern talking-to."

"I'll grab a basket," Billie says. "And ignore the fact that most of you are fucking my brothers. Because no. That's horrible. When you're finished taking it, put your test in this basket on the counter back here, and *no peeking*."

"Why am I suddenly nervous?" Skyla asks. "I know I'm not pregnant."

"Because you just never *truly* know," Ava says with a wink and smiles smugly at me. "I love these girls. They feed into my crazy."

One by one, we take turns in the bathroom at the back of the store, then deposit our test in the basket, results-side down.

We wait for five minutes, all of us hovering over the basket like it holds the secrets of the universe, and then Ava says, "Okay, let's check them."

"I'm going to mix them up first," Billie says, giving the basket a little shake.

"I'm sweating," I mutter, flapping my arms like wings, trying to get some air to my armpits. "Book Club is supposed to be fun, Ava. Not stressful."

Ava giggles, and Billie pulls out the first stick.

"Negative."

We collectively breathe a sigh of relief.

"Next one," Billie says, "negative."

"Thank God. I hope that was mine," Skyla says.

"Positive."

We all freeze at that one word uttered from Billie's perfectly painted lips.

"Fucking hell," I grumble, shaking my head.

"Negative. Negative," Billie continues, but now we're

all eyeing each other as if we can tell who's knocked up just from looking in each other's eyes.

"Positive."

"Wait." Alex holds up a hand. "Are you fucking telling me that *two* of us are pregnant?"

Unease slips through my gut. I can*not* be pregnant. Neither Blake nor I want kids. We've only been together for like six minutes.

No.

"Okay." Ava doesn't sound so sure of herself now. "I guess we're all taking another test."

"I hate you," Dani says to Ava. "Like, not *really*, but I hate you right this minute."

"I think we all do," Alex agrees, and then we file into the bathroom, one by one, as if we're walking the plank to our doom.

This time, we hold on to our tests.

Dani breathes a sigh of relief when hers is negative.

Skyla does a little dance in her seat. "Not it."

"Alex?" Billie asks, and Alex shakes her head.

"Not me," Alex says.

Billie checks her test and then goes stone still.

"No," she whispers, shaking her head. Her eyes fill, and her eyes fly up to Dani. "Are you kidding me?"

"Finally!" Dani jumps up and claps her hands, then attacks her best friend in the tightest hug, holding on tight. "I told you it would happen. You just had to give it time."

"We've been trying." Billie wipes at her tears. "And

we were going to go see a specialist because it wasn't working. But it *worked.*"

"I'm calling my brother right now," Skyla says, wiping at her own tears. "Hello, brother. You should come to the bookshop to see your wife."

"Is she hurt?" we hear him ask.

"No, she's not hurt. But she could use a wee hug from her man."

"I'm on my way. If someone hurt her feelings, they're going to pay."

We all chuckle at that, and while everyone is distracted, Ava swaps her test with mine. I frown at her, and she winks at me.

"Okay, who's the other pregnant one?" Dani asks, looking over our way.

"Me," Ava says, holding up *my* test.

Oh my God.

Oh my God, *no.*

"Ava, are you okay?" My friend is bombarded with questions, and she just shrugs and deflects, acting as cool as a cucumber while I silently freak the fuck out. Connor storms in, and everyone is distracted by the incredibly handsome billionaire sweeping his wife off her feet and kissing the hell out of her.

"What's wrong, *a ghrá*?" He hooks her hair behind her ear and nuzzles her nose, as if none of the rest of us are even in the room.

"Nothing's wrong," she says through fresh tears. "But I have news."

"We'll be fine, bumble, no matter what it is."

Billie smiles and rests her forehead against her husband's, and my own eyes fill with tears.

They're so sweet together.

"You're going to be a daddy, billionaire."

Connor blinks at her, then lifts her right off her feet, hugging her so hard and so close.

"Jesus, that's beautiful," Ava mutters, wiping a tear from her eye, and all I can do is nod.

I have to talk to Blake.

Because I'm going to have a freaking baby.

And it's official. I'm really *not* a fan of a surprise baby.

Chapter Twenty-Nine
HARPER

"Why did you swap tests with me?" I ask Ava as we walk into Blake's house and dump my bags on the kitchen island. We were dead quiet on the drive home because I think I'm numb.

What the fuck is going on?

"Uh, *duh*." She rests her hands on her hips and tilts her head to the side. "You're clearly not thinking straight, which is valid. Honey, Billie is Blake's *sister*, and the others are all either with his brothers or are good friends with him. If they found out that you're pregnant *before* Blake does, you can't control that information. They might call him immediately. I mean, I like them all, but I don't know them very well. I bought you time, babe."

"Shit, you're right." I lean against the countertop and feel faint. "Ava. Holy mother of fuck, I'm *pregnant*."

The word doesn't even make sense to me right now.

"How did this even *happen*?"

Her eyebrows climb. "Well, when a mommy and a daddy—"

"Shut the fuck up." I roll my eyes as she snickers, and I pace away. "I know *how*. But I don't know *how*."

"Because that makes sense."

"I've had an implant in my arm for four years, Ava. They last five years. Mine hasn't expired."

"Are you sure? Because maybe you counted wrong. You've been pretty busy the past few years, you know."

I frown and think back. "I got it the year before Nathan and I got together, and we were together for two years—"

"That's three."

"And I've been away from him for two years—"

"That's five."

I blink at her.

"Babe, it expired."

"But ... *fuck*."

"Yeah, you fucked, and now you're knocked up."

I hang my head and moan.

"He's going to be so mad."

"Whoa." Ava hurries around the island and wraps her arm around me. "You don't know that. He's a doctor, and I may not know him well, but he seems level-headed. Not to mention, the man worships the ground you walk on. It's almost disgusting. I'm totally jealous, by the way."

"Aves, Blake and I have had these conversations. Neither of us really wants kids. Hell, neither of us really wanted a serious relationship."

"Well, you have both." She leans her head on my shoulder. "Unless you don't. You know, you have options. You have choices. But you really need to talk to your man about this because he deserves to know."

"I won't keep it from him." The mere thought makes me so uncomfortable that it's not even an option. "I wouldn't do that. I'm not scared of him or anything. I just hate the idea of disappointing him or having him think that I'm trapping him."

"He asked you to live with him," she reminds me. "That was his idea. He's smarter than that, Harper. Give both of you some credit."

"I know." I let out a breath that I didn't realize I was holding and feel the thump of my heart in my ears since it's beating so hard. "I'm kind of freaking out."

"Of course, you are, babe. But we're going to figure this out. If need be, I'll raise this baby with you. You have a village. You're not alone."

I pause and frown down at her. "I don't feel alone, you weirdo. And *yes,* you're going to help me raise this baby because you're Auntie Ava, and you're the cool aunt who lets her eat ice cream for dinner and takes her to Seattle on the weekend for a Swiftie concert."

"Oh my God, I can't wait to do that. What do we need to do to make sure it's a girl? Do you need to like hang upside down during a full moon or what, because I'll get the rope."

I shake her off and pace to the other side of the kitchen.

"I'm not hanging upside down. Jesus, we went off on a tangent. Ava, *I'm pregnant.*"

"I know. I'm actually a little excited and grateful that it's not me. What's next?"

I cringe. "Well, Blake's working late again tonight and he works at the clinic tomorrow, and I start nights for two nights, but then we get three days off together, so I'll tell him then. I think I should probably see a doctor and get an ultrasound and stuff."

Ava's nodding. "Do you want me to go with you?"

No, I want Blake with me.

I want my man. I want him so bad right now, but he's busy saving lives, and I need to suck it up and deal like a big girl. Because if we're going to make this work, I'll be dealing with his schedule for a long, long time. How can we possibly do this? How are we going to raise a baby together when we hardly see enough of each other as it is?

I shake my head and feel the energy move right out of me. "No, I'll do it. It'll be okay."

"I have to say, you might think you're freaking out on the inside, but you seem to be taking this remarkably well. Do you want to yell? Cry? Break something?"

"I don't think it's real yet," I admit. "I think the major freak-out is still to come."

Chapter Thirty
BLAKE

It never ceases to amaze me the horrible destruction that humans are capable of inflicting on each other. The way they can literally tear each other apart and leave nothing behind.

Not even life itself.

That some people can take a life without thought. Without remorse.

I don't often see humanity at its worst, but tonight was one of those nights, and I'm sick to my stomach as I pull into the garage next to Harper's car and cut the engine.

There's a light on in the kitchen. I'd normally come home to a dark house, but my girl left a light on for me, and it loosens the knot in my gut for the first time in hours.

I need her.

I changed out of my bloody scrubs and showered at the hospital, so I didn't bring that mess home with me, and I'm glad because I don't want to wait long enough to shower to touch her. I need her *now*.

Walking through the mudroom and into the kitchen, I smile when I see the note on the counter next to a plate of cookies, illuminated by the soft glow of the light above the stovetop.

> *B-*
> *Missed you today. I made you some cookies.*
> **Heart**
> *-H*

Leaving the cookies where they are, I shut off the light and carry the note with me to the bedroom, where I tuck it safely away in my bedside table and strip out of my clothes. Harper is sleeping peacefully, her hands tucked under her chin, all that gorgeous dark hair fanned out on the pillow behind her, and I've never needed to get my hands on someone so badly in my life.

Slipping between the sheets, I wrap myself around my girl and pull her against my chest, press my nose to her hair, and just hang on.

"Hmm." She nuzzles into me and loops her arm around my waist. Finally, my nervous system calms down, and I can take a deep breath. "You okay?"

I love her sleepy voice and her warm skin against me.

"Better now. Don't wake up, baby."

"Need to talk," she whispers, burrowing into me even tighter.

"Is it life or death?" Christ, I'm tired.

"No."

"Can we just have this for tonight?"

She blinks her eyes open, looking up at me in the moonlight. "Of course. Are you really okay?"

She cups my cheek, and I lean into it, soaking in her touch.

"Bad night." I press my lips to her forehead. "Go back to sleep, sugar."

With a sigh, Harper kisses my lips gently, then wraps her arms around my neck and hugs me to her, her hands in my hair, my face against her neck, offering me comfort in her sweet way.

"I'm right here," she whispers against my ear, and it cracks my chest wide open.

God, I fucking love her so much.

"Need you," I whisper, my hands gliding down her bare skin to her ass. "And I like finding you naked and warm in my bed, sugar."

Rolling her onto her back, I press wet kisses along her jaw, down her neck, and cover her lips with mine and melt into her. This is *exactly* what I need to forget everything I saw tonight.

She wraps her legs around my hips, opening herself beautifully for me, and she reaches down to guide my hard cock to her already wet pussy.

"Christ, baby."

"Take whatever you need," she says, and I sink inside her, groaning with every inch. "I'm all yours, Blake."

"Harper." I start to move. Long, deep, steady strokes

that fuel the fire burning inside me. I want to be gentle with her, to make love to her, but I'm on edge.

"I won't break," she says and nips at my chin. "Fuck me, babe."

She doesn't have to tell me twice. My hips move hard and quick, slamming into her tight heat, erasing the last of the shitty night from my mind. She reaches down between us and covers her clit with her fingertips. Her already snug pussy tightens more, and she starts to quiver around me.

"Come for me." I pluck her nipple with my teeth, making her back arch. "Fucking come, Harper. Go over for me."

"Oh God." She fists the sheets, but I shake my head.

"Grab onto *me*."

Her hands find purchase in my ass, squeezing as she falls apart beneath me, and I don't try to hold back. I *can't* hold back. I rock into her, riding out my own orgasm, so fucking grateful that I have this amazing woman in my life.

"Stay," I whisper before I pull out and walk into the bathroom, get a warm wet washcloth. I return to her to clean her up, and then hug her to me. "Sleep, beautiful girl."

"Are you okay now?"

I smile and kiss the top of her head. "I'm okay."

Chapter Thirty-One

HARPER

He was gone before I even woke up this morning. I reached for him, needing to have him hold me for a few minutes, but he wasn't there, and he'd left me a text message.

> Blake: I need to go to the hospital before the clinic today. I kissed the fuck out of you before I left, but you were sleeping so well. Love you, sugar.

I love him, too. And something wasn't right with him last night when he woke me up. The sex was spectacular, as always, but something hurt him, and now I wish I knew what it was.

Not to mention, we need to talk about a certain pregnant woman.

That would be me.

But I want to do it when we can sit down and really have a conversation without fitting it in around patients or right before or after a shift at the hospital. I don't want to have to rush it.

It's too important.

I can wait two more days. Maybe. I don't like feeling as though I'm keeping secrets from my man. Even though this is truly better talked about when we have time to work through our feelings.

I have a couple of hours until my night shift starts, but I need to hunt down one of the OB/GYN doctors I've come to know since I've been here to see if she'll do a quick ultrasound on me. There's only one medical clinic in town, and Blake works there.

I want to keep this on the down low for just two more days.

I'm on my way down to obstetrics, the hospital rather quiet for this time of day, and press my hand to my still-flat stomach. According to my research, this little one is about the size of a raspberry and doesn't quite look human yet.

"Harper?"

I pause at the sound of my name and then let out a little squeal.

"Hannah?" The other woman throws her arms around me and hugs me close. Hannah Hull is an incredible OB/GYN from Cunningham Falls. I worked with her when I had an assignment there last year. "What are you doing here?"

"I'm consulting on a case. I'm only here for the day."

She grins at me. "I heard you took a position here. They're lucky to have you."

"Thanks. I love it here." I clear my throat as an idea forms in my mind. "Hey, would you be against helping me with something?"

"Never. What's going on?"

I press my lips together and look around, making sure no one is listening. "I took a test. It's positive, but I need an ultrasound to make sure—"

"Follow me." Taking my hand, she leads me down the hallway and into a room. She locks the door and gestures to the bed next to the ultrasound machine.

"Wow. Just like that?"

"This is the easiest favor you could have ever asked me for," she replies with a grin. Hannah's gorgeous, with red hair and a sweet smile, and we share a love for hiking. When I lived in Cunningham Falls, which is just about four hours from here, we hiked together often. She's married to the police chief and is one of the best people I know. "Unfortunately, it's pretty early, so this will have to be a vaginal ultrasound."

"I figured." I shimmy out of my pants, drape the little sheet over my bottom half, and lie down on the bed. "I'm not shy."

Hannah grins and gets to work. It's not comfortable, but it's not the worst thing that's ever happened to me.

"I have an implant in my arm, but I think it must have expired," I inform her. "Can you take it out for me?"

"Sure, that's easy enough," she says, studying the screen. "You're definitely pregnant, my friend."

I stare at the black-and-white screen, seeing a black circle with a little blob in the middle and a racing heartbeat.

Hannah turns on the sound, and I can hear that heart, and everything in me goes soft.

Blake should be here with me.

"Well, shit." Tears fill my eyes as I stare at that little blob. "Wow."

"I'd say you're about nine weeks along. Everything looks normal to me."

I swallow hard and brush a tear off my face.

"Who's the daddy, friend?"

"Blake Blackwell."

Hannah's eyes widen, and then she grins at me. "Well, good for you. Blake's not only one sexy guy—don't tell my husband I said that—but he's also one hell of a doctor. Now I know why you wanted this on the down low."

I nod, and when she removes the wand and starts to clean up, I put my pants back on and then sit on the side of the bed.

"Is it okay to keep having sex?"

Hannah smiles. "Absolutely. You can do everything you've previously done—just stay away from alcohol, limit your caffeine and fish, and listen to your body. That little one is safe in there. Have all the fun sex you want."

I nod and take a deep breath. "I should be more terrified than I am."

"Why?"

"Because this wasn't planned."

Hannah shrugs. "Sometimes the best things in life aren't planned. You're going to be a great mom, Harper."

"Will I?" I bite my lower lip. "I don't know. I hope so. Mine was pretty shitty, so I don't know what it's like to have a good mom in my life. But I already love her. And her daddy and I will figure it out."

"You think it's a girl?"

"I'm just calling her a her. I don't really have any intuition one way or the other."

Hannah passes me a print out of the image from the ultrasound, and I kiss it before tucking it safely in my pocket.

"Thank you." Hannah pulls me in for a hug. "I appreciate the help. And I'm glad I got to see you while you were here."

"I'll be sure to call you next time, and we'll plan dinner or something. If you have questions about anything at all, don't hesitate to reach out."

"Thanks. Do you have a doctor here who you recommend?"

"Absolutely. I'll text you names. You'll want to get established with someone right away."

After a few more minutes with Hannah, I head up to my unit, ready to clock in for my shift. I wish I had time to run down and see Blake, even if it's just to hug him. I *really* want to show him the ultrasound picture.

But we're busy, and I'm thrown right into the middle of my duties as soon as I set foot in the unit.

"Baby Matthew needs to be fed," Amy tells me with a smile. "And I'm heading into bay 6."

I nod and set off to see how Baby Matthew's doing. He came in the other day, so tiny and sweet. His is another situation where his parents aren't able to come in for every feeding, so we take care of it when they can't be here.

"Hey there, little guy." I spend time with the preemie, change his diaper and give him a bottle, rocking him in the chair as he sucks and stares up at me with bright blue eyes. "You're pretty darn cute."

That's the only quiet moment of the night because after that, I have to be on hand for delivery of a sick baby, and then I have to cover lunch breaks for my staff.

It's almost midnight when I come up for air and check my phone, smiling when I see a text from Blake that came in an hour ago.

> Blake: Miss you, baby. How's work?

> Me: I miss you, too. It's been busy up here tonight. Is it a full moon?

Slipping my phone in my pocket, I walk into little Oliver's room to check on him. His mom is asleep in the chair next to him, and I let her rest as I check his monitors. It's almost time for a blood draw on the little man, so I turn to get some supplies for that when I'm suddenly hit across the side of the head and slammed into a cart, knocking the breath from me.

"Stay away from my kid!"

Fuck, the pain. My entire right side throbs from where I hit the cart, and I'm dizzy and disoriented from being hit in the head.

"No!" I think that's Oliver's mom yelling out right before I take another hit to the face and then a kick in the side. "Stop! Help!"

I hear running feet and more yelling, but *shit*, my side hurts.

Someone—another dad?—grabs the man who shouldn't even be here, holding him against the wall with his arms pulled behind his back, and then security comes running in to restrain him and haul him away.

"I'm so sorry," the baby's mom says. "He promised he wouldn't lose it again."

"He's not welcome here," I tell her, trying to climb to my feet. "If you let him in again, you're both out for good. I'm pressing assault charges against him."

"Oh, please—"

"You won't talk me out of this."

Shit, I'm so achy. But I'm not on the verge of a panic attack. This was so different from before. I'm just good and pissed off now.

And fuck, do I hurt.

"Amy," I say as the fellow nurse helps me get my balance. "I need you to get me down to the ER."

She frowns but doesn't ask any questions as she loops her arm through mine.

"Do you need a wheelchair?"

"No. Just take it slow. I'm a little dizzy from that knock to the head."

"Your lip is bleeding," she says. "Dr. Blackwell will freak out."

"Yeah, well, this is the least of his worries." I walk slow, my right hip and side absolutely killing me, but I'm most worried about the baby.

God, let my little raspberry be okay.

Chapter Thirty-Two
BLAKE

There will be moments in my life that are seared into my brain and haunt me until my dying breath.

One of them will be seeing Harper hobble into my ER with a black eye and a split lip, her hair in disarray, and her blue scrub top torn at the sleeve.

"Jesus, baby," I rush over to her and lift her in my arms, but she winces and cries out in pain.

"Christ, that hurts," she says, a tear falling down her cheek. "The right side is probably bruised pretty bad. Hip, too."

"Fuck." Two nurses rush after me as I get her on a gurney in a room, and we immediately start working on her, but Harper holds her hands up, stopping us.

"Everyone out," she barks, her pain-filled eyes holding mine. "I need to talk to you alone."

"Let us get you—"

"No." She closes her eyes with a wince, and it takes

everything in me not to reach for her. I need to help my girl. "You don't have my consent to touch me until after I talk with you alone."

Unease slithers through my core, but I nod at the nurses. "Out. Close the door."

Harper shifts on the bed, wincing again, and it's killing me.

"Baby, let me help you."

"Oh, I plan to. Get over here."

I rush to her side and take her offered hand, bringing it to my lips. "What happened?"

"Fucking pissed-off dad happened. Motherfucker hit me from behind, threw me into a cart, and I fell to the floor. My right side is a mess, but Blake, we need to *talk*."

She swallows hard, making all of the hairs stand up on my body.

"Just tell me, Harper. What's wrong? Talk to me."

"Okay." She blows out a breath. "So we're having a surprise baby."

I'm pretty sure the Earth just shifted on its axis.

"What?"

"I'm sorry." I pull my hand out of hers and cross my arms over my chest, and the immediate hurt in her eyes makes my gut clench. "I swear to God, Blake, I planned to tell you on Wednesday when we had the day off together so we could talk and not be interrupted or rushed. But that's not going to happen now, and that pisses me off. I *just* found out last night. I have not been hiding this from you."

The knot around my chest loosens as tears fill her gorgeous gray eyes.

"I swear, I wasn't hiding it. You got home late, and then you were gone this morning, and our schedules—"

I remember when I climbed into bed, and she said we needed to talk.

"Okay." I can't stand it. I pull her against me, careful of her right side and press my lips to her hair. "Okay, baby. You weren't keeping secrets."

"*No.* I wouldn't do that. I think my implant expired. But I saw the baby today because I got an ultrasound to be sure"—she pulls ultrasound images out of her pocket—"and there's a baby."

"I need to examine you, and we need to get another ultrasound to make sure that fucker didn't hurt the baby, then we can talk about the rest, Harper."

I know I sound detached and hard, but I'm in doctor mode. I need to make sure she's okay before I can dive into the emotions of what this all means.

My God, she's pregnant.

"I get it," she says with a nod, and she lets me tug her scrubs top up over her head so I can see her side.

Bruises bloom in angry purple and black over her ribs and down her hip.

"Christ, baby."

"I don't think anything's broken," she says. "But fuck if it doesn't hurt."

"It looks like agony. Are you dizzy?"

"I was, but that's better now. He hit me on the head twice. Once on the side, and one punch to the face."

Rage coils in my belly, and I clench my teeth together.

"I'm going to kill that motherfucker."

"I'll press charges. I just needed you first. I really needed you, Blake."

"I'm right here," I reply, then poke my head out the door. "I need an ultrasound machine in here now. Let's get an IV going with warm fluids."

I glance over and see Harper's teeth chattering.

"And warm blankets. Move."

We hustle, and within minutes, my girl is hooked up to an IV, a heart monitor, and a blood pressure cuff, which she glares at.

No one loves the blood pressure cuff.

"Do they have to stay?" she asks when I get ready to do the ultrasound.

"I'm going to go check on room 3," my nurse says, and takes the tech with her, leaving just Harper and me in the room.

"Thanks," she says softly, her eyes pinned to the screen as I start the ultrasound.

The heartbeat starts right away, shifting something in my soul, and then it's on the screen, beating strong.

"Is everything okay?" Harper asks. "Tell me it's okay, Blake."

That's our baby. I study the screen and take measurements. Nine weeks. This little one has existed for nine weeks, and we didn't know.

"It all looks good to me. We'll watch for bleeding

over the next few days, but I'd say that everything is just fine, sugar."

And now that the adrenaline is wearing off, I take a second to just stare at my girl, the heartbeat still sounding in the room.

"I don't want you to think I'm trapping you or something stupid like that," she says softly.

"By all means, trap me."

Her eyes widen, and then she starts to cry. I clean up from the imaging and pull her against me, kissing her forehead, her temple, and then her lips.

"I'm so sorry." God, she's breaking my heart.

"What are you sorry for?" I cup her face and rest my forehead against hers.

"I didn't mean to get pregnant, and I told you that I had the birth control handled. You trusted me."

"I still trust you, Harper."

"You shouldn't," she whispers. "Because I fucked up."

"I want to get you home, and then we can sleep, or talk, or whatever you need."

"I should go back to work."

Fuck that.

"Neither of us is going back to work. You're going to finish that bag of fluids, and I'm going to make some calls. I want you to rest, Harper."

"Blake, I can handle my own—"

"Let me." Cupping her face, I brush my lips over hers and let myself take a moment to soak her in, knowing she's safe. "Let me handle this for you. I know you're a badass and as tough as nails, but let me deal with this, okay? You and the bean are mine to take care of, sugar."

Harper's shoulders fall, and she nods as she bites that lower lip. "Thank you."

"Just relax. I'll be right back."

Rushing out of the room, I pull my phone out and start making calls, starting with administration. I want to make sure that piece of shit isn't allowed anywhere near this hospital again.

Within twenty minutes, I have my shift covered, along with Harper's, and I'm taking the IV out of her arm.

"I'm so freaking tired," she says, barely holding her eyes open.

"That's pretty normal, baby. You're coming off the adrenaline of a scary episode. But I've got you." Helping her to her feet, I keep my arm around her shoulders and lead her out of the ER and out to the parking lot where my car is.

"My purse. My car—"

"I'll have someone get it for you." I press my lips to her head. "Do you want me to carry you?"

"No, I'm going to keep my dignity intact and walk," she says, making me smile. "But when we get home, you can carry me all you want."

"Deal." I keep pace with her, not rushing her as she walks to the vehicle, then help her into the passenger seat.

The ride home is quiet. Harper dozes next to me but wakes up when I pull into the garage. True to her word, she doesn't put up a fight when I lift her into my arms and carry her inside.

"Bed or couch?" I ask.

"Couch. We need to talk."

I nod and set her down on the sofa, then walk into the kitchen to get a couple of waters and bring her one, then sit facing her.

"I want it to be known right now that I'm super salty that all of my plans got ruined," she says with a frown. "I mean, I wasn't going to do anything cheesy because that's not me, but still. I wanted to talk to you on my own terms and not spring it on you in the middle of a crisis at work. That's fucked up."

"I'm glad that you're mad and not upset anymore." I reach for her hand and steel myself for the answer to my next question. "What do you want to do, Harper?"

She blinks at me, and then she's up and in my lap, hugging me close, and I finally breathe a sigh of relief.

"Shit, did you think I wouldn't—" She shakes her head, not completing the thought. "I know I said I didn't want kids. And neither do you—"

"I said I didn't see myself with a family," I correct her, brushing her hair back from her face. "But I didn't have you yet, sugar."

She bites her lip. "I was afraid that you'd be so mad, but you don't seem mad at all."

"I'm not mad. Surprised. Pissed off that someone put his hands on you. Worried about you. But no, I'm not at all mad at you, baby."

"I'm really scared that you're going to think I did this on purpose. That I'd try to trap you—"

"You said that before, and I hate that fucking word." I tug her lip out of her teeth and run my thumb over the soft skin. "We're consenting adults, Harper. I can't keep my hands off you. You believed that your birth control was working, and if I was worried about that, I could have used condoms. I told you that I love you before we had any inkling that you could be pregnant. You moved in with me. We're a team, sugar, so no. I don't feel trapped in any way. I want you. I *need* you in my life."

"It's really soon for a baby." She licks her lips. "I'm not trying to talk anyone out of anything. I'm just talking."

"I understand. Go ahead."

"We haven't been together long, and I *just* moved in. I would have liked some more time with you, all to myself, before we started thinking about adding more people to the mix."

Her fingers are in my hair, brushing through the strands. You'd never know we're talking about bringing a life into this world. We're both so calm.

I'd say that means that everything about this is right.

"The fact that you're not running, that you want to be here with me, is all I need to know. I don't disagree with you. More time would have been ideal, but we have roughly seven-ish months to get used to the idea." I press my hand to her stomach, and a ghost of a smile spreads over her lips.

My clinical brain knows there's a baby in there. I

know all the medical nuances about everything happening in Harper's body. The how and why and when.

But this is my girl, the woman who I'm so in love with, it's a living, breathing emotion in every cell of my body, carrying *my child*. And that makes every bit of my medical degree go right out the window.

"What are we going to do?" she whispers, watching my fingers splay over her abdomen. "We both work so much, Blake. We hardly have time for each other."

"What we've been doing." I lift my eyes to hers and cradle her face. My thumb drifts over the apple of her cheek. "I'm going to keep loving you and take care of you as much as you'll let me. We'll figure out all of the logistics."

I'm going to marry you.

She's not ready to hear that yet.

"And we're going to get ready for a baby."

She wrinkles her nose. "That's a crazy statement."

"It's a little overwhelming," I admit with a chuckle.

"Oh, thank God you're overwhelmed, too. I thought it was just me."

"No, it's not just you. Harper, there is no one else in the world that I'd want to do this with."

"Same." Her finger drifts over my lips. "I never thought I wanted kids, and while I'm definitely a little ... *concerned*, and I was a little scared of your reaction, I'm not freaking out about this. Ava—"

"Ava knows?"

She pauses and nods. "She was with me. And even

though I had no intention of keeping it from you, she made sure to remind me that I needed to tell you ASAP. She also offered to take our girl to Seattle for the weekend for a Swift concert."

I blink at her, feeling like I've just missed fifteen years in there somewhere.

"Uh, I think that's a few years off."

Harper grins. "I know. She's going to be an awesome auntie. Anyway, Ava was shocked at how calm I was. And I think that under any other circumstances, I would *not* be calm. But it's you. And despite the bad timing, I can't be upset about it, Blake."

I hug her to me and kiss her hair, and Harper clings to me.

"We have to think of B names," she says, making me smile.

"We don't *have* to," I reply, shaking my head. "We have enough of those already. Hey, did you know that Billie's pregnant? She called me at work this morning ..."

I trail off when I see the look on her face.

"You knew."

"We kind of found out at the same time."

"Okay, what the hell happened last night, Harper?"

"We had a pregnancy test party because of the surprise baby in the book. It was Ava's idea. Turned out, two of us were pregnant, and neither of us knew about it."

"You had a *pregnancy test party*."

"Ava's the wild one," she says, holding up her hands in surrender. "It was her idea. But it's good that we did it because your sister is so over the moon, and I'm glad we know, too."

"My sister isn't the only one over the moon."

Her eyes fill with so much hope as she stares at me. "Really?"

"Absolutely. You're what I want. I have no doubts about that. You moving in here was just the beginning, and when you're ready, we'll talk about more."

"I mean, I'm *pregnant*, Blake. Wow, that's still weird to say. I don't know how much *more* there can be?"

I lift a brow and tap her ring finger.

"I don't want you to propose just because—"

"Don't even finish that sentence." I press my finger to her mouth and frown down at her. "In case you missed it, I love you. *That's* why I'll propose one day, sugar."

But first, I need you to tell me you love me, too.

Chapter Thirty-Three

HARPER

It seems like Blake and I just dozed off when I hear rustling coming from the room across from our bedroom, pulling me out of sleep. My side is *so sore,* and when I bend my knee and bring my leg up to my chest, my hip sings in agony.

Christ, that asshole threw me hard.

I don't want to take any pain meds because of the baby, so I need to rest and let it heal.

Dammit.

I hear more rustling and decide to get out of bed to see what's going on. After tugging on one of Blake's T-shirts, I get to the doorway of the guest room, and find my man, dressed only in gray sweatpants, with a tape measure in his hands, staring at the wall with his back to me.

His dark hair is all messed up from my fingers and bed, and his back muscles tighten my core.

The muscles on this man.

"Crib over there," he whispers, making my breath catch.

He's figuring out the baby's room.

"Shelves here. Changing table. She'll want a rocking chair. Do I need to open that wall and make this room bigger?"

He sighs, seeming to work it out in his head.

"She should be here with me. We'll do whatever she wants."

Without thinking twice, I step up behind him, wrap my arms around his stomach, and kiss his spine, right between his shoulder blades.

"Did I wake you?" he asks as his hand covers mine.

"No." Resting my cheek against his back, I lean on him, soaking in his warmth. "I love you so much, it scares the shit out of me."

He starts to move, but I hold him tight.

"Let me say this part."

Bringing my hand up to his lips, he whispers, "Okay."

"Being in love with you is so easy, Blake. You're incredible. I couldn't respect you any more than I do. You're everything I've ever needed and wanted in my life, and now that I have you, I'm terrified that I'll lose you."

"I'm not going anywhere, sugar."

"I think I've loved you since the minute I saw you on the plane. I recognized you, and I'd never seen you before in my life."

He turns in my arms and cups my face in his hands, kissing my lips so tenderly, it brings tears to my eyes.

"I can't stand the thought of you thinking that just because the words are hard for me, that I don't love you so much," I whisper against his lips. "I've *never* said them before to anyone. But Blake, you're the beginning and end for me. When I need to talk, you're who I want. Last night, when Ava was here talking to me about the positive test, all I could think was, *Blake should be here.*"

"Baby." He drags his knuckles down my cheek and presses his lips to my forehead.

"And earlier, when Hannah Hull, who was in town today, did my ultrasound, I just wanted you to be with me. It *killed* me that our schedules were so jacked up that I couldn't tell you right away. But tonight, after that ... after I got hurt, all I needed was you."

"You never have to wait for my schedule to clear, baby."

"I know that. I know that in an emergency, I can count on you. And even though it wasn't ideal, I was okay with waiting a couple of days to talk to you about the little bean. I just need you to know that *you're* my person. You're everything. I'm going to work on saying the words more because you deserve to hear that I love you every fucking day. You're so damn good to me."

His hand glides over my hip, and I can't stop the wince that comes, making him scowl.

"Are you hurting, baby?"

"I'm sore. I'll take it easy, and I'll be fine."

"Come on." He takes my hand and leads me back to the bedroom, helps me into the bed and tucks me up against his side, and we curl together, making sure I'm off my right side. "I love you."

He kisses my head, and I smile, feeling braver. Saying the words isn't hard when the love is spilling out of every fucking pore of my body. "I love you, too."

Seeing him in that room, in the dark, planning our baby's safe place just kicked my heart over the edge.

How can I *not* tell him how I feel?

After an exhale, he tips my chin up and smiles softly. "Please say it again."

"I'm so crazy in love with you, Blake Blackwell."

"I need my car and my purse."

Blake's already shaking his head as he follows me out to the garage, and I sit in the passenger seat of his SUV. "You need to stay home and heal."

"Blake. *Please* take me to the hospital so I can at least get my purse and fill out the forms with legal for the asshole who bruised my body." I bat my eyelashes at him. "Please. I'm not running any marathons here. I just have to go in for a few minutes. Then we can get lunch—"

"No, then I'm bringing you home."

"—to go from Juliet's place. Just a grab-and-go salad or something."

I bite my lip, but he narrows his eyes.

He's not caving.

"The *baby* is craving a salad from Juliet's place, Blake."

"You are absolutely *not* going to use that excuse for the next seven months, sugar." He grips my chin in his fingers and lowers his lips to mine, then he bites my lower lip and makes me grin. "But yes, we'll stop and get you whatever you want."

I brush my nose against his. "I love you."

"Fuck, I'm so screwed when it comes to you."

With a shake of his head, Blake walks around the car and climbs in next to me, then pulls out of the garage and heads to the hospital.

"Your wounds are fresh," he grumbles. "I don't like the look of that bruise on your hip, and I'd rather you were lying down."

"I'm using arnica salve on the bruises," I remind him. "And it does help. Don't worry, I'm not going to throw a clot or something—"

"Don't fucking say shit like that, Harper." His voice is so hard and angry, all I can do is blink at him. "It's not funny, and it happens every goddamn day from bruises less severe than yours."

"You're right." Reaching for his hand, I lace my fingers through his and squeeze. "It's not funny, and the bruises suck ass. I'm really sore today, and I'm moving slow, which I hate. I'm using the arnica. I'm taking it easy. I'm just going to go to the legal office, and I've already texted someone in my unit and asked them to bring me my purse so I'm not walking all over the hospital."

Blake lets out a sigh of relief and nods. "Thank you."

"I talked with Chase Wild this morning, the policeman assigned to the case, and gave him my statement."

"Good. Chase will do a good job."

"I know. He's already got the asshole in custody, and he hasn't been able to post bail. I'm filing a restraining order, so he's extra banned from the hospital."

Blake nods, his shoulders loosening up a little with each step that I explain to him.

I know he's worried. He'd be worried if I wasn't pregnant, but add in that not-so-little detail, and he's obsessed.

Any of my brothers would be the same. I can't fault him for hovering.

When we arrive at the hospital, Blake parks as close to the door as possible, and we walk slowly to the legal offices on the first floor, not far from the emergency room.

Signing the paperwork only takes a couple of minutes. My purse and keys are already waiting for me, and before long, we're walking back out again.

"See? Didn't take long. Now, I'll follow you—"

"No." His voice is calm again, and he plants his lips at my temple. "Your car will stay here. You're not driving for a few days."

"I can drive."

"I understand that you're capable. But you don't have to. Give me just a few more days, baby."

"Will you at least ask someone to bring it home for me?"

"That I can do." Blake finds a parking spot in front of Sage & Salt, and the restaurant is quiet when we walk in, which isn't too surprising at just after two in the afternoon.

I wasn't kidding earlier. I'd do a lot of illegal things for the chopped chef salad that Juliet keeps stocked in her grab-and-go section, which I grab two of, along with some bread for sandwiches and some chocolate chip cookies.

"What do you want to grab?" I ask Blake, holding my finds to my chest like they're my treasure and I refuse to share.

Because that's exactly what they are.

He smirks and grabs his own salad. We approach the counter to pay, but I frown when I see Juliet brush a tear from her cheek before forcing a smile at us.

"Hey, guys."

"Whoa. What's wrong?" I set my stuff down and walk around the counter, not giving a shit that I don't even work here, and take her hand. "Who do I have to kill?"

Jules shakes her head and sniffs. "No one. I'm fine. You seriously love that salad."

"Who made you cry?" I ask her, not giving in, and she side-eyes Blake, and I immediately know. "Ah. A stubborn Blackwell man."

"I haven't even *seen* Jules," Blake insists, making us both chuckle.

"I had to call a tow truck this morning," she says, and Blake nods. "He wasn't happy about that."

"You know, you live here, too," I tell her. "You can't just hide from him and stay out of his way so you don't piss him off. I don't know what the story is there, but it's not fair of him to expect you not to live your life, Juliet."

"Yeah, it is," she whispers, then shakes her head. "I'm going to be just fine. Thanks for asking, though. It means a lot. I don't have a lot of friends here anymore."

"I'm your friend," I remind her. "Ava is, too. I like Brooks, and his brother is mine, but that doesn't mean I can't be a good friend to you, too. Now, ring me up because I'm starving, and if I don't eat that salad in the next thirty minutes, I will become someone who Blake doesn't want to see."

Jules laughs and bags up our food but shakes her head when we try to pay.

"Enjoy it. You made me feel better, and that's all the payment I need today."

"Jules," Blake begins, but she shakes her head.

"I won't take your money today." She winks, and more customers file in behind us, and we leave so she can get back to work.

"I hate that," I mutter when we're back in the car headed home. "Brooks isn't a mean guy."

"He can be an asshole," Blake says. "But no, not as a rule. He's stubborn when it comes to her."

"Blake, I like her a lot. She's my friend. Is that going to be a problem?"

"Not for me." He pulls my hand up and kisses my

knuckles. "I like her too. But there's more there than either of us knows about it. And at the end of the day, it's none of our business."

"I know. I feel bad for them." I clear my throat and shift in the seat. My side is a little better today, but this hip is aching like a bitch.

When we get home, we eat our lunch and then end up on the couch to watch a movie and make out.

It's not a bad way to spend an afternoon.

Chapter Thirty-Four
BLAKE

"How are you feeling, sugar?"

Harper's fixing her makeup in our bathroom, and I brace my hands on the counter on either side of her hips and press my lips to her bare shoulder. She's in a gorgeous little green sundress that doesn't have any straps, showing off her toned and tanned shoulders, and fuck if I can keep my hands, or my lips, to myself. She smells amazing, like roses and clean air. I could breathe her in all fucking day.

"I'm nervous," she admits, meeting my gaze in the mirror. I wrap my arms around her and tug her against me and press my lips to the crown of her head. "I kind of liked having this secret to ourselves for a while. For the most part, anyway."

Come to find out, when Harper and my sister found out they were pregnant a month ago, Ava claimed Harper's test as her own to take the focus off my girl and to buy her time.

I was grateful to Ava for protecting Harper, but for the past month, everyone in their friend group thought that Ava was pregnant. The girls didn't spread the news, but still. Ava finally came over for dinner last night and asked us to set the record straight so she could go to book club without deflecting pregnancy questions.

"It's time to tell the family," I remind her, dragging my hands down her sides to her hips. She's all healed up after the incident at work that left her bruised and beaten, thank fuck. The asshole is serving some time for assault and battery.

"I know," she replies, leaning back into me, and I'm immediately on fire for her. "I've always been so damn attracted to you, but these pregnancy hormones are making me *feral*, Blake."

"I can help with that." Nibbling my way down her shoulder, I gather her skirt in my hands until it's bunched up around her waist. "We have time."

"I think we're already late."

I grin against her skin and push her panties down her legs, letting them pool at her feet. I brush my fingers through her already sopping wet pussy and growl against her neck.

"Fuck, baby."

"Told you." Her breaths are coming faster, and she pushes her ass out, silently begging for more. "I need you to fuck me, okay? Hard."

"You never need to ask twice. You want my cock, Harper? You want me to fill you up?"

"God, yes." Her head rolls forward, but I reach around and grip her throat, lifting her chin.

"Keep those pretty eyes on me."

Her gray orbs flare with need and lust. She loves it when I take control.

"Blake."

"Mm, yes, baby?" Brushing her hair over her shoulder, my lips wander down her neck, making her shiver. "What do you need? Use your words."

"I need you."

"Keep talking." With one hand, I unbuckle my belt and unfasten my jeans, then work them and my briefs down my hips, letting my hard, weeping cock spring free.

But I don't slip my dick inside her yet.

First, she gets my fingers, and that has her biting her lip on a moan.

"Tell me," I demand, my voice hard.

"I need you to make me come. *Please.*"

"I love it when you beg," I whisper against the back of her neck, and she shivers again. Her pussy clenches around my fingers before I pull them free and lick them clean, still holding her gaze in the mirror. "Fuck, you're beautiful."

"Blake."

I know what she needs, what she's asking for.

And I'll happily give it to her, as often as she wants, for the rest of my goddamn life.

"Please," she whispers, and that's all I need.

I lift her left leg, and she rests it on the counter, opening herself to me beautifully. I bend my knees, line my cock up with her dripping opening, and slide inside, making us both moan.

"*Yes,*" she sobs, pushing back against me. "More."

"Hard and fast?"

She nods and reaches back to grab my hip.

"Need to touch you."

Pulling out, I quickly turn her around, boost her up on the counter and sink back inside her. Her hands glide up my chest and into my hair, holding on while I fuck her, my hips moving fast and steady.

"Fucking perfect," I say against her lips, drinking her in. "Every bit of you was made for me. Only me."

"Only you."

My mouth dives for her neck, and she holds me to her as I increase the pace and intensity. I'll never get enough of her.

This body that I love so much is already changing. Her breasts are fuller, and her stomach is starting to round ever so slightly.

It's goddamn magic.

"Blake." She bites my shoulder over my shirt, and her whole body tenses. "I'm right there. Oh God, I'm right there."

"Fuck yes. I'm with you, baby." I grind into her, pushing against her sensitive clit, and as her climax rolls through her, she pulls my own out of me.

"Holy shit." She's panting, clinging to me, and then, to my horror, she starts to cry.

"What's wrong? Oh, God, did I hurt you? Baby, talk to me."

"Nothing's wrong. It was exactly what I needed." She buries her face in my chest and proceeds to break down as if I hit her dog with my car, and *I'm still inside her.*

"Help me, Harper."

"Hormones." Her voice is muffled against my chest, but I relax a little. "Christ, what's wrong with me? I'm not a crier."

"You're pregnant."

Now her head pops up, and she glares at me. "I *know* I'm pregnant, Blake. Trust me, I'm well aware. Shit, I'm sorry I snapped at you. You just gave me the best sex ever"—the tears start again—"and I snapped at you. I'm a monster."

"Ah, sugar, you're not a monster. I'm sorry. What can I do?"

She shakes her head, and I slip out of her, then get to work cleaning us both up before righting our clothes, and she hops off the counter.

"Just be patient with me because I don't mean to be mean to you."

"You're not being mean."

"You should have heard what was left unsaid." She laughs at that and then boosts up on her toes so she can brush her lips over mine. "I love you, Blake."

She's said it a hundred times over the past month, and it never fails to steal the breath from my lungs.

"I love you too. Come on, let's go have dinner with the family and let my parents get excited about another baby."

"I like your family," she says with a smile as she fixes

her mascara, then runs a brush through her long dark hair. She slides her hand into mine as we leave the bathroom. "I feel bad that Ava took the heat all this time. I swear, I kind of forgot. I haven't been at a book club meeting all month because it just didn't fall right with my work schedule, and when she mentioned it last night at dinner, I could have thrown up."

Luckily, that's one symptom my girl hasn't struggled with.

"She laughed it off," I remind her. "Ava's a good sport."

"She's the best." Harper sighs and grabs the dessert she's bringing for dinner. She's always mindful to make sure everything she brings for the family is safe for Birdie, and that just makes me fall in love with her more. "I hope everyone likes carrot cake."

"What's not to like?"

"Harper, you look gorgeous," Mom says with a big smile as she hugs my girl to her and winks at me over Harper's shoulder. "Of course, you always look amazing. Dare I say, green is your color."

"You're too nice," Harper says with a smile. "I hope you like carrot cake."

Mom takes the cake from me as we walk through the

farmhouse that I grew up in, but that Beckett and Skyla live in now, leading us to the kitchen.

"There won't be a bit of this left over," Mom informs Harper.

It looks like a normal Sunday family dinner at the ranch. Everyone's spread out through the kitchen and outside on the back deck. Birdie's standing on a chair, helping Skyla stir something on the stove, and Bridger's holding the sleeping baby against his shoulder, rocking back and forth.

Dani, Skyla, and Billie have their heads together, and when they see Harper, they wave her over to join in.

My family loves my girl. Of course, what's not to love? She fits in perfectly. I couldn't have asked for anyone better to bring into our fold.

"I love her," Mom murmurs next to me as she slips her arm through mine. "She's a sweetheart, my boy."

"I know." I kiss Mom's head. "Can I please have Grandma's ring?"

Her eyes fly up to mine, and they mist over.

Christ, I'm dealing with a lot of emotional women today.

"Of course. It's yours. Just swing by the house anytime to get it."

I nod, watching as Harper and Billie cackle together. Bee's eyes catch mine, and she smiles bigger.

Connor and Beckett come in from outside, along with my dad and Brooks, and since everyone's in one place, I gesture for Harper to join me. She immediately links her hand with mine.

"We have news," I say, getting everyone's attention.

Harper bites her lip nervously, but I'm not nervous at all.

"We're having a baby." I grin at the moment of silence, and then it's chaos as everyone asks questions, and the girls run over to hug us both.

"Wait, I thought *Ava* was pregnant," Skyla says, and Harper winces.

"She was covering for me," my girl admits. "Don't be mad at her. It was a shock, and *so* unplanned, and—"

"No need to explain," Bee says, shaking her head. "Also, that means we get to be pregnant together."

"So many babies and weddings," Mom says, wiping at her eyes. "I'm *so* glad we moved home. I wouldn't miss this for the world."

"Speaking of weddings." Skyla glances up at Beckett, who nods and wraps his arm around her shoulders. "Should we tell them now?"

"Tell them, Irish," he says.

"Now you have to tell us," Bridger adds.

"We were going to have the wedding this fall, but I can't wait that long," Skyla says. "So we're going to have it here, at the ranch, in two months. Charlie swears we can pull it off."

Charlie is Dani's younger sister, and she's a highly sought-after event coordinator in Bitterroot Valley.

"She can," Dani assures Skyla. "She's so excited."

Suddenly, Billie covers her mouth, her eyes widen, and then she dashes off to the bathroom.

My sister has not been as lucky as Harper in the getting sick side of things.

"I'll go," Mom assures Connor when he went to follow his wife. "You sit this one out."

"I fucking hate it for her," Connor says. "But she doesn't complain."

"Oh, she complains," Dani says with a laugh. "Just not to you. Because even though it's hard, she's so excited."

"There's a lot to be excited about." Harper smiles up at me and then leans her head on my biceps. "It's going to be a busy year."

You have no idea, sugar.

Chapter Thirty-Five
HARPER

"Did I tell you that I have to get my dress taken out for Beck and Skyla's wedding?" Blake and I are hiking on the same trail we hiked all those months ago when I first moved back to town. It's one of our favorites because the views are amazing and it's not too far from our house. "My stomach decided to basically pop out overnight, and there's no way I'll fit into that dress next month."

I can't believe that the wedding is only a month away. The summer is flying by, and I'm only a few weeks from being halfway through this pregnancy.

"I'm sure that Polly can help you out at her shop," Blake says, moving a tree branch out of my way.

"I have an appointment with her in a couple of days."

We're moving at a fast clip, which has me breathing hard, and Blake has hardly even broken a sweat.

"Oh, guess what?"

Blake grins down at me and brushes his hand down my back. "What, baby?"

"Amy's retiring." I stick my lip out in a pout. "I don't want her to go. She's so freaking good at her job, but her daughter is having a baby in Texas, and she's going to move down there to be near them."

One of the things I love most about our days out hiking is all of the talking we do. I swear, I still have diarrhea of the mouth around this man. My brain just never stops.

"Good for her," Blake says. "I have news, too."

"Tell me."

A trail runner comes down toward us, and Blake and I move out of the way so he doesn't have to slow down. When we're back on our way up, my man takes my hand and threads our fingers together.

"The hospital has hired another ER doctor. I'll still be working in the clinic four days a week, likely about forty hours, but now I'll only be in the ER for one shift a week."

I stop and frown up at him, not wanting to get too excited until I ask some questions.

Because this is exactly what I want.

But does he?

"Blake—"

"This is what I want, baby." He tucks a stray piece of hair behind my ear. "I need to cut back on my hours so I have more time with you and the bean. Yes, my job is important, but it'll never be more important than my family."

His hand covers my baby bump, and he smiles softly.

I'm taking six months off after I have the baby, and then I'm slowly easing back into work. I know that I'm lucky to be able to spend so much time with the baby.

"As long as you're sure, and you won't resent us because you work less."

"How could I ever resent the best part of my life?" He shakes his head and kisses my forehead, and then we're off once more. "My schedule changes before the end of the month."

"So we get about five months together before she's born." I grin up at him and realize what I just said and feel my eyes widen. "You know what I mean."

"Harper."

"It could be a boy," I insist as we climb over the last ridge that opens up to an amazing view of the mountains and a small lake.

"Harper."

I stop and face him, my hands on my hips, and feel like such a jerk.

"What happened to it being a surprise?"

I bite my lip as guilt settles heavily over my shoulders.

"Hey." Blake tips my face up, but instead of anger or annoyance, he grins at me. "Talk to me."

"Blake, I'm not good at surprises. It sounded good when I was first pregnant, but it's taking *forever*, and we need to decorate the nursery. I didn't mean to find out without you. At my last appointment, it was noted in my chart, and I saw it. Don't be mad."

"Look at my face." He steps closer and traces my lips

with his fingertip. "Do I look mad, baby? Haven't you figured out by now that it would take a lot to make me *truly* pissed at you?"

"So can I tell you?"

He laughs and kisses my nose. "I think you already did."

"We're having a girl." The giddiness bubbles up within me, and I bounce on the balls of my feet. "A little baby girl. And I think she's going to be spicy."

"Of course, she is." He kisses me so softly, so gently, that it makes my knees weak. "Let's take a selfie."

Just like the first time.

I smile and open my phone. Blake shifts us so the mountains and lake are in the background, and we smile at the lens. He takes a few, then kisses my temple and takes another.

"One more," he says. I look up at him, and he kisses my lips, snapping that moment as well.

And then, when I shove my phone back in my pocket, I turn to find my sexy man down on one knee, with a gorgeous ring clutched in his fingers.

"I love you so much, Harper. I can't believe I endured the bare minimum for so long when you existed the entire time. You've shown me what it means to truly be in love, be best friends with the one person you can't wait to see at the end of the day, and be with the one you trust above all else."

Tears flow freely down my cheeks as I listen to every single beautiful word flowing out of his lips.

I don't want to forget *anything*.

"I love the life we're building together. No one gets me like you do. You set me on fire, and you soothe me all at the same time."

God, at this rate, I'll never stop crying.

"You're everything good in this life, and I'd love nothing more than for you to be my wife. The mother of my children. I will do everything in my power, every single day, to make sure you never forget how much I fucking worship you."

I squat in front of him, and my hands cover his. "I love you, and I feel so lucky that I found you. Of *course*, I'll marry you."

He wraps his arms around me, and we rise to our feet as his lips cover mine, kissing me almost desperately.

And then, he slips the ring on my finger, and more tears come.

"It was my grandmother's," he says, looking down at my hand. "Until I found you, she was my favorite person. She and my grandpa were married for sixty years, so I think this ring has good luck. But if you want something new, we can get you whatever you want."

I have to swallow three times before I can manage to talk.

"I don't have family heirlooms," I say, the words barely above a whisper. "So the fact that you are giving this to me is really fucking big, babe."

"She'd love you." He kisses my temple and rubs his big hand up and down my back. "And I like to think she's already held our baby."

And now, I'm a blubbering mess.

"What was her name?" I ask him as I look up and see a tear in the corner of his eye.

"Isabelle."

I nod and feel the baby kick next to my belly button, so I yank Blake's hand against my abdomen. "Wait for it."

I nudge the other side, and Blake's eyes go round in awe as they hold mine.

"Do you feel that?"

"It's a little flutter." His voice is rough and low, and I cover his hand with my own, just as the baby kicks again. "Christ, we're having a baby."

I grin up at him. "I think her name is Isabelle. We'll call her Belle, keeping with the B tradition. Is that okay with you?"

His smile could light up the night sky. "Yeah, baby. Yeah, that's more than okay with me. Now, what kind of wedding do you want?"

"Small. Just our families and closest friends."

"Shit, that's not small, sugar."

I chuckle with him as he rests his forehead against mine.

"I guess it's not. Can we wait to do it until after the baby comes, so I can wear a pretty dress that isn't a tent, and Belle can be there, too?"

"Baby, you can have whatever you want. Always. But maybe we take care of the legalities before she's born."

I cup his cheek, loving him so much. "Justice of the

peace, you and me, before she's born, and a celebration after."

"It's going to be a great life, Harper."

"It already is."

Epilogue
BROOKS BLACKWELL

"We wanted a small get-together to announce our engagement, and it turned into a party for fifty people," Blake says, shaking his head as we stand outside our sister Billie's house, taking everything in.

Billie and Connor's place is the biggest out of all of ours, and Billie immediately volunteered to host this party. She and Harper have become close this year.

Of course, Harper's also become friends with the one woman who turns me inside out just by existing.

The only woman I've ever loved.

And the one who makes me want to burn the world to the motherfucking ground.

Right now, Jules, my wildfire, is dancing with my sisters, either by blood or by marriage, laughing and acting like she belongs here.

She fucking *doesn't*.

"I warned you she'd be here," Blake says, his face grim as he watches the group of them. "Harper wouldn't leave her out, and—"

"You already told me." I shake my head and sip my beer. "I'm fine."

"Neither of you is *fine*," Beckett says.

"I said I'm fine." If I thought I could get away with it without hurting my brother's feelings, I wouldn't be here. I'm not big on crowds anyway, and if *she's* within a mile, I steer clear of it, but this is Blake's engagement party, and I love my brother.

I'm thrilled for him. Despite his woman's poor taste in friends, I'm crazy about her. She's excellent for my reformed workaholic brother.

So I'll stay and celebrate with them and ignore the gorgeous little blonde who's set my soul on fire since I was sixteen fucking years old.

More than twenty years of loving her.

Fifteen of hating her.

It's a fucking mess.

She's been back in town for almost a year, and I was doing so well at ignoring that she even existed.

Until that goddamn day at the resort when I found her bent over the cooler, and every memory I have of her flashed through my mind as if no time had passed at all.

Her sweet laughter.

A body that would make the gods weep.

Every whispered secret, every second of being inside her, and the goddamn torment she caused.

She's off. Fucking. Limits.

"So the wedding's in two weeks," I say to Beckett, trying to shift my focus.

"Twelve days," he says with a nod. "I'd do it today. I just want to marry her. I don't care about the party or any of the hype."

"Women care," Blake says. "Shit, I'm being flagged over. Sorry, guys."

Blake hurries over to his fiancée, kisses her passionately right there in the middle of the dance floor, and everyone whoops.

Beckett's pulled away, and I walk to a table and have a seat by myself, then check the time.

I've only been here for thirty minutes.

"Hi, Uncle Brooks." Birdie climbs in my lap as if it's as normal as breathing for her.

Which it is. This peanut knows that she has all of us wrapped around her little six-year-old finger.

"Hey, baby girl. Why aren't you out there dancing with the others?"

She looks out at the dance floor and shrugs. "Because you looked sad."

I nudge her chin up and smile down at her. "I'm not sad, sweet girl. It's a happy day. Uncle Blake's going to get married."

"I know. I like Harper. She's a baby nurse."

Nodding, I kiss her hair.

"Now it's your turn."

Sure that I've misheard her, I raise an eyebrow. "Excuse me?"

"Everyone's getting married, Uncle Brooks. Now it's

your turn."

"Why do you sound like my mother?"

Birdie giggles and lays her head on my chest. Christ, I love this little girl.

"You know, not everyone ends up getting married. Sometimes, people are happy staying single."

"Why?" She frowns up at me. "It's so much more fun to have people around."

"Not always." I pat her back for a few seconds, then scoot her off my lap. "Go dance. You're so good at it. Go show them how it's done."

"Will you watch me?"

"Of course, I'm right here."

She smiles big, showing off a gap in her teeth where she recently lost one of them, and runs off to the dance floor.

I sense her before I see her, and every muscle tightens.

Juliet sits across from me and takes her shoe off, rubbing the arch of her foot.

"You can't keep hating me," she says, and just the sound of her voice sets every hair on my body on end.

I don't reply. I can't. Something is lodged in my throat.

"It's been fifteen years. I live here, Brooks. This is my home, and these are my friends."

I cross my arms over my chest as resentment bubbles up in my stomach.

"I mean, I get it. We don't have to be friends."

"We're nothing," I finally grind out, and her face falls.

Fuck.

I don't want to feel anything for her. I don't want to feel bad for her. I don't want to *want* her.

"I can't hide away when I'm not at work and have no life. That's what I'm trying to say." She slides her shoe back on and leans back in the chair, mirroring me with her arms crossed under breasts that have only gotten better with time. "I won't hide. I didn't do what—"

"I don't want your fucking words." I lean forward, sure to keep my voice low so only she can hear me. "I don't give a shit what you have to say. You're right. It's been a long time. Live your life, Jules, I don't fucking care. Just ignore me. If we're in the same place at the same time, *I don't exist for you.* Do you hear me? I don't want to talk to you. I don't feel anything for you."

She blinks, swallows, and then nods. "Okay."

"You're nothing." *You were everything.* "And that's the way it's going to stay."

Are you excited for Brooks and Juliet's story in Where You Belong? You can get more info here: https://www.kristenprobyauthor.com/where-you-belong

Alex, Adam and Gabe's story can be found here: https://www.kristenprobyauthor.com/when-we-breathe

. . .

If you'd like to read Hannah Hull's story (the doctor friend of Harper's), you can find it here: https://www.kristenprobyauthor.com/charming-hannah

Turn the page for a preview of Where You Belong:

Where You Belong Preview
JULIET

Present Day

After making sure the deadbolt on my apartment is engaged, I turn to walk down the steps but then spin back around to check that the door is locked again.

I do that three more times before I finally feel confident enough to walk down the stairs to the alley behind my restaurant, Sage & Citrus, and start my morning walk.

I never have anything in my ears during my walks. I don't own earbuds or headphones. I never listen to podcasts or audiobooks or music when I'm on my walks. I know that Bitterroot Valley is safe, and that the odds of being mugged during the early morning hours here in town are very low, but that habit has been ingrained in me for years.

I don't like surprises.

I don't do well with being startled.

Besides, this way I can hear the birds waking up, the *tick-tick-tick* of the lawn sprinklers, and the occasional car drive by. I like the way my town sounds so early in the day.

I know this town like the back of my hand, yet it's still so foreign to me. I had been away for almost two decades before I finally made my way home. And that's what this tiny town in Montana is.

Home.

But I don't really belong here anymore. I definitely don't fit in. I'm an outsider, a move-in, despite being born here and coming from three generations of Bitterroot Valley citizens. The friendships I had as a child are all gone. I don't have family since Mom passed away about ten years ago, and Dad ... Well, Dad's been gone for a long time.

So it doesn't necessarily make sense that when I finally found my freedom and could go anywhere to start over, I chose to come to the place where I was born, where there seems to be nothing but ghosts of the past that haunt me.

Taunts me.

Reminds me that I was stupid and made choices that destroyed me.

However, I knew, deep in my soul, that Bitterroot Valley was the one place on this godforsaken rock hurling through space that could heal me. I need the mountains, the fresh air, and even if they don't want to have anything to do with me, the people who live here, whether they're familiar to me or not. Just knowing that they're nearby is soothing.

Making my way down the block and into the oldest residential neighborhood in town, I take a deep breath. Fall is fast approaching, but summer is holding on by its fingernails. There's a slight nip in the air this morning, but flowers still bloom, and none of the trees have started to turn quite yet.

I slow my stride just a bit when I get to the corner where my favorite house in town sits. It's funny how when you're a kid, things look bigger. Or, maybe, it's just the memory that's skewed. If you'd have asked me when I was sixteen about this house, I would have told you it's a mansion.

But I've lived in a mansion three times this size, and this house is so much better in every way. So much more a home than the cold fortress I spent all of my marriage in.

In reality, the house before me is a large older home, white with a red roof and black trim, and sits on a huge corner lot. Whomever owns it now doesn't seem to like flowers, as there's no landscaping to speak of, but the lawn is cut religiously every Sunday.

This house needs rose bushes and hydrangeas. Maybe lilacs on that one side. A pretty mixed garden in that corner. And in the back, I'd plant a garden with herbs and veggies.

Brooks and I used to talk about this place all the time. We took a lot of walks, or went for rides through town, and we often came this way.

"How many bedrooms do you think it has?" I ask as I lean on the open passenger window, letting the cool wind blow through my hair.

"I dunno," Brooks says. "Maybe four? Five?"

"That's a lot of bedrooms. We'd have to have a lot of kids to fill it up."

"Not really. There are five of us at my house, so four bedrooms wouldn't be enough. Why, how many kids do you want, Wildfire?"

I grin back at him, see him watching me with those gorgeous hazel eyes. "The right amount to fill up that house."

I shake my head and keep walking. It seems like there are memories in every corner of this town. But that's the price I have to pay to be here.

To feel safe.

So I'll pay it.

Pulling myself out of *that* funk, I start making a mental list of everything I need to order for the restaurant today. It's ordering day, and because my place has become so popular this summer, it will be a big order.

That makes me almost giddy.

I've wanted to open a restaurant like this for as long as I can remember. I have gluten sensitivities. I suspect I have celiac disease, but I've never been diagnosed. However, since I've been working in and using a clean kitchen, I've had minimal issues.

Feeling good is a luxury I'll never take for granted again.

On my way back through downtown, I come across

Jackie, the owner of the Sugar Studio, as she sets her chalkboard on the sidewalk.

"Good morning," she says with a big smile. Jackie and my mom were good friends, and she's been one of the few people who's been sincerely excited to have me back home. "How are you, beautiful girl?"

I let her hug me close even though touch is something I'm still getting used to again, and I give her a smile when I pull away.

"I'm doing well, thanks. How are you, Jackie? How's your knee?"

"Meh." Jackie shrugs. "It hurts like a bitch most days, but who has time for knee replacement surgery?"

"Um, *you* need to make time. You're on your feet every day, remember?"

"Oh, trust me, this knee doesn't let me forget it. But I'm okay, sweetie. It's nothing a little ibuprofen doesn't help. I have a new gluten-free scone recipe for you. Or, if you want, I can come by one evening, and we can make them in your kitchen."

I love this woman. I know she'd make it for me in *her* kitchen—Jackie makes the best pastries in the state—but her facility isn't gluten-free, and it might make me sick.

Instead, we've spent plenty of time in my kitchen, and her recipes never miss.

"I'd love that. Anytime works for me. I've decided to start closing at four on Sundays."

She tilts her head to the side. "Why's that?"

"Well, working from seven in the morning until nine

at night makes for a long-ass day." I chuckle and brush some hair behind my ear.

"You have girls who work for you," she reminds me. "Let them handle a day by themselves so you can take a day off."

I wrinkle my nose. "I don't need a whole day. What would I do with myself? But a half day would be great. Plus, I'd get to see you. I can't wait to try those scones."

She grins at me, but I see the worry in her eyes. "You work too hard, baby girl. Your mama would tell me to make you slow down."

"My mama worked two jobs all my life," I remind her and turn to leave. "So she'd have no room to talk. I'll see you later."

When I get down the block to my place, and before I can walk around to the alley, where the stairwell that leads to my apartment is, movement across the street catches my eye. I see Brooks walking out of Bitterroot Valley Coffee Co, with a cup in hand. He doesn't see me at first, and I'm able to take him in.

God, he's beautiful.

Taller and more muscular than he was when I was in college, Brooks grew up very well. Okay, that's the understatement of the year. His jawline is firm and chiseled, and his dark hair a little too long and tousled, as if he just rolled out of bed.

Or had sex.

Fuck, don't think about that.

He's wearing jeans, and his deep red T-shirt is tucked

into them, showcasing a narrow waist and sculpted abs. But it's always been his arms that make me weak in the knees. That shirt looks like it's a second skin around his biceps.

I know how it feels to have those arms wrapped around me, and there's nothing like it in the whole world.

Suddenly, his eyes come up to mine, and his stride slows, just a smidge. His eyes harden. His jaw clenches.

And then he turns the other way and walks to his garage, as if I don't even exist.

That's the part that tears my heart out.

"You're nothing." His eyes bore into mine, so much anger shooting through him, and landing right on me.

I was invited to his brother, Blake's engagement party by Harper, Blake's fiancée. She's a sweetheart, and a loyal customer of mine. I love her to death.

She's my friend, and I don't have many of those.

But it's shitty luck that she's marrying Blake because that means that I'll have to be very careful to pick and choose which invitations to accept from her. I don't want to be anywhere I'm not wanted.

That's the last thing I want.

***

"Holy shit, this salad is *so good*," Harper says with a moan. She sits back and closes her eyes, enjoying her mouthful of salad, and it makes me smile.

My friend is pregnant, and she's been craving this salad every day.

I finally stopped charging her for them. They don't

cost me much to make, and I didn't want her to go broke.

"So good," Ava, Harper's best friend, echoes. "Like, smack my ass and call me Sally good."

I snort out a laugh and shake my head. "I'm glad you like them. I'm thinking about adding artichoke hearts to that one. What do you think?"

"Yes," Harper says, nodding enthusiastically.

"No," Ava says at the same time and wrinkles her nose. "It's the texture for me. I can't do it."

"Maybe I'll offer it as an add-on." I wink at them and leave them to their lunch. I clear off a table and wipe it down, then head back behind the counter.

This is a full-service restaurant offering breakfast, lunch, and dinner. Everything is gluten-free, including the bread and pastries, and is safe for anyone with celiac disease to eat here.

Including me.

The food is pretty good, if I do say so myself.

And I try to rotate things through with the seasons. Now that summer is coming to a close, I'm starting to come up with ideas for fall, but clearly, that salad that Harper's in love with will have to stay forever.

My phone pings in my pocket with a text, making me scowl. Only one person ever texts me these days, and I only keep my phone on me for emergencies.

Pulling it out, I sigh at the message.

Unknown Number: *I need two grand.*

I keep blocking her number, but she just gets a new

one. It's constant. And exhausting. She knows she's only supposed to email me, but she doesn't care.

She's not good with boundaries.

Without replying, I block this one, too, and then shove the phone back in my pocket.

"You okay?" Christy asks with a frown.

"I'm great, just a spam text." I shrug and get to work filling an order for the shrimp tacos that came in through the take-out app. "Hazel's coming in at noon today, and Tandy said she'd be in at four to help with dinner."

"Actually, Tandy just called." Christy winces. "She sprained her ankle."

I close my eyes and sigh. "I'll call Erica in."

"Erica is at Yellowstone with her boyfriend," Christy reminds me. "Don't worry about it. I'll stay."

"You've been working doubles all week."

"So have you, boss lady," she says with a wink. "It's fine, I can use the overtime. I've got my eye on a pair of shoes that will most likely maim me and make me bleed, but they're *so pretty*."

"Then it sounds like you need them." I pat her on the shoulder. "Thanks for staying. I'll stay, too, and the three of us will be good to go. I have three new hires coming in throughout the month, as long as they don't back out on me. They all want different hours, so I can stagger them throughout the week. I don't think we'll have much of a shoulder season, but I'm not complaining about that."

"This is exactly what this town needed," Christy says. "It's different and fresh, and the food is amazing. So it doesn't surprise me that we're busy. Tandy felt so bad, especially because she knows Erica's gone."

"We'll be fine."

I will never complain about having to put in extra hours or being exhausted from running this place.

It's something I never thought I'd have, and it's all mine. I bought the building, free and clear, and I own everything inside it.

No one can take any of it away from me.

And the fact that I'm already doing so well just boosts my confidence and reminds me that despite having moments of doubt, this really is where I'm supposed to be.

Newsletter Sign Up

I hope you enjoyed reading this story as much as I enjoyed writing it! For upcoming book news, be sure to join my newsletter! I promise I will only send you news-filled mail, and none of the spam. You can sign up here:

https://mailchi.mp/kristenproby.com/newsletter-sign-up

Also by Kristen Proby:

ALSO BY KRISTEN PROBY:

Other Books by Kristen Proby

The Wilds of Montana Series
Wild for You - Remington & Erin
Chasing Wild - Chase & Summer
Wildest Dreams - Ryan & Polly
On the Wild Side - Brady & Abbi
She's a Wild One - Holden & Millie

The Blackwells of Montana
When We Burn - Bridger & Dani
When We Break - Beckett & Skyla
Where We Bloom - Connor & Billie

Get more information on the series here: https://www.kristenprobyauthor.com/the-wilds-of-montana

Single in Seattle Series
The Secret - Vaughn & Olivia
The Scandal - Gray & Stella
The Score - Ike & Sophie
The Setup - Keaton & Sidney
The Stand-In - Drew & London

Check out the full series here: https://www.kristenprobyauthor.com/single-in-seattle

Huckleberry Bay Series

Lighthouse Way

ALSO BY KRISTEN PROBY:

Fernhill Lane
Chapel Bend
Cherry Lane

The With Me In Seattle Series

Come Away With Me - Luke & Natalie
Under The Mistletoe With Me - Isaac & Stacy
Fight With Me - Nate & Jules
Play With Me - Will & Meg
Rock With Me - Leo & Sam
Safe With Me - Caleb & Brynna
Tied With Me - Matt & Nic
Breathe With Me - Mark & Meredith
Forever With Me - Dominic & Alecia
Stay With Me - Wyatt & Amelia
Indulge With Me
Love With Me - Jace & Joy
Dance With Me Levi & Starla
You Belong With Me - Archer & Elena
Dream With Me - Kane & Anastasia
Imagine With Me - Shawn & Lexi
Escape With Me - Keegan & Isabella
Flirt With Me - Hunter & Maeve
Take a Chance With Me - Cameron & Maggie

Check out the full series here: https://www.kristenprobyauthor.com/with-me-in-seattle

The Big Sky Universe

ALSO BY KRISTEN PROBY:

Love Under the Big Sky
Loving Cara
Seducing Lauren
Falling for Jillian
Saving Grace

The Big Sky
Charming Hannah
Kissing Jenna
Waiting for Willa
Soaring With Fallon

Big Sky Royal
Enchanting Sebastian
Enticing Liam
Taunting Callum

Heroes of Big Sky
Honor
Courage
Shelter

Check out the full Big Sky universe here: https://www.kristenprobyauthor.com/under-the-big-sky

Bayou Magic

Shadows
Spells
Serendipity

ALSO BY KRISTEN PROBY:

Check out the full series here: https://www.kristenprobyauthor.com/bayou-magic

The Curse of the Blood Moon Series

Hallows End
Cauldrons Call
Salems Song

The Romancing Manhattan Series

All the Way
All it Takes
After All

Check out the full series here: https://www.kristenprobyauthor.com/romancing-manhattan

The Boudreaux Series

Easy Love
Easy Charm
Easy Melody
Easy Kisses
Easy Magic
Easy Fortune
Easy Nights

Check out the full series here: https://www.kristenprobyauthor.com/boudreaux

ALSO BY KRISTEN PROBY:

The Fusion Series

Listen to Me
Close to You
Blush for Me
The Beauty of Us
Savor You

Check out the full series here: https://www.kristenprobyauthor.com/fusion

From 1001 Dark Nights

Easy With You
Easy For Keeps
No Reservations
Tempting Brooke
Wonder With Me
Shine With Me
Change With Me
The Scramble
Cherry Lane

Kristen Proby's Crossover Collection

Soaring with Fallon, A Big Sky Novel

Wicked Force: A Wicked Horse Vegas/Big Sky Novella
By Sawyer Bennett

ALSO BY KRISTEN PROBY:

All Stars Fall: A Seaside Pictures/Big Sky Novella
By Rachel Van Dyken

Hold On: A Play On/Big Sky Novella
By Samantha Young

Worth Fighting For: A Warrior Fight Club/Big Sky Novella
By Laura Kaye

Crazy Imperfect Love: A Dirty Dicks/Big Sky Novella
By K.L. Grayson

Nothing Without You: A Forever Yours/Big Sky Novella
By Monica Murphy

Check out the entire Crossover Collection here:
https://www.kristenprobyauthor.com/kristen-proby-crossover-collection

About the Author

Kristen Proby is a *New York Times*, *USA Today*, and *Wall Street Journal* bestselling author of over seventy published titles. She debuted in 2012, captivating fans with spicy contemporary romance about families and friends with plenty of swoony love. She also writes paranormal romance and suggests you keep the lights on while reading them.

When not under deadline, Kristen enjoys spending time with her husband and their fur babies, riding her bike, relaxing with embroidery, trying her hand at painting, and, of course, enjoying her beautiful home in the mountains of Montana.